Praise for the *Fifi Cutter* series

"A deceptively goofy thriller filled with dead pan one-liners and punchy humor that would be the envy of many a stand-up comic."
— Book Pleasures

"A briskly paced mystery that will even surprise seasoned mystery readers."
— Authors Den

"When a novel's principal characters are a currently unemployed insurance investigator named Fifi Cutter and her usually unemployed half brother, Bosco Dorff, you know you're in for a bit of weirdness... The characters grab us from the moment we meet them, and the story... is well constructed... The novel is billed as 'A Fifi Cutter Mystery,' which gives the impression that more will follow. Let's hope so."
— David Pitt, *Booklist*

"There is a sly sophistication lurking behind the laughter created by Fifi Cutter, the scrappy heroine of *Murder...Suicide...Whatever...*, the witty debut novel of Gwen Freeman. This first in her mystery series may be set in the guise of a traditional locked-door, but Ms. Freeman wrestles a generation of self-absorbed Los Angelinos flat to the mat before they know the match has begun."
— Robert Fate, Anthony nominee, *Baby Shark* and
Baby Shark's Beaumont Blues

"Fifi Cutter has outrageous 'tude. She is the most entertaining amateur sleuth since Stephanie Plum. Although Ms. Freeman begins from a standard whodunit set-up, this is not your Aunt Mabel's mystery."
— Bruce Cook, National Best Books Finalist,
Phillipine Fever

CRAZY FOOL
KILLS FIVE

CRAZY FOOL KILLS FIVE

GWEN FREEMAN

CAPITAL CRIME PRESS
FORT COLLINS, COLORADO

First edition published in the United States by Capital Crime Press. Printed in Canada. Cover art by Gwen Freeman. Cover design by Nick Zelinger.

Capital Crime Press is a registered trademark.

Library of Congress Control Number: 2008921434
ISBN-13: 978-0-9799960-0-9
ISBN-10: 0-9799960-0-7

www.capitalcrimepress.com

To all those who helped make this happen
and a special thanks to my Baby Daddy.

Chapter One

I *had* him!

I had him dead.

I adjusted the lens on the antiquated video camera, so excited I forgot to hold still. The image went all jiggly and I steadied the camera against the lowered car window, slowing the borrowed Volvo to a halt. This maneuver annoyed the driver of a yellow Tercel, who pulled impatiently around me, further spoiling my view of the sidewalk across the street and the man who was striding down it.

Son of a bitch, I thought to myself, he is actually going to the gym!

Mr. Steven Randolf Burton, file clerk and workers' compensation claimant (temporary total disability due to a back injury allegedly suffered while lifting a box of toys collected by the office do-gooders for needy families last Christmas) was heading toward Work Out World and I had a clear shot of him from across the street.

His employer, the Chinatown law firm of Wong, Wu & Chu, who had hired me to conduct this *sub rosa* surveillance, was going to be delighted.

I re-focused the camera just as Burton bent down to tie his New Balance cross-trainers. A tall, shapely redhead, walking north, stepped into the frame and fell into the arms of a broadly built guy with helmet hair walking south. Their enthusiastic embrace completely obscured my shot of Burton. I silently urged the amorous pair to *just get a room already*, but they began talking earnestly, heads together, hands waving. The bright Southern California sun lit them up like they were on stage.

Burton straightened up and gave a start. I ducked down. Had he seen me? I lifted my head a fraction, but his gaze seemed to be directed to Helmet Hair and the Redhead. *Whew*, I thought, he's just offended by Public Displays of Affection. And really, who isn't?

I sat up, but before I could get back into position, Burton had disappeared into Work Out World. My opportunity to get the killer shot was gone.

Fuming, I waited a few minutes before moving the wagon down Fair Oaks in search of legal parking. I found a metered space within two blocks, deposited the twenty-five cents required by the City of Pasadena for 30 minutes automotive respite, and made a note in my log. Tuesday morning, 10:13 AM.

I hustled back along the sidewalk, cramming my camera into my brand new, bright pink, Mandarina Duck bag. Not a great fit.

The plate glass windows of Work Out World showcased three buff specimens stationary-bicycling, stair-stepping and tread-milling. I tried not to stare as I sashayed through the front door, and presented myself to the front desk.

I don't spend a lot of time in gyms. They smell bad, even the upscale ones like this one. Come on now, people, why can't you sweat in the privacy of your own home? Nobody really needs a $1,200 treadmill, do they? Can't you just jog in one spot in the kitchen? And time yourself with the little clock on the oven? You wouldn't even have to buy a $270 spandex outfit. You could wear your faded Bermuda shorts and old college sweatshirt. And best of all, I'd never have to see you.

I didn't, however, say this to the spandex-suited, pony-tailed blond at the front desk.

"Membership card, please," she said.

"I don't actually have a card," I began, raising my voice over the clanking, whirring, squeaking din.

The blond looked momentarily less perky until I added, "I'm thinking of joining, though." That cheered her right up.

"Oh, do allow me to show you around and demonstrate our state-of-the-art body-awareness facilities. Ricardo, take over for me here, I have a prospect," she announced to the unnaturally cut Hispanic man who would have been so handsome but for the steroid acne.

"No, no, I don't want to bother you, it's okay," I protested. "Maybe I can just spend a few minutes looking around by myself, you know just to get an idea—"

"I'm happy to be of assistance. I take it you're not presently a member of any other gym, are you?" she asked, but she wasn't really asking. She could tell by the toothpick arms sticking out of my white T-shirt, and the pencil-thin legs sticking out of my denim miniskirt.

"By the way, I'm Mindy," she chirped. "Tell me your name. I'll fill out an application for you." She fixed me with bright blue eyes, pen poised over clipboard. I realized with dismay that Mindy must get a commission on any new sign-ups. There was no way she was going to let me get away.

"Fifi Cutter," I reluctantly replied.

"Fifi! What a cute name!"

I smiled. I didn't want to, but I did.

"Age?"

"Twenty-seven."

"Oh, that's so cool, that's the same as me." Mindy beamed. "And where do you live?"

"Mt. Washington," I dutifully replied, adding, "It's one hill over from Dodger Stadium," since nobody ever knew where Mt. Washington was, even though it is one of the oldest neighborhoods in Los Angeles and not fifteen minutes from where we were standing.

"And what do you do?"

"Uh, I'm in insurance." No reason to explain to her what an independent insurance adjustor was, much less that it involved tailing sleazy insurance cheats who worked out at her gym. Usually, telling people you are in insurance cuts off all further inquiry. It worked this time too, as Mindy began extolling the benefits of Lifetime Membership, for only $34.99 a month.

"Here we have our aromatherapy and skin-care products. We carry only organically based formulas, with the very purest of ingredients. And we offer massage services, shiatsu, Swedish, deep tissue. Here is the room where we do step and spinning—that's Rita in there now, and she is, like, the best step leader ever. And she has a beginner class that's not too challenging," she added, as if doubting my ability to step quickly and repeatedly in place.

"Now here we have a free-weight station, just for women. Sometimes women feel they shouldn't work with free weights, but that's so wrong." Mindy gestured toward a rack of barbells with apricot, peach, and mauve colored weights on either end.

"Very dainty," I said with as much seriousness as I could muster, while I surreptitiously scanned the room looking for Burton.

Mindy bent over and picked up a barbell, demonstrating how easily she could hold it over her head.

God damn it, where was he? There! Settling down for some bench presses. I squinted at him, and missed what Mindy was saying.

"Huh?"

"Here, you try, let me take your bag." She replaced the barbell on the floor and lifted my bulging purse off my shoulder. The bag gapped open, and that's when things got ugly.

"A video camera!" Mindy's pretty little face wrinkled up. "Who brings a video camera into a gym?"

"Oh, I just need it for my job," I hastily explained and stuffed it back into the bag.

"Your job? I thought you said you were in insurance."

"Right. That's right. So can you show me again how to do a curl?"

Mindy was not to be so easily dissuaded. "I think you should tell me what you were doing with that video camera."

"It's not illegal to have a video camera."

"If you had a good reason, you'd tell me." Mindy's voice was getting shrill.

"You are so overreacting."

"You're, like, a paparazzi, aren't you?"

"No." I was insulted. "What celebrities come here anyway?"

"For your information plenty of celebrities come here. This is, like, the most popular gym in Pasadena."

"Well, I'm not a paparazzi." My own voice had started to get louder.

"Don't shout at me."

"I am not shouting!" I was shouting a little.

"Get out of here!"

"Calm down!"

"Look, for all I know you want to sneak in the locker room and video our guests undressing and sell the video to *Access Hollywood* or something." Mindy grabbed at my purse, and we engaged in a very one-sided tug of war.

"Give me back my purse, you freak, I'm not going to sneak—"

Mindy interrupted. "You could be, like, putting together a porno tape or something."

"I'm not doing porno!" I yelled, instantly freezing the room. The slowly diminishing whir of the wheels on the stationary bikes was the only noise, as all eyes turned to me. Holy crap. If he hadn't seen me before, Burton was sure looking at me now.

Before I could even begin to think of anything to say, Mindy was yelling for Ricardo and some other guy, even bigger than Ricardo, whose name I didn't catch. Ricardo gripped my right arm, Bigger-Than-Ricardo gripped my left, and they whisked me toward the entrance, my toes tapping on the floor. At the door, they hoisted my five foot two inch frame up another few inches, and without any unnecessary motion, tossed me out onto the pavement. I landed as gently as could be expected.

A few seconds later, Ricardo came out with my purse and the video camera and silently handed them to me. He crossed his massive arms in front of his chest and waited for me to depart. I briefly considered waiting and trying to get a shot of Burton leaving the gym, but what would that show? He could claim he went in there for a whirlpool bath.

Humiliated, and deeply worried about how I was going to put a positive spin on this when I reported to Reginald Wong, I headed for home.

As I wound up San Rafael, the acid green of the canyons glittering in the April sun, I pondered my predicament. Mr. Wong was taking this particular case very seriously. I'd only been on the job for four days, and Wong had already left me several messages inquiring as to my progress. He seemed very worried about his workers' compensation premiums going up.

I sighed. I would just have to send him whatever video footage I had so far—which included Burton taking out the trash and Burton unloading the groceries from his car. Not great, but it did tend to disprove his doctor's conclusion that "Claimant suffers excruciating pain upon minor exertion and is unable to lift over three pounds at the present time." What BS!

Maybe I could still get the gym footage, I thought. It was a fair assumption that Burton worked out at around ten, maybe not every day, but at least every Tuesday. People tend to be regular about their gym attendance. I just had to wait a week. Obviously, I couldn't do it myself, not now that Burton had seen me, but I had someone in mind.

Chapter Two

"Are you crazy?" said my worthless brother. Half-brother.

"Of course I'm crazy. I let you live here in my house. You borrow money, you never pay it back. You don't have a job, and I can't keep food and beer in the refrigerator without you sucking it down like some—some—some giant food and beer-sucking swamp creature."

Bosco leaned back in the kitchen chair and smiled his most sincere what-a-great-guy-I-am smile. "You're very generous, Fifi. I say that all the time, don't I? Don't I say, 'Fifi is a good and generous sister and I am lucky we share a mom'?"

I plopped the pink purse onto the counter and sat down hard in the chair opposite Bosco. "Generous is your word for stupid." I glared and pushed on. "You're a leech, Bosco, nothing but a sponging, useless leech. And don't get me sidetracked. I had a point to make. The point is that you owe me."

"Fifi, you're upset. I understand—you had a horrible experience. You're emotionally scarred. But you're not looking at the big picture. If you think you had a bad time when you were discovered with a video camera, can you even imagine what Ricardo would do to a guy he caught carrying a video camera?" Bosco shook his head regretfully.

"But they wouldn't catch you, would they? You're an actor, aren't you? You're really good at this sneaky stuff." Bosco had a horrible role in a pukey sitcom twenty years ago when he was a kid, before his dad won the custody battle and whisked him off to New York. He hadn't had an acting job since. Or any kind of job. Still, actors are vain and I thought if guilt didn't work, maybe flattery would.

No such luck. "That's exactly why I can't risk your plan," Bosco explained. "My looks are my life, Fifi. How would I manage my career if the profile got damaged?" He pretended to consider it. "No, no, I can't risk it. It really wouldn't be prudent." Bosco went back to reading the Business section. Did I mention I'd arrived home at 11:37 and he had just that minute gotten up?

"What am I supposed to do?" I demanded.

"What about VJ? Why doesn't she help you out?"

VJ, a.k.a. Victoria Jane Smith, was my best friend. Shit, she was my only friend. See, if I were older, and whiter, and male, I'd be a curmudgeon.

But VJ was my friend because we'd known each other since she moved to LA from London and we were the only two black girls in our class at a prestigious private high school, long before she'd become a "Young Lawyer to Watch" and I had become a person everyone pretended not to notice.

"VJ has done enough. She's the one who asked Reg Wong to give me this job in the first place, you moron. And she lent me her parents' car while they're in England. If I ask her for any more favors, she's going to have to adopt me." My own car—well, the car I regularly borrowed—had gotten blown up just before Christmas. Super long story, don't even.

"I was just thinking," Bosco shrugged. "She's a big, tall girl. She could give that Ricardo a run for his money and I don't think your pal Mindy would have a chance."

"Well, forget it," I snapped. "VJ is starting the trial from hell next week. That crazy fool that killed five people. VJ's not going to be doing much else for a long time."

I contemplated my pasty brother with a great deal of dissatisfaction. He and our Mutual Mother were two of the laziest white people on the planet. I didn't get it. Weren't white people supposed to be all Puritan work ethic? But no, Pop used to say slavery came back when he married Mother. And it was true. Mother had been perfectly happy to grind my poor father to death, keeping her in bodacious baubles and Botox. Well, actually Mother had only been Pop's second wife. His third wife should probably get credit for actually finishing him off. But still—

"Bosco," I said, trying another tack. "You know I'm running low on funds here. It's hard to be an independent. I work out of my house, how lame is that? And it's not getting any better. We may have to start considering cutting back on some luxuries."

Bosco cocked a skeptical eyebrow. "Luxuries?"

"Yeah," I said, momentarily flailing to think of something we had that resembled a luxury. Then it hit me. "Like—like—cable! We may have to drop cable."

Bosco started to look perturbed. Mother had recently given us a high-def television—and don't go thinking she did it out of the goodness of her heart, because you would be making the mistake Bosco keeps making, which is thinking she has a heart. But I still had to pay the cable bill.

"Well, look, I'm sure as shit not sneaking in there with a video camera, but maybe I could think of something," he admitted. I waited. Bosco closed his eyes and turned his head, giving me the precious profile.

"Okay," he said, opening his eyes. "What you did wrong was try to hide the video camera."

"Oh, really," I replied. "I was supposed to walk right in and announce to Mindy that I had a little business to take care of, and I'm sure she wouldn't mind if I took some film of one of their clients, 'cause he's a workers' comp cheat, and I'm an insurance adjustor working for his employer, and I have no doubt that Work Out World would want to help me out? Is that what you plan to do?"

"No," Bosco waved airily, "I'm going to tell them that I'm Dante Wildman, nationally celebrated photographer, and that I want to take a few preliminary video clips because I'm thinking of a series set inside a gym. That particular gym."

"Dante Wildman? Isn't he the guy who does those shots of Dalmatian dogs, set in weird backgrounds?"

"Exactly. His dog's name is Sparky. He gets these art shots of Sparky next to a sunflower or waiting in front of a school. All in black and white, you know what I'm talking about. Guy makes millions with his coffee table books, calendars, greeting cards."

"They're nauseatingly cute."

"He's huge."

"He doesn't do gyms, he does places that have a sickeningly charming ambience."

"He's going in a new direction. Trust me," Bosco said. "It'll be perfect."

I wouldn't call it perfect, but I did call it good enough. I sat down to write the interim report when the phone rang.

"Fifi Cutter Adjusting."

"Hello, Ms. Cutter, this is Reg Wong."

"Oh hello, Mr. Wong. I just this minute got back from my surveillance of Mr. Burton. I think I got some great footage."

Reg Wong's voice was deep and resonant, which probably kept the jurors in the back row awake but was less pleasant over the phone.

"Good," Wong cooed. "I want to catch that little cheat."

"I understand."

"Can you bring the tape over to the office tomorrow? Around three?"

"Tomorrow?" I squeaked. "I was thinking of sometime

next week. I think I could really nail him if I had a little more time."

"That's great, but I'd like to see what you've got so far. I won't have time to look at anything next week. I'm extremely busy right now. You know the Skyblu case is going to trial next week. I assume Victoria told you about it?"

"Yeah, a little bit." A charter airplane carrying two Chinese businessmen had crashed three-quarters of an hour after takeoff from Van Nuys. Investigation afterward showed the pilot had been shot. The pilot, copilot, both businessmen, and the mentally unstable disgruntled Skyblu ex-employee—who had snuck on board and presumably effectuated the shooting of the pilot—were all dead. Wong represented the families of the dead passengers, but VJ's firm had picked up a client too, the widow of a guy who was sitting at home, having a beer in his Winnebago when he got smooshed by the main fuselage, a wing, and the better part of the left engine.

Crazy fool kills five.

"It could be the case I retire on," Wong said. "We have two defendants with lots of insurance. Skyblu, the charter company, and Grund Aviation Technologies, for not putting a locking door from the cabin into the cockpit."

"Locking cockpit door? I didn't know they put those in private jets."

I'd apparently touched on a sore spot as Wong was testy in his response. "They don't. But they should. That's our point. They should. If they had a locking door, the perpetrator could maybe have gotten onto the plane, but he couldn't shoot the pilot."

"But if the locked cockpit door stopped him from shooting the pilot, couldn't he have still shot your Chinese businessmen? I can see your case against Skyblu for letting the guy on the plane, but your case against Grund seems weak." Silence at the other end told me I had put my dainty size fives right in my mouth. I tried to make amends.

"What am I saying here? Why would he shoot the Chinese businessmen? It was Skyblu he was mad at. Right? Of course he wouldn't shoot the Chinese businessmen. That would have just been insane." More silence. "Well, then. I guess I'll see you at three tomorrow."

Wong disconnected.

I must have had a tact lobotomy sometime in my teens. I would make it up to him by preparing a detailed report. I watched the tape, noted the salient features, documented time and place, and made a copy of the report and tape for my file before turning to the latest home improvement project: painting what I still optimistically call the guest bathroom, although I haven't had a guest since Bosco moved in last October. Unless you count the members of his harem, who occasionally spend the night and greet me cheerfully when I walk into the kitchen for my morning coffee. Which I don't.

By 8:37, my curly, wispy, loam-brown hair was streaked with latex semigloss the color of pale butterscotch. I jumped into the shower, half wishing that Pop had left the damn house to someone else. But not really.

Chapter Three

The office of Wong, Wu & Chu was located on the top floor of a modest office building, Chinatown adjacent, with not quite enough parking. I arrived at 2:54 Wednesday afternoon. After circling the underground parking twice, I stuck the Volvo in the farthest handicap spot, consoling myself with the fact that there were still three empty handicap spots, and the chances of four seriously handicapped people all driving in and needing to park in the brief time I was there were very small.

The elevator opened directly into the cramped waiting room. Three low chairs wrestled for space with a two-person sofa. The walls were dotted with oriental florals, and frequently-handled Chinese language magazines crowded the blocky red coffee table. The receptionist, a pudgy Asian woman, looked up and smiled.

"You want to see Mr. Wong?" she said in a heavy Chinese accent. "You supposed to tail Stevie Ray?"

I nodded, not too happy to find out my super-secret mission was common knowledge. I guess I should have expected it. It wasn't a big office, probably fifteen lawyers total and maybe twenty staff employees. One of those employees might still be on good terms with Burton and might tip him off. I needed to keep the gossip mill from screwing everything up until after next Tuesday, when we would have all we needed.

"MR. WONG, LADY WHO TAIL MR. BURTON HERE."

A deep voice I recognized as Reg Wong's came from the first office on the left. "Send her in, Judy."

Judy waved me through and I found myself in a large, neat office, furnished in office-set bland.

Reg Wong was sitting behind the desk, a thin man, approaching seventy with energy undiminished. He was of medium height, with high cheekbones and thick, iron-grey hair, cut very short. He rose as I entered.

"Thank you for coming in to see me, Ms. Cutter, and accommodating our trial schedule." He shook my hand. "Did you get him?"

"I think so," I waffled. "A few good views of him bringing groceries into the house, that type of thing. He certainly isn't as injured as his doctor claims."

Wong frowned. "That son of a bitch isn't injured at all. I was there when he lifted that box, he was fine. He didn't say anything, he just lifted it. He's a scammer."

"Well, you can give this to your comp carrier, and it should help at the hearing," I said handing over the packet. "You can keep the tape. I have a copy. And I may be able to get some additional footage next week. I have a tip that he works out on Tuesday mornings at the gym." The great thing about dusky skin is the almost total inability to blush.

"Sounds good." Wong stuck the tape into a VCR player in the corner of the office. "Let's see what we have here." A clear shot of Burton emerging from his apartment with a backpack slung over his shoulder appeared on the screen. Wong shook his head. "You know, he worked here for two years. He was basically a good guy. He was a good document clerk, and he worked hard. Worked on this Skyblu case, as a matter of fact, and we could sure use him now. I don't know what happened to make him try some cheap workers' comp swindle." He turned and gave me the benefit of his serious-matters frown. "Personally, I think it was his new girlfriend. She's a hostess at The Back Room."

The Back Room. The nightspot of the moment. A dark, semi-scary place where the nouveau hip of Hollywood could go to drink too much, spend too much, and show way too much skin while rubbing shoulders with A-list celebrities and those on lists farther down the alphabet who made up for their lack of status by behaving even more outrageously. The hostesses were part of the draw, edgy Lonelygirl15 types.

"Thinks she's the bomb?"

"Yes she does. I'm guessing all of this was probably her idea. She came here a few times to pick him up from work. Nadia, that was her name. She struck me as a bad influence."

"Maybe I could get some footage at The Back Room?" I suggested. I deeply deplored the superficiality of people who paid fifty-dollar cover charges and scarfed down drinks that were priced so high that if you had to ask, you couldn't afford them. But if I could go at a client's expense...

"No way." Wong scoffed. "They'd never let you in. You have to be somebody."

I reminded myself that I was already on thin ice with Wong, allowed myself to overlook the obvious implication, and politely departed.

As I walked into the waiting room, a young Chinese woman brushed past me on her way into Wong's office. I caught an impression of tall and willowy. The faint fragrance of sandalwood and citrus lingered in her wake.

I turned back to find Judy the receptionist on her feet, her hands on her sturdy hips. "Ms. Fang, I have to announce you. Please." The door to Wong's office slammed shut.

I gave a sympathetic glance. "Who was that?"

The receptionist sighed. "That was Violet Fang. She's a client. She always does that. And he lets her. I know it's a big case, but still—"

"The Skyblu case?"

"Yes. Her father was on the plane. I should feel sorry for her. But Ms. Fang so bossy. She American girl." Sitting back down and straightening her desk, the stout sentinel confided. "Ms. Fang come here all the time. She want to sit through the whole trial. Fine for her. Not like she has a real job." The phone rang, reminding Judy of her own real job. I waggled my fingers goodbye.

* * *

When I got home, I found that Bosco had conned one of his many girlfriends into taking him shopping. He had, it seemed, bought one of every Dante Wildman product on the market and was chortling over his cache at the kitchen table, his leggy blond chauffeur/financier standing uncertainly beside him.

"Hi, Bosco. Hello, Alexandra." I nodded politely to the blonde.

Bosco looked up. "This is Lindsey."

"Hello, Lindsey," I amended.

She turned to Bosco. "Who's Alexandra?"

We ignored her. I picked up one of the bags and pulled out a full-color wall calendar. It was marked half-price (after all, we were half-way through April) and I saw, as I riffled through it, the clownish face of Sparky, the Dalmatian, posed in holiday-of-the-month-themed locations. In front of a Ferris wheel by the beach, pretend-driving a mail truck in the snow, nose to nose with a caged turkey. Like that.

There were also note cards, glossy, with thick, cream envelopes. Must have set Lindsey back more than she expected, I thought. But they would come in handy in case anyone we knew was sick, had a baby, got married, or graduated from high school.

Not to mention a set of four coffee mugs and Dalmatian-spotted paper napkins and party plates.

I started to feel bad for poor Lindsey.

"And I've read up on him, too," Bosco announced. "Got his start right here in Los Angeles. West-side guy."

"A West-side guy? Really? I would have never guessed." I displayed a photo of Dante, complete with fedora, soul patch, and sunglasses.

"That's right," Bosco beamed, oblivious to sarcasm. "This is going to be a piece of cake."

"What exactly are you going to do with all this stuff?" Lindsey asked.

We continued to ignore her. Really. It was kinder that way.

Chapter Four

Thursday I spent interviewing witnesses to a red light/green light smash-up in West Hollywood. Two of the witnesses said the Toyota had the green light, two said the Ford had the green light, and the Nicaraguan nanny out on a stroll with her charge told me to give her $200 and she'd say whatever I wanted.

Friday afternoon found me sitting in my office, a room that had been the dark-paneled dining room of the old Craftsman house. My PC was balanced on a card table and my files were laid out in an intricate filing system over the hardwood floor. When my father had left me the house, it had been full of beautiful furniture, rugs, collectibles, lamps—all the usual stuff. But Mother, a.k.a. the second Mrs. Cutter, and her replacement, Mrs. Cutter the Third, sued each other and spent a ferocious eleven months litigating who got what. At the end of it all, Mother and stepmother split up everything the lawyers didn't sell to pay their fees, and I got nothing. I sleep on a pool raft. Bosco has the futon.

The message light of the phone was already blinking when I sat down.

"Hello Fifi, this is Carlotta Anelli at Colchester Casualty. Jack told me you're doing freelance? I have a job for you if you would give me a call."

I took the number down, speculating as I dialed, why Carlotta would be giving me a job. Carlotta hated me.

"Hello, Carlotta, Fifi here. I got your message."

"Hello Fifi, how are you doing? Long time no see. I was so happy when Jack told me you had this little home business set up."

Jack was my old boss at Colchester Casualty. He was a company man who didn't stick up for me when the pink slip landed on my desk. I yelled at him for that, but he shook his head and said, "Wouldn't have done any good." On the other hand, Jack was the one who made my "little home business" possible by sending me freelance assignments, which, as he pointed out, actually did do me some good.

"I'm doing fine, Carlotta."

"I am so happy to hear that, Fifi. When you were fired, I felt so bad. I mean, I heard you got your car repossessed and everything. I pictured you wandering around, homeless, and hungry." She chuckled merrily.

"Nope," I replied, gritting my teeth, "As I said, I'm doing fine. I take it you have a job for me?"

"I do," Carlotta's musical tone put me on guard. I could just see her—short and chubby and overly made up—smirking into the phone. "It's in your neighborhood, too. In Eagle Rock. A simple rear-ender, but they're claiming total loss. Bent frame. Need you to go take a look and get some photos before we total it out." She gave me the address and faxed over the loss report.

I glanced at the clock. It was 2:05. I decided I might as well check it out. It wasn't like I had to do anything else.

In fact, this was way too easy, I thought as I carefully edged the Volvo out into traffic. The repair shop was only about fifteen minutes away and I found it with no trouble and parked in the front lot.

I spied the car, a 1999 Cadillac El Dorado Coupe, sitting around the side. I went into the office to introduce myself, but no one was there. I stuck my head into the bay and spoke to the pair of legs sticking out from under a Lexus.

"Pardon me. I'm Fifi Cutter, adjusting this claim for

Colchester. Here's my card. OK if I have a look at the Cadillac outside?"

The legs slid out to reveal a tall muscular man of about thirty-five. He stood up and walked over, looking me up and down. He gave me a superior little smile, to let me know that he knew that I noticed how handsome he was. I gave him a smile to let him know that I thought he needed dental work, but I don't think I conveyed my message.

"Wade Brockett," he said. "My friends call me Wade Rockhard."

"Oh, I doubt that." I ignored his outstretched hand. "Can I go look at the car?"

"Sure, you can look at my car. You can look at my shop. You can look at my tools. You can look at anything you want." This lame double entendre was accompanied by a grin that reinforced my opinion regarding his immediate need for a full set of porcelain veneers.

Of course, I now understood what possessed Carlotta to land me with this gig. But if she thought I couldn't handle old Rockhead, she would find out how wrong she was. It's not like I hadn't put up with jerks before. I have an advanced degree in putting up with jerks.

"Colchester wants me to document the owner's claim of frame damage," I informed Wade as we walked outside to where the Caddy was parked. "Did you have it up on the lift?"

"Sure did, darlin'. It's totaled all right. Bad frame damage. See that here?" He pointed to the left wheel, which was not connected to the car in any way the manufacturer had intended. "Shows you right there."

No, I thought to myself, that just shows me you took the wheel off. As I bent down to look, I felt Wade's hand pass firmly across my ass. I jumped up, whirled, and glared. Wade looked at me blankly, pretending nothing had happened.

"See that right there," he pointed at the dented bumper.

"Impact from the back caused the frame to buckle. Nothin' you can do about it. Cost more to fix than the car's worth. Just total it out. I'll buy it from the company," he offered. "I can use the parts. Although," he leered, "I already got pretty good parts myself."

"I need pictures. Actual photos," I said, wondering how to get the shots I needed without bending down again. Wade moved closer. As he cast his shadow over me, I realized that there was no foot traffic on this stretch of the road and the high chain link fence at my back surrounded an unoccupied junkyard. It appeared no one else was working at the repair shop.

I tried not to step back, but his breath was onion-y and his shirt was on Week Two of not being washed. I stepped back. He advanced until the mesh of the fence imprinted on my sweat shirt.

"I got something you'll like, sweetheart. Right here in my pants." Wade leaned in and placed his hand against the fence over my head. He tried to stare into my eyes. I looked down to see if I could knee him in the crotch, wishing I had paid more attention to Mindy's moves at the gym.

He stuck his hand into his back pocket and pulled out a thick white envelope. "Here you go, Fifi. I took a bunch of shots when I had it up."

He handed me the packet and I pulled out the pictures. Just glancing at the top two, I could see they were taken with a cheap camera, but were well lit, sharply focused, and showed the bent frame with clarity.

I slid out from under his arm and scooted over to the Volvo.

"Hey, where's my thank you?" Wade called.

"I don't know," I yelled over my shoulder. "Maybe you can find it if you bend over."

I arrived home, badly in need of a large drink and a little sympathy. But when I related the story to Bosco, all he said was, "So the guy thought you were hot. You should be flattered."

"He did not think I was hot, you idiot. If he'd really thought I was hot he would never have had the stones to talk to me like that."

"Cut him some slack. He was just trying to flirt with you. Some guys aren't very smooth. You should try to be more friendly. Maybe you'd get a date."

Seeing I wasn't going to get any sympathy, I dropped the subject. But I put a little "IOU" for Wade into my mental filing cabinet, as Bosco followed me into the kitchen.

I grabbed a Taj Mahal out of the refrigerator and handed one to Bosco. "I wonder how VJ made out in court today?"

* * *

"You wouldn't believe what happened in court today," VJ's voice came over the phone. I checked the time. It was 10:46, and I'd downed two-and-a-half beers. "We spent all day arguing motions and then, at four-thirty, when we were just getting ready to wrap it up and go home, Judge Stein starts yelling at us. 'I don't care what you say,' as if that were not already perfectly obvious, 'I'm not going to try this case for two weeks without sending you to a settlement conference.' He meant right then. At four-thirty in the afternoon. I believe the man drinks."

"Well, it would be good to settle the case, wouldn't it?"

"Of course it would be good, but the case wasn't going to settle. Judge Stein made me call up my client and she had to drive all the way down from Oxnard. She moved there after the accident, and it's a terrible drive in traffic."

"What about the defendants? What about Wong's clients?"

"Daniel Boatwright, Skyblu's lawyer, had Mr. Czypiesky, the president of Skyblu, there and Jan Porter—she represents

Grund—was able to get Mr. Grund there too. The insurance people were already there. Apparently they're going to sit through the whole trial."

"Did you settle?"

"We didn't even come close. Judge Stein sent us down to Judge Newman, who agreed to stay late and tried her best. But we stayed there until after nine o'clock and made no headway at all. Mr. Czypiesky and Mr. Grund would rather prance around West Hollywood naked in G-strings than admit they did anything wrong."

I laughed. "Yeah, but it's not up to them, is it? The insurance adjustors decide whether or not to settle."

"They aren't any more reasonable. Walton Yarborough, big bald guy, was there for Brunswick Insurance, Skyblu's insurance carrier. He looks like Mr. Clean's accountant. And Cissie McMull, who was there for Grund's insurance carrier, stood around all day making lame jokes and fiddling with her Blackberry. A right wanker."

"Who does she work for?"

"Get this: it's a consortium of various insurance carriers called Insurance Coverage for Aviation Risks U.S."

I worked it out. "ICARUS? You're kidding me?"

"Totally serious. It's just too precious. But Cissie was hard as nails when it came to negotiating, in a latter-day-cheerleader-from-a-lower-income-school kind of way. Although I can't blame the defendants entirely for the failure to settle. Reg Wong announced that his clients won't take less than sixty million. So there we were. Skyblu won't offer anything unless Grund offers at least half. Grund will never offer anything approaching half. Neither will even talk settlement with me unless they can settle with Reg. Reg's clients won't take less than sixty million, and Reg has decided that we won't settle with one defendant without the other, anyway."

"What did you ask for?"

"I started the bidding at three million, signaling clearly

that I would take one point five. Very fair, but they wouldn't even listen."

"So what happens now?"

"What else can happen? The case is going to trial."

"That's not all bad, though, is it? I mean, this could be your big chance. If you win this case, they may even make you a partner."

"Sure, if Reg Wong allowed me to do anything other than carry his briefcase. He's treating me like his personal servant. They never replaced Burton, you know. Now I'm getting stuck doing all the drudge work. I've told Reg he had to hire another document clerk, but he can't find anyone."

"What about me?" My heart rose at the thought of making some extra money.

"What do you mean, what about you?"

"You know how I used to help Pop with trial work, when I was in high school. I know what a document clerk does."

"Gee, thanks, but no, I don't think so. What about Bosco?"

"What do you mean, what about Bosco?"

"I mean..."

"Okay, I know what you meant. But Bosco doesn't know anything about trial preparation. He doesn't know anything about any real job. I could do it. Come on, VJ."

"Uh, well, I think maybe this is beneath you, Fifi."

"Beneath me? VJ, I'm trying to hold onto this house and support my worthless brother. Dancing on a street corner dressed up as a hot dog with a sandwich board around my neck isn't beneath me."

"Yeah well, it's just that you can be kind of, well, abrasive."

I swallowed the retort that sprang to my lips. It was a little abrasive. "I'm not abrasive, VJ. I'm candid. And you recommended me to Wong for the surveillance job."

"That's different. You don't have to actually interact with anyone when you're on surveillance."

"I interact with Reg Wong just fine."

"It's only going to be like twenty bucks an hour." She was weakening, I could tell.

"Twenty bucks an hour is great."

"But it's only temporary work, so there's no benefits."

"That's perfect. I only want temporary work, just while Cutter Adjusting Services is having a short-term setback."

"If I know Reg Wong, he won't pay for parking or anything."

"Mighty white of him," I replied. "Come on. Tell him to hire me."

"Promise me you won't piss him off, Fifi. You have to promise me that."

"I promise I won't piss him off."

VJ was silent for fifteen seconds while I held my breath. "Okay. I'll put in the word. But you'll have to start on Saturday. I'm afraid there will be lots of weekends on this case."

I closed my eyes. VJ knew how much I hated to work on the weekend, so I had to concentrate on keeping my tone just right. I didn't want to sound put out, but I didn't want to sound too suck-butty either, she'd only take it as sarcasm.

"Alrighty then. Excellent. That's a go for Saturday."

"Stop being so sarcastic. Be at Wong's office by nine-thirty. I'll see to it that they have a conference room set up for your use, and that Judy, the receptionist, will be there to let you in. Norman Chu will be there as well. He's the junior partner."

"Great."

"Oh, and by the way, Mum and Dad are coming back from London on Tuesday. I'll need the Volvo back."

"Great," I said, with all the sarcasm hanging out.

Chapter Five

I arrived at the office at 9:34 on Saturday morning, late. I left home extra early, but you can't control the traffic. An accident had blocked Figueroa and I couldn't get on the freeway, so I had to take surface streets—which were jammed from people trying to avoid the accident. I was in a terrible mood.

Judy showed me to the conference room, a few doors down the hall from Wong's office. It was windowless and the walls were grimy, but the table was large. My mood lightened when I saw there was a pot of fresh coffee on the battered credenza. Judy became my new best friend.

As I poured myself a cup, Norman Chu arrived. We eyed each other politely. He was, I decided, the most serious-looking guy on the West Coast. He could have been a funeral director from Minneapolis, he was so serious. Except that, other than his formal demeanor, he looked about twelve, painfully thin, with an abnormally big forehead. I glanced at his left hand. Married. Not that I was interested, believe me. It was just a reflex.

"It's good to have you on the team, Ms. Cutter," he said.

"Fifi," I smiled. He stared as if he didn't know what language I was speaking. "Call me Fifi." I clarified. The stare ended in an embarrassed blink. "Really, Norman, it's my name. You can call me Fifi."

"OK," he said, but I knew he wouldn't. All I had done was create a situation where he couldn't call me Ms. Cutter, and he wouldn't bring himself to call me Fifi. He'd end up never addressing me directly.

"Let me summarize the known evidence for you," he said. "You know what this case is about, don't you? Generally? A fixed wing aircraft—"

"You mean a plane?"

"A private charter jet. A Cessna, modified by Grund Aviation Technologies. It went down in Tulare County. Owned and operated by Skyblu Aviation. Our clients, Mr. Fang and Mr. Han, were very successful businessmen based in Singapore. They were on their way to view underdeveloped land in the outer part of the county. The other plaintiff— uh—your friend's client," he paused, and I wondered if VJ had committed the mistake of asking him to call her Victoria. "Her husband was unfortunately at home in their trailer that day. The plane, or rather parts of the plane, flattened the trailer. There was almost nothing left of it." Norman's face became, if anything, more severe. "The cause of the crash is almost certainly the actions of an ex-employee, who snuck onto the plane and shot the pilot. Guy named Jim Farnswell."

I gave the expected headshake. It was one of those inexplicable murder-suicides. Don't these dumb fucks ever think how awkward it's going to be when they arrive at the Pearly Gates at the exact same time as the fifteen other people they just killed? With all those folks standing right there, how do they think they're gonna talk their way in?

Chu continued. "It will be our position at trial that liability lies with both defendants. The only question is who is more at fault, Grund for not having locking cabin doors on a plane refurbished for charter use, or Skyblu, the charter service, for not realizing this man was a threat to air safety when they employed him, gave him access to the premises, and then permitted him clandestine entrance to the aircraft."

I marveled at the phrase "clandestine entrance."

"And, of course," he cleared his throat, "the question of how much it's worth."

"Sounds simple. And," I recalled my previous faux pas when talking to Wong, "you guys win either way. I mean it wasn't the passengers' fault and it sure wasn't the fault of that poor bastard microwaving a hot dog in his double-wide when the sky fell in."

Chu almost smiled, and I caught a gleam in his eye. "It's our strategy in this matter to induce the defendants to point the finger at each other. The claims of liability will be even more credible when repeated by the defendants themselves."

I nodded. "All you have to do is parade the grief-stricken widows and children, pump up the hard numbers, and pocket the money at the end of the day. How much are you going to be asking for?"

"A total of sixty million. It's mostly a matter of selling our lost-earnings claims. We have highly significant loss of earnings. Of course, Ms. Porter for Grund and Mr. Boatwright for Skyblu are arguing the claims are speculative. We have a very good expert. They're trying to exclude his testimony." He leaned forward and his voice became even more earnest. "It's because they don't understand the Chinese markets. Cash flow here translates into profits there."

"Big numbers," I commented.

He shrugged. "Your friend won't be able to sustain comparable figures on the part of her client. Her client's husband didn't really have a significant amount of taxable income."

I was momentarily saddened. Why should Earl Dean Rayburn, who liked to drink his beer out of a can, eat beef on a bun, and play penny-ante gin rummy, be worth less than Wong's clients, who liked to drink appletinis, eat beef only if it came from Kobe, and play the world markets?

I started to haul the cartons onto the table. "These are the documents produced by Skyblu?"

"Yes. To be precise, these are the documents they tried to hide and produced late. We had to bring a motion to compel them to comply with their discovery obligations. The judge granted our motion and we just got these a few weeks ago. No one has had time to review them yet."

I flipped up the box tops and peered in. There were seven boxes; each seemed pretty full. "I think I can get through them all today, and if not, then by tomorrow. I'll do an index and flag anything of particular importance, okay?"

"I would appreciate that very much." He stood. "I will be down the hall. I've been tasked with preparing the opposition to the motion to exclude our expert. You can come down if you need me, or just dial 3447 on that phone."

I glanced over at him. "Can I ask one thing? Your case is so good, seems like you could have settled out before trial."

Chu blinked. "You'd think so, but unfortunately the defendants seem to be intractable. Neither Grund nor Skyblu want to admit that they have made mistakes. Mistakes that cost five lives."

"Six, if you count the crazy guy."

"I don't count him." Chu sketched a slight bow and withdrew, closing the door behind him.

Sighing, I turned to the task. The boxes weren't numbered and the documents didn't seem to be in any order. I selected the nearest box and started in. After about fifteen minutes of puzzling over what I was seeing, I realized that I was looking at Skyblu's financial information. The company was doing well, but the four jets had been heavily mortgaged and business had dropped off considerably after the crash. Well, duh, I thought. It was a good thing they had insurance. Curious, I pawed through to see if a copy of the policy was included. It wasn't, but a letter from the bank referenced the limits. My eyes widened. A hundred million dollars. Nice.

If Wong convinced the judge to let his expert testify, and the jury bought it, there would be enough insurance money to pay a verdict of sixty million dollars. Okay, this was a big, important case.

Two-and-a-half hours later, I had a headache. The room had become uncomfortably warm. The coffee was gone. I had to pee. I opened the door and stuck my head out. I could hear Chu in his office down the hall. He had one of those programs that allowed him to dictate into his word processor. "Dragon Naturally Speaking." Very cool.

Or was he talking to somebody? I decided not to disturb him, and went on a bathroom safari. I eventually found not only the bathroom, but also a vending machine and the office first-aid kit, from which I extracted two aspirin. I was good to go.

Three hours and forty-five minutes later, I had to pee again, I had a headache again, and the room had become uncomfortably cold. I decided to take the last box home with me and finish my review tomorrow. A person could only take so much, and I could just as easily review whatever the box contained in the comfort of my own dining room, at my card table/desk.

I walked down to Chu's office, but he'd already left. I noticed the light under the door of the office next to his, but there was no name plate. I hesitated, and gave a tiny knock.

"Who is it?" An unknown male voice, slightly accented, more than slightly hostile.

"I just wanted to tell someone I was leaving, and taking one of the boxes with me," I called.

"Who are you?" The voice asked, but meant "Who the hell are you."

Talking through the door was awkward. "Fifi Cutter. I'm the new document clerk. Working on the Skyblu case."

The silence lengthened. "What are you taking home?"

"Just the last box of Skyblu documents that I didn't get a chance to review." We were now beyond awkward. "It's mostly financial information so far, and plane maintenance records, which are pretty irrelevant."

"Then what do I care?"

"Can't answer that. Thank you, door, have a good evening, and give my best to the window." I hoisted the box on my hip and turned to leave.

* * *

I came into the kitchen Sunday morning, still drowsy as I had worked late going through the documents in the last box. I was startled to see Bosco, dressed in a black silk shirt and a fedora. I was even more surprised to see a large, painfully thin, white dog at his side.

"What the hell are you doing? Why are you awake? It's only 9:43. Why are you dressed like that? And get that thing out of here. I am not living with a dog."

"Relax, I'm getting into my role. I'm up at this hour because I had to pick up the dog, but I'm just borrowing him. He's my prop. He's a Dalmatian." Bosco slipped the drooling monster a crust of toast

"That's not a Dalmatian, bonehead."

"I couldn't get anyone to loan me their Dalmatian. Sketch here is half Dalmatian."

I looked closer and discerned six or seven small dots on the animal's back and legs. "Yeah, well, whatever it is, it's starving to death."

"No, the other half is greyhound, that's why you can see his ribs. But look at his legs," Bosco proudly displayed the dog's long, muscular limbs.

"You don't actually need a dog to get into the gym, Bosco. You tell them you're just scouring locations. I don't want a dog, and if I did want a dog, I wouldn't want that dog. I'd want a cute dog. Give it back to whoever you borrowed it from."

"No can do. At least not yet. See, I didn't exactly borrow him. I'm babysitting him while the owners are on vacation. Just for a few weeks." Seeing my expression, he hastened to add, "Hey, it's $200. I'll give you half."

"Oh, gee, thanks, that'll really help. Do you realize that as of Tuesday, we're going to be carless again? Do you think you can find a car to babysit?"

"I'll get right on it, sis," replied Bosco, ignoring my tone. "And next time you're at the store, better get some dog food."

I headed for the living room, ready to pick up where I had left off on the Skyblu documents. I opened the door and lost my breath. Someone had ransacked my dining room office.

I fell to my knees, frantically gathering up the papers that were strewn among the office impedimenta on the floor—pens, paper clips, my stapler. Some files had been flung aside untouched, but some had been shredded. Shredded. As I scrambled around, I jammed my knee on a broken bit of something plastic. I yelped in pain, jerked back and landed on a chewed-up sneaker.

I removed the item from my backside and stopped.

A chewed-up sneaker.

Not that many burglars stop what they're doing to chew up a sneaker.

"Bosco!" I drew breath to bellow again when he appeared at the doorway, holding Sketch by the collar. "That dog—" I pointed, "That dog—!"

Bosco took advantage of my inarticulate fury to begin picking things up, wincing as a leaky pen dripped ink on the hardwood floor.

"I'll help you get this stuff up," he said, sweeping detritus into a pile.

"Can you tell which papers go into which file?"

"No," Bosco admitted.

"Then you can't help. Unless you get that dog out of here, that would help." I batted at Sketch, who had found a cassette tape of a witness interview on one of my red light/green light cases. He was munching with gusto. I pulled what was left of it out of his mouth, hoping it had already been transcribed.

The Skyblu documents hadn't been disturbed, beyond a few slobber splats on the first sheets. I lifted up the pages and began carefully wiping them off. My eyes focused on the words.

"Bosco, I think I found something."

Chapter Six

VJ phoned at 6:42 Monday morning. I was up. Sketch had come into my room during the night and curled up next to me on the pool raft. I snuggled against his warmth and he licked me gently on the ear. Eventually, he'd noodged me off the raft onto the floor. By 5:15 he had also taken the covers.

"Good morning, Fifi. Just wanted to know if you came up with anything?"

I cleared my throat. "Just one thing I thought was pretty interesting. Skyblu produced a copy of the employee telephone tree. You know, companies put together phone lists, in case of emergencies?"

"Yes, Fifi, I know what a telephone tree is. Well, we did ask for all employee records, and I guess that a telephone tree is an employee record. So why is a telephone tree important?"

"It has numbers for all the employees, plus the numbers of emergency contacts. Farnswell doesn't have an emergency contact listed, but next to his name and number is the word "grandmother" in parentheses. Like she didn't have a different telephone number. You see?"

"No, not really."

"Okay, look. Other people have the name of their spouses in parentheses."

"That means what?"

"I'm guessing it means Farnswell lived with his grand-mother."

"Lived with her? That could be very important, Fifi." VJ paused. "God, if he actually lived with her, she would know all about his mental condition. If Farnswell was acting out or off his meds, she would know."

"Exactly," I replied.

"All the Skyblu employees are company tools who are saying that Farnswell was acting just as normal as could be until the day he was fired. The Skyblu story is that Farnswell was fired because business was bad, not because he was bonkers. They all say they had no way to know he was mentally unstable.

"But if the grandmother could testify that he had a history of being a nut ball, or even just that he was acting strangely around the time he died, the jury could infer that he must have been acting weirdly at work too. And they could find that Skyblu should have known he was a security risk. And if they should have known, they would be liable."

"I'm liking the sound of that, VJ."

"We need to talk this over with Reg, and I could use you to take notes while we're picking the jury, anyway. Meet us at the courthouse."

* * *

I parked at the new cathedral and walked over to the courthouse, getting through security with only a modicum of problems. I wore a navy suit and kept the jewelry light, but my low-heeled pumps set off the metal detector. I was duly wanded, allowed in, and finally found the courtroom, up several flights of escalator on the seventh floor.

I slipped into the courtroom as the judge was barking out, "State your appearances. Let's get started. We're already late and I have a lunch appointment." VJ waved me over to sit right behind her.

At the left-side table, away from the jury, a tallish, thinnish guy pushed himself leisurely out of his chair. "Daniel Carter Boatwright for Skyblu Aviation, your honor, here with my client, Mr. Paul Czypiesky, president of Skyblu Charter Flights." Boatwright had a honeydew Southern accent, and from my rear perspective, looked altogether fine. His client had a less prepossessing appearance: sloppy, big and hunched over in defensive mode.

Next to him, a statuesque woman in a dark wool suit rose. Her hair was swept into an elegant French twist and she tossed the end of a silk scarf over one shoulder. "Janet Porter for Grund Aviation Technologies, with my client, Herbert Grund." Herbert Grund was a small man, with a military haircut and unfashionable glasses that glinted as he briefly turned to survey the courtroom.

"Victoria Jane Smith, here with my client, the widow of the deceased Earl Dean Rayburn, Mrs. Ruth Rayburn." Victoria's accent was at its very British best, emphasizing the momentousness of the occasion.

Elegant in his silver-grey suit, precisely matching the color of his hair, Reg Wong stood and paused a moment, establishing his presence. "Reginald Wong, of Wong, Wu & Chu for the heirs of George Han and Bobby Fang." They had made a strategic decision to use the "American" names of the decedents. "Representing the family of the victims here today is Violet Fang." I recognized the young Asian woman sitting next to him. She briefly ducked her head. Her black hair hung to her elbows. "Ms. Fang's mother is also here, as is the family of Mr. Han." Wong turned to gesture.

I glanced over the aisle and saw two older Chinese women, one still very beautiful, the other not so much.

VJ looked great in a midnight blue suit; she had to be six foot one in heels. The judge pointed at her and gave a head nod. Show time.

"Call the panel in," Judge Stein ordered his clerk, an

unjovial fat woman who moved to comply with greater speed than I had thought possible.

A mere six hours later, the jury was picked.

Juror Number One was a stocky plumber from Culver City. I liked him; he was blue collar. He'd relate to VJ's client, Mrs. Rayburn, I thought. I had met her over the lunch break. Ruth Rayburn was a nice-looking, no-nonsense, salt-of-the-earth woman in her late fifties.

Juror Two was a hard-eyed Asian woman and an accountant, to boot. Reg Wong wanted her, to ensure that no one in the jury room would feel free to let loose with their assorted ethnic prejudices against his clients, but she wouldn't help VJ. Asian women and accountants were notoriously tight-fisted.

Jurors Three, Five, and Six were of a kind—women over sixty, well—if unflatteringly—dressed. Over-sprayed hair, chunky jewelry, and pantsuits in primary colors. The "Golden Girls," I dubbed them. I could already tell they would be a voting block. What Juror Number Five thought, they would all think.

Juror Four was a middle-aged Hispanic man with thick spectacles.

Number Seven was a Bible carrier. Quite literally. Wong voiced serious reservations about her, but VJ finally got to override him. Seven looked up from her Bible on more than one occasion during the proceedings to beam kindly at Mrs. Rayburn.

But Number Eight was the primary hope—a sixty-ish organic farmer with a ponytail. A ponytail! Under questioning on voir dire, Eight admitted to reading The Nation and watching The Daily Show With Jon Stewart. Why had the defense lawyers left him on? VJ was busy concentrating, but I was watching Dan Boatwright and I saw him start to speak, no doubt to "thank and excuse" Old Hippie Dude. But Janet Porter, the defense counsel for Grund Aviation, bent toward him and stopped him. They argued fiercely, his mouth a thin line, her beady eyes blazing. She won, and Eight was left on.

Number Nine was an African American woman. While VJ would never rely on the sisterhood, I figured it couldn't hurt.

Number Ten was a ditzy-looking white girl, a blond in every possible way. She would be a non-factor.

Number Eleven was Engineer Guy.

Juror Number Twelve was the wild card. He was a handsome man, pierced eyebrow, fitted shirt, and Italian shoes. He could be a free-thinking liberal. Or he could be a free-market libertarian, the worst possible juror in a product liability case. But the alternates, next in line, were abysmal—an older man who kept carping that "government regulation was out of hand" and a bitter-faced woman who, when asked what her only daughter did for a living, replied, "I don't know and I don't care."

As we were walking back to our cars Monday evening, Wong told me to come to court Tuesday as well. "I may need you," he said. "We've got a lot of exhibits."

"He really doesn't like to carry his own briefcase," I remarked to VJ, as Wong got in his car and drove away.

"He's paying you," she pointed out. "And he's old-fashioned. He doesn't do electronic. He likes to pass notes. And don't forget, I need the car back tomorrow, too. I'm getting a ride in so I can drive it home. You need to get a ride home."

I relayed all this to Bosco over dinner. He just smiled. "I have a little something up my sleeve," he said.

"A little car up your sleeve?" I asked.

"You'll see. What time do you need to be picked up?"

"I guess around noon, when we break for lunch." I peered at him suspiciously, but he pretended not to see.

✱ ✱ ✱

47

That evening, after dinner and after the dishes had been left unwashed in the sink, I seated myself on a pillow on the floor in the living room. I flipped on the television, to catch what passes for the news. I had just missed the weather report; the inappropriately dressed Latina was saying, "And that's the seven-day forecast. Back to you, John."

John, the Great White Hope of this particular news show, replied in a suitably deep voice. "Thank you, Elena, and now for the business report. Disturbing news for stockholders of Brunswick Insurance Company, facing an audit by insurance regulators, amid growing concern that reserves are insufficient to meet projected losses."

I snapped to attention. Brunswick was Skyblu's carrier. That was not good.

"Company executives have been accused of applying inappropriate pressure on claims adjustors to keep reserves artificially low on large-loss claims."

Yeah, like two dead Chinese guys and one dead Earl Ray, I thought. No wonder they couldn't settle. Before I could decide what to do, my attention was driven back to the screen by a name I knew. John hadn't done with me yet.

"The body of Steven Randolph Burton was discovered Monday in his apartment at the Altadena Arms." A picture of a nondescript apartment building flashed on the screen. "Burton, twenty-nine, was found by his live-in companion at approximately 4:30 AM." A closeup of a craggy-faced detective. "We believe that Mr. Burton was the victim of an intruder. He appears at this time to have been shot twice." The detective continued. "It does not appear that anything is missing from his apartment, but due to the wounds, suicide has been ruled out. It's possible that the perpetrator feared discovery and fled before achieving his purpose. However, at present, there are no leads."

John's face loomed back on the screen. "Thank you, we'll be keeping an eye on that story. In other news, one hundred people feared dead in a bombing in a Basra marketplace yesterday—"

Shit, I thought to myself. There goes my paying gig. I've got to be the unluckiest person in the world.

I called VJ on her cell, not knowing if she would be at home or still in her office.

"VJ, something awful has happened. That Burton guy? He died."

"Jesus, Fifi, what the bloody hell did you do?"

"I didn't do anything." This was so unfair. "He just got killed. Shot in some burglary gone bad. I wasn't even there."

"Oh well. Then it's just sad," VJ acknowledged.

"Burton isn't the only sad thing, either." I told her the news about Brunswick. She was silent for several seconds. "That makes it all the more important to hit Grund. They're insured by the ICARUS consortium of insurance companies. Unlikely they'll all go belly up. Harder case though. Much harder case."

When I hung up, I had to tell Bosco the bad news that his star role as Dante Wildman would never see the silver screen.

He slapped his forehead and blurted out, "I've got to be the unluckiest guy in the world!"

See, that's how shallow he is.

Tuesday morning, I drove the Volvo in and parked in the cathedral parking again. I got to the courtroom at 10:32, just as the opening statements were over. I slid into my place behind VJ and Wong.

By 10:54 Mrs. Rayburn was on the stand. I thought she looked good. A bit heavy, but she carried her weight with confidence. I noted her powder-blue blouse; it was a blouse you'd want your mother to wear to church if your mother ever went to church, which mine certainly never did. A small diamond glittered from a chain around her neck, a modest ornament. It told the jury that someone very sweet and perhaps shy had loved her. I got it at Target over the weekend on VJ's instructions. Apparently, Mrs. Rayburn never wore jewelry, and that wouldn't do.

"Mrs. Rayburn, could you please tell the jury how long you were married to Earl Dean?" VJ stood at the lectern.

"Twelve years," Mrs. Rayburn replied.

"Happy years?"

"The best. Earl Dean was the love of my life and my best friend." Mrs. Rayburn paused. "I know the difference too. I was married before. It didn't work out. I moved around a lot, had an interesting life you could say. But I was ready to settle down and that's when I met Earl Dean."

I knew VJ would be pleased with how naturally Mrs. Rayburn mentioned that she had been married before. Boatwright and Porter would try to make a big deal of Ruth's very ugly divorce from her first husband, and the fact that she hadn't been married to Earl Dean for all that long. Getting it out first took some of the sting out of it and turned the briefness of their marriage into a poignant plus.

"You and Earl Dean were retired?" VJ continued.

"Yes. I had worked for years in the hotel industry; different places, you know. Earl Dean was the manager at a metal fabricating plant. He'd put in his thirty years, and was just getting all set to enjoy his life and take it easy for a change."

As Norman Chu had told me, Earl Dean had very little to claim in the way of lost earnings. I knew VJ had pinned her hopes on creating a picture of an idyllic retirement that he had worked so hard for and didn't get very long to enjoy. If the jury couldn't award very much for economic harm, maybe they'd award more in general damages.

"Can you tell the jury how you met?"

Mrs. Rayburn began telling the story. A cute meet at a gun show. They both tried to buy the same World War Two Luger.

"Objection, your honor," Porter snapped. "This is irrelevant and prejudicial."

Judge Stein snapped right back. "If you keep interrupting, Ms. Porter, I'll show you some prejudice. Plaintiff has a right to establish the nature and quality of her relationship to the decedent. Just have a seat."

Porter sat down, having achieved her objective—breaking up the touching moment when the future Mrs. Earl Dean Rayburn came close to plugging her soon-to-be husband with a rusty Luger.

At 12:02 Judge Stein rapped his gavel. "We will break for lunch. Be back in sixty minutes. And I mean sixty minutes exactly. I don't want to have to wait for anyone to show up. That means you, too," he growled at the jury before flouncing off the bench.

"What a jerk," I leaned forward and whispered to VJ. "Real control issues."

"Tell me about it," she whispered back. Wong bent his head and monopolized VJ's other ear as I resumed my study of Dan Boatwright's back. There was something about the quality of his voice and the set of those lean shoulders that intrigued me.

"Fifi, can you come here for a minute?" VJ motioned me to counsel table, and I snuck another peek as I pushed past the swinging gate and threaded my way past boxes of exhibits, demonstrative boards, and a projection screen. A longish face, generous mouth, amused eyes that were a little too close together, in a good way. He gave me a ghost of a smile as he passed me on his way out. I held his gaze a fraction of a second too long.

VJ looked up. "We have an assignment for you. Reg will explain what you need to do. I've got to go through some exhibits here."

"Fine." I lowered my voice. "By the way, VJ, that Boatwright dude is cute. Can you introduce me?"

"He's the enemy, you brainless twit." VJ brushed me away.

Miffed, I turned to Reg Wong. He was standing near the swinging gate separating the gallery, when Ms. Porter edged by. The look of cold hate that those two exchanged could have solved global warming.

Chapter Seven

"Here's the deal." Wong took my arm and pulled me close as we walked out of the courtroom into the hall. "We need you to track down that witness. Grandma. The way I see it, everyone who worked with Farnswell probably knew that he lived with his grandmother. He was there for seven years, for God's sake. But in all of the depositions we took, no one mentioned it, and Skyblu never listed her as a witness. That means she's very important. You see that?"

I tried to look intelligent. Wong frowned.

"Either Granny was bad for them and they don't want us to find her, or she was good for them and they're going to try to spring her on us right at the end. We gotta know which way the wind is blowing here." He rubbed his hands together. "She may or may not still live at the house. And we don't know her name. It may not be Farnswell at all."

"You want me to find her and interview her?"

"Yeah, I want to see just how crazy Jimmy Farnswell was before the big meltdown. If he was seeing a psychiatrist, if he was acting funny. Anything that would have given Skyblu reason to know that he was a whack job. Anything that would have put them on notice, you get me?"

"Yeah, I get you." I made a note on my pad to emphasize how much I got him. I looked around to see if anyone was in earshot. "So, what's the story on that lawyer for Skyblu? Boatwright?"

"Danny Boatwright. Piece of work. He made the list of Best Lawyers Under Thirty last year, and now his head's too big to fit in the courtroom door. Graduated from University of Virginia, could have gone to any big firm, but he likes trying cases. He joined Stellhoffer, Wickham and then took the client right out from under the senior partner. Four years out of law school and he started his own firm. He is always at his office, I tell you, he once sent me an e-mail at 3:30 in the morning."

Hmm, I thought to myself, he's ambitious, successful and hard working, and all that is in addition to the lock of straight brown hair that falls across his forehead, just begging to be gently brushed back.

I would have asked more questions but Wong was, strangely, not as interested in Daniel Boatwright as I was. He wanted to talk about Burton, but I had seen the same newscast he had and didn't know anything more.

I tried out a few platitudes. "I guess he was just in the wrong place at the wrong time. You know, when your number's up, it's up."

Wong responded. "I guess it's just one of those things."

I was going to counter with "you just never know," when Wong raised his hand.

"Hey, there's Violet." She wafted her way out of the courtroom and drifted in our direction. "Violet, come here. This is the investigator we hired. Name's Cutter."

Violet stared at me. "I thought she was a document clerk."

"She's also an investigator. Ms. Cutter is the investigator who took that video of Steve Burton."

"I'm sorry for your loss, Violet." I struck out my hand. "My father died last year. I know how it is."

She gave me a scornful look, flipped her hair, and ignored my outstretched hand. "You have no idea how it is. My father was a complete A-hole."

"Violet," Wong yelped. "Don't talk like that. You gotta

testify about how much you loved your father, and you gotta sell it. You hear me?"

Violet gave a pout.

I was about to take my leave, just as Bosco rushed up.

"Hey, Fifi, hoped I'd make it," he began before catching sight of Violet. He stood, mouth slightly open, staring at the perfect oval face, the gleaming blue-black hair, the delicate eyebrows. I think they're called "moth" eyebrows, so much in contrast to my own, angry caterpillar eyebrows.

Violet visibly thawed.

Bosco smiled. "I'm Bosco Dorff, by the way. I take it you know my sister?"

"Actually, we just met. I guess Ms. Cutter's going to be helping us locate a witness."

"That's great," Bosco beamed. "Maybe she mentioned that I'm her partner? We run kind of a family business. Insurance adjusting. Investigation. Litigation support. I'll certainly be glad to do all I can to assist you in locating your witness. I'm sure it's a very important witness."

"Bosco," I interrupted, "You have transportation for us?"

Bosco glanced at Violet and smiled even more brightly. "Yes, they picked up the Mercedes this morning, and gave me a loaner. It's a little smaller than what I'm used to," he gave a shrug. "But not a bad little ride."

"Really?" I asked. "And just what kind of car did the Mercedes-Benz dealership lend you, Bosco?"

Wong elbowed in and shook Bosco's hand. "Nice to meet you. Come on Violet, we gotta go. We got things to do."

"I'll call you with results." I turned back to my brother. He had a bemused expression on his face. That made me uneasy. Bosco is not easily impressed.

"Snap out of it," I snarled. "And tell me how you really got here."

Bosco dangled a key chain with a single tiny key on it. "You asked me if I could babysit a car, didn't you?"

"That doesn't look like a car key," I pointed out. "That looks like the key to a safety deposit box."

"Oh, it's a car key, little sister. This is your key to freedom."

"You shouldn't be driving," I reminded him. "You don't have a license. What kind of loser would give a car to a guy who doesn't even have a license?"

Bosco refused to be drawn, until we made it downstairs, where a teeny station wagon waited for us. Illegally parked right in front of the courthouse. It was no longer or wider than a Mini-Cooper, but a lot taller and it looked like it had to be fifty years old.

I glanced up and saw a zaftig meter maid—more of a meter mama—three-fourths of a block away with her eye on our so-called car.

Bosco saw her too. "Hurry," he yelled and I leaped into what I thought was the driver's seat.

"Shit!" I said when I realized that the steering wheel was on the other side. With the determined meter maid bearing down on us, frantically trying to write the ticket as she waddled along, we jumped out, bumped into each other running around the car, and changed seats.

I put the key in and nothing happened.

"Shit!" I said. The car had a pushbutton starter. I stabbed at the button with my finger and the little car sprang to life. I revved the engine and tried to put it into first. We bucked backward and stalled.

"Shit! Shit! Shit!" I said as the meter maid rapped angrily on the window.

"You can't park here," she was yelling. "I got to give you a ticket."

I restarted the car. Bosco breathlessly informed me that reverse was first and first was second. I slammed the stick shift down to the left and gave it gas. We jerked forward. I pulled away from the curb, ground it into second, and took off. I had a great view of the meter maid in the rearview mirror, and she didn't look happy.

"What the fuck is this piece of crap?" I yelled over the noise of the engine. The little car was beginning to fill up with fumes.

"It's a '57 Squire, Ford-built for the British market," said Bosco enthusiastically. "It's a classic."

I grunted as I tried to get from second to third. The gears screeched in protest.

"Double clutch into third," Bosco instructed, rolling down the window. I did and we swerved onto the entrance ramp to the 110 freeway.

"It gets up to about forty miles per hour," Bosco informed me as I tried to merge into traffic.

"Where did you get this ridiculous car?" I demanded. "It's not a real car, it's a toy. No, it's not even a toy, it's a cartoon. How can I be seen driving this car in LA?"

"People love it," Bosco assured me. "It's different."

It was that, I agreed. "Are you going to tell me how you got it?"

"Belongs to a friend of D'Metree's. Guy named Dino. He rents it out to movies, but it needs work. I offered to fix it," Bosco said.

D'Metree is my cousin, on my father's side. He's not quite the relentlessly amoral screw-up Bosco is, but he's not above pulling a fast one on friend or foe.

"What do you mean you offered to fix it?" I fished around for a seat belt, in vain. "You don't know anything about fixing cars. Did I mention you don't even have a driver's license?"

"Yes, I do."

"I mean a valid driver's license."

"Alright, that's true, but I don't have to tell Dino that. I told him it might take two weeks to get the parts, and then in two weeks I'll just tell him that I tried really hard, but the parts aren't available any more." Bosco smiled. "By then you'll have earned more money and maybe we can put something down on a really cool car. Something that would impress Violet. Maybe a Porsche."

We were approaching our exit.

"So what needs to be fixed?" I asked.

"The brakes," Bosco replied.

* * *

We got home safely, after I had perfected the choreography of stopping the car—a delicate ritual of pumping the pedal, slipping into second gear, and, where necessary, pulling up the hand brake, only to find that Sketch had gotten tired of waiting and taken a dump on the floor. Bosco and I argued about who would clean it up. He pointed out that he had scored the car and therefore I owed him. I argued that if he didn't clean it up, I would whack him four times in his head with the Webster's Unabridged Dictionary (third edition).

I won.

Chapter Eight

"Wake up! Wake up!" I pounded on Bosco's door Wednesday morning.

He stumbled out, bleary-eyed and wearing Calvin Klein pajamas.

"Jesus, it's the crack of dawn, I just got to sleep, what the hell's a matter with you?"

"You told Violet you were my partner, so it's time for you to go ahead and be my partner."

"I don't wanna," Bosco protested, but forty-seven minutes later he was showered and dressed and drinking coffee at the old green Formica table in the kitchen.

"I can't find out Farnswell's grandmother's last name," I said. "I've run all the records I can online. I know she married Lewis Cranford, but they got divorced after Farnswell's mother was born, and I can't find any record of her after that. She may have gotten remarried in some other state and changed her name."

"What about the house?" Bosco asked. "Wouldn't she be on the title?"

I shook my head. "No, they just rented and the lease was in Farnswell's name. The easiest thing is to go over there and ask the neighbors. It's been two years since the plane crash, but I think it was big enough news that people will remember."

We drove out to Riverside in the Squire, which usually would take about an hour, but took two hours and fourteen minutes, stuck in the slow lane the whole way. No radio. Sketch in the back seat slobbering all over the windows. Worse, we didn't have air-conditioning. I had dressed in a lightweight beige pantsuit, but it looked like a used brown bag by the time we arrived. Bosco didn't look much better in black linen slacks and a light-grey button-down.

Okay, I'll be honest. He still looked much better.

"Here." I gave Bosco a clipboard, then locked Sketch in with a pan of water. "This will make you look more official. I'll start at their old house, you take the other side of the street."

The neighborhood was lower income. Small, poorly constructed ranch houses sat on small, poorly maintained lots. Farnswell's old house was no worse than the others and no better.

The new occupants, a young Burmese couple, had only been there for three months. They had no idea they were living in the erstwhile home of a notorious murderer. They seemed upset to find out.

I had better luck at the puce house immediately to the east. An older white man opened the door, his beaked nose laced with red veins.

"I've lived here thirty-two years," he informed me in response to my first question. "I used to own a pawn shop in town. Did okay till the divorce."

"Do you remember Jim Farnswell? Next door?"

"Sure do. Coulda knocked me down with a feather when I heard what he did. Saw him that very morning, I did, I'll never forget it. Didn't say nothin'; just waved and got into his car."

"You were friendly with him?" My hopes rose.

"No, not to say friendly. Knew him. You know, to wave to."

"But you knew his grandmother? She lived with him?"

My luck skidded to a halt as the old man shook his head. "Nope. Knew she lived there, but she didn't get out much."

"Did you know her name?"

The old man scratched his head before allowing that he couldn't say that he did.

I thanked him and went to the next house. A frazzled stay-at-home in her early thirties answered the door just long enough to scream "You woke the baby!" before slamming it again.

Nobody was home at the next two houses. I turned and walked back, starting all over again at the Farnswell's neighbor to the west. A nice enough woman, but she didn't speak English.

The next house over was light blue, freshly painted and newly roofed. The yard was a bit cramped with plastic flamingoes, but the pansies made a cheerful display. I knocked and waited. A white-haired woman opened the door. She was wearing a cotton housedress, an eye-popping orange and yellow flower print. I wondered how anyone could have seen that particular dress on the rack at Wal-Mart and said "Orange and yellow! I gotta have it!"

"Are you here to sell me Girl Scout cookies? 'Cause I already bought them from my niece. I bought ten boxes and I really can't use any more."

"No, no, I just wanted to ask you a few questions." I smiled and tried to look a little older.

"Like a survey? I gotta tell you I don't follow politics. It's all a bunch of foolishness, as far as I'm concerned."

"No, I'm trying to find an ex-neighbor of yours. I work for a law firm, and we think she may be a witness in a trial that's going on."

The woman's eyes became shrewd. "I heard that plane crash case was finally going to trial. Is that it?"

"Yes, that's exactly it. May I get your name? I take it you knew Mr. Farnswell?"

"My name's Clara Deere. But I don't wanna be a witness. I really didn't know the man at all."

"Actually, it's his grandmother we were looking for," I

explained. "We know she lived with him, but we don't have her name or where to find her."

"She moved out right after the crash happened. She aged a hundred years that week. Can't think what her name was. I was still working at the time, I only just retired, so I didn't spend a lot of time talking with her. Nice lady though. She had the cutest little poodle dog. I remember his name. It was Beanie."

She went on like that. I patiently tried various ploys to jog Clara's memory, but finally had to give up. The name wasn't going to come to her.

I met up with Bosco at the car. He hadn't had any luck either, except for the naughty housewife in the negligee who had invited him in and offered him a drink.

We let Sketch out to pee and got yelled at by the Burmese husband, who apparently thought dog pee was death to hydrangeas. We hurriedly got back into the car.

Flustered, I turned left instead of right and had to go around the block. As I passed the house that was back-to-back with the Farnswell's place, an old man came down the walk with a fluffy little poodle on a leash. Sketch went wild, lunging onto my lap and barking ferociously. The man slowed, although the poodle seemed unconcerned. I tried to beat the big dog back and, without thinking, slammed on the brakes. My foot went all the way to floor without any visible effect. I let up and pumped slowly. Halfway down the block I finally stopped. We really had to get the brakes fixed.

"Go back and talk to him," I snapped at Bosco. "That's her poodle. He must have taken it in."

"Whose poodle?"

"The grandmother's poodle, you jerkoff. Beanie, that's Beanie." Sketch's tail whapped me in the face as he frantically tried to find a way out of the car and on to the poodle.

"How do you know it's her poodle?"

"I just know, you dipshit, now go. Go."

Bosco got out and I managed to tie Sketch to the back-seat door handle with an old bungee cord.

When Bosco came back, order had more or less been restored.

"Wow, you were right. The guy's name is Rudy Dunlap. Friend of the grandmother. He said her name was Edna Wegliecki, W-e-g-l-i-e-c-k-i. Married a Polish guy in Chicago and then moved back out here when he died. She had been married three times, actually. And that was her dog."

"Great. It'll be a lot easier to find her with the right name."

"It's even easier than that. He visits her every month. Takes the dog to see her. She's at the Villa Flora Assisted Living Home in Corona."

Jazzed, we drove off. Bosco figured out the quickest route by looking at the Thomas Guide. I headed for the freeway and hopped on the 91.

It was all good until a black and silver big rig appeared in my rearview mirror, going sixty miles an hour and not slowing down.

I floored it, but I was already going forty-five and that was all the speed the Squire had. I glanced to my right to see if I could safely pull off, but the side of the freeway was a construction zone and the shoulder was missing, replaced by a freshly dug trench. Orange traffic cones were lined up at regular intervals as far as I could see.

"Damn, what's that nut doing?" I gripped the wheel as the grill of the truck loomed right behind me.

"Change lanes," Bosco croaked. The Squire was not equipped with sideview mirrors, but I edged out into the center lane, only to have another black and silver tractor-trailer combo zoom up. I eased back into the slow lane.

"Look out the window; when that truck passes, tell me

if anyone else is coming." I cursed the right-hand drive, and all things English.

"He's not passing," Bosco informed me. I glanced over. The behemoth to my left had boxed us in. The guy in back was about an inch away from my bumper. I spared a moment of regret for Sketch, peacefully asleep on the back seat, unaware that his narrowly focused, but generally pleasant, life was about to come to a horrific end.

"Faster, faster," screamed Bosco.

"This is as fast as this piece of shit car will go," I screamed back. "If he hits me, I'm gonna have to put it in the ditch." I momentarily lost my grip on the wheel and clipped several orange cones. I closed my eyes.

Just before contact, we came to a slight incline. The Squire, having little relative weight and chugging at full power, didn't slow down, but the multi-ton rig that was crawling up our ass eased off several inches, pulled back by its own load. I could hear the son of a bitch change gears as he prepared to speed up and ram.

But he didn't. I opened my eyes and saw a black and silver blur move forward and hastily disappear up the center lane. In the rearview mirror I saw his twin laboriously change lanes and follow suit.

I let out a gasp of relief until I noticed the previously invisible motorcycle cop, who stayed right behind me until I had cleared the construction zone. Then he pulled me over.

When the cop started toward us, Sketch woke up and mistook him for a poodle. I tightened the bungee cord and tried to smile reassuringly at the officer whose hand was now hovering over his holster.

When he came level with Bosco's window, he bent down and did a double take. Steering wheel not on that side. He stomped around the front of the Squire to my side. "Let me see your license and registration. You knock those cones over back there?" he demanded.

I figured that if the trucks blocked my view of him, then they must have blocked his view of me. "What cones?"

"Those cones back there that are now all over the damn freeway, ma'am."

"I don't know anything about any orange cones."

"That so? And how fast do you think you were going?"

"Why don't you tell me how fast you think I was going? That strikes me as being more in line with the spirit and letter of the Fifth Amendment."

"Fifth Amendment? What are you talking about? This is a traffic stop." The cop was starting to sweat, and his voice was getting loud.

"I was not exceeding the speed limit, I know that." I spoke with authority.

"I didn't stop you for exceeding the speed limit." He was bellowing now. "I stopped you because you knocked over those cones."

"What cones?" I asked, getting us back full circle.

I got tagged for driving too slow, but avoided any reckless or dangerous driving charges. All in all, I considered myself lucky.

"What just happened here?" Bosco said wonderingly as we resumed our stately progress.

"I'll tell you what just happened. I just got a not-speeding ticket, that's what happened. It's seventy-five bucks. We could have rented a real car for two days for seventy-five bucks."

Bosco declined to comment on my economic analysis. "Just as soon as we get our first big lead, a couple of long-haulers try to dump us in a ditch. Man, don't you think that's weird?"

"Of course I think it's weird, Bosco, but I think a lot of things are weird. Reality TV. The concept of the fatwa. Non-dairy creamer. I could go on."

Chapter Nine

Villa Flora Assisted Living was a rambling, low-slung, flat-roofed, cinderblock structure. The landscaping was utilitarian and not well kept. Bald spots marred the gazania beds, and the hot pink impatiens were leggy. We entered the glass double doors, bracing ourselves for the old-person-and-disinfectant smell. The anteroom was narrow and long, with a high counter at the far end. Two Philippine nurses chatted in Tagalog. The shorter one pushed the clipboard to us without looking in our direction. The taller one glanced up, saw Bosco and smoothly elbowed her less observant sister to the side.

"Are you here to see a patient?" she cooed, leaning over the counter and letting the fluorescent light catch the sizeable zircon-encrusted cross which rested on her considerable bust. She twirled a stray lock of flyaway black hair.

"Uh, a friend, yes, Edna Wegliecki." Bosco smiled back.

"Oh, Mrs. Wegliecki is just the nicest little lady. Is she expecting you today? She don't get a lot of visitors, you know, no family left. Very sad." The breasts crept forward across the counter as the nurse bent her head toward Bosco. "You know about her grandson, yes? Crazy as a loon. Lost his job at the airline, became totally unhinged. He took a gun and brought down a whole plane. It was like a hundred people killed and everything."

"Is that right? God, how awful," Bosco leaned right back at her. "Does she ever talk about it?"

The nurse looked up as if consulting the acoustic tiles. "Does she ever talk about anything else—oh my God!"

The second nurse elbowed back into view. "Don't say that. It's not nice. These people are friends of Mrs. Wegliecki's. Mrs. Wegliecki is so sweet, she's like my special patient." Lashes fluttered.

"She's my special patient, too," our informant flared up.

"Maybe we could sign in and talk to the special patient ourselves," I suggested. The first nurse placed a pen on the clipboard and we signed our names.

"I'll just need your telephone number too, Mr.—," she consulted the sign in sheet, "Mr. Dorff." He recited our number and First Nurse said, "Mrs. Wegliecki will be in the rec room now, I'll take you there. Maria, you mind the front desk. My name is Dolores, by the way," said Nurse One, again a little quicker on the uptake than her shorter friend.

The hallways were narrow, so I was relegated to trailing after Dolores and Bosco. We turned left, right, went through the double doors, then turned to the right again. I pointedly said thank you and good-bye to our guide before entering. We didn't need an audience.

The rec room was crowded and uncomfortably warm. I counted seven television sets, each tuned to a different show and each surrounded by a little cluster of geezers sitting on metal folding chairs, crammed as close as they could get to the screen. The volume on all the sets was way up.

A bent munchkin of a woman stood guard at the door, splayfooted. The expression of keen watchfulness on her face was belied by her milky eyes.

"Can I help you?" the sentinel snapped.

"Yeah, we're looking for Edna Wegliecki," I replied.

"You're not family. She's got no family."

"What are you, like the security guard?"

"That's right girlie. Ex-army. WAC in World War Two. That's me." She cocked an eyebrow. Well, not an eyebrow, but a few stray gray hairs where her eyebrow used to be. "Civilians. Sitting ducks. Anybody could walk in here. I keep an eye out. I'm not much, but I'm all they got."

I was about to point out that she probably couldn't see a Nazi tank brigade if it plowed into the side of the building when Bosco interrupted.

"They're lucky to have you, ma'am. Women make great soldiers. I've always said it. Like the Amazons. Or the Valkyries."

"I don't know who they are, but I can tell you they don't have nothing on the women of the United States Army."

Bosco was about to about to launch into hosannas about the women of the United States Army, when I interrupted back. "Don't bother, Bosco. She's blind, not senile. With your permission, ma'am, maybe we could talk to Mrs. Wegliecki?"

"Hehe. Girl after my own heart. Speak your mind, doncha? You in the Army?"

"No."

She peered closer at me. "Don't suppose you could fill out a uniform."

"Why does everyone feel entitled to comment on my stature? I'm short. I'm skinny. I get it. Could we please get back to Mrs. Wegliecki?"

"What do you want to talk to her about?"

"Her grandson. You know, the one who—"

The old bird nodded and gestured toward the second television on our left. "That's her there watching the telly. I'll tell you what I told the other one. Offer to take her to the cafeteria and buy her a piece of pie. She likes the mincemeat pie. She's pretty much the only one here who does."

We did as ordered, and Mrs. Wegliecki gladly accompanied us through an oversized metal door, down another hall, to a large room with a buffet line. I glanced at the clock on the wall: 3:23. No meals were being served, and the place was empty except for two cafeteria workers drinking coffee. They glanced up as we came in and one of them, an unsmiling black woman with malevolent eyes, got to her feet, lumbered around to the cash register, and sold us a thin piece of gluey, brown pie. I pocketed the receipt and made a quick note of the expense.

"Meals come with the room," Mrs. Wegliecki explained, "but you have to pay for anything extra."

We sat down at a sticky wood-veneer table. I flicked away an empty straw wrapper.

"You like it here?" I asked.

"It's okay," she replied, digging into the pie with gusto. She was a husky woman, but looked like she used to be bigger. "I get to see Beanie. Love that doggie. You're here to talk about Jimmy?" she asked "Everybody wants to talk about Jimmy."

"You mean other people have been here to talk to you?" I asked, picking up on what the old soldier had mentioned.

"Yep," she agreed. "Some guy. I'll tell you the same thing I told him."

"Which was?"

"Not much. He wanted to know whether Jimmy was a moody boy. If he ever talked about suicide. But he never did. Not at all."

She took a huge bite of the unappetizing pie.

"Just a normal guy?"

"That's right. Just a normal, good boy."

"Was he upset about having been laid off?"

"Just in a normal way. He'd worked there for seven years. No write-ups, no trouble, no nothing. But they didn't have enough business, that's what it was. Nothing to do with anything Jimmy'd done wrong; Jimmy was a good worker. He'da gotten another job, don't you worry about that."

I tried to wrap my mind around how pleasant a guy

who killed five people could be. "No violence of any kind before?"

"Nosirreebob. That cat, that wasn't Jimmy's fault," she added cryptically, as she scarfed down the last bit of pie.

Whoa, I thought. This can't be good for VJ's case. VJ and Wong needed Skyblu to be on notice of Jimmy's whacko tendencies, or there wouldn't be any liability.

But wait a minute. Assuming the man who came to talk to her was Boatwright, Skyblu's attorney, then it made no sense for him to hide Mrs. Wegliecki. It was like Wong thought. Boatwright would put our Edna on the witness list—on the star witness list. Something was not right.

"Mrs. Wegliecki, what was that you were saying about the cat?"

She pushed herself away from the table and made a face. "I didn't say nothing about no cat. Ummph, got a little acid reflux," she mumbled tapping her chest. "Comes right up on ya, you know? Pie's pretty rich, I guess. Don't have the digestion I used to have."

I pretended I didn't hear. She bitched about it all the way back to the rec room, by which time she really wasn't looking too good.

"Thanks for coming," she smiled weakly, as Bosco helped ease her back onto her chair in front of the television. The old soldier looked keenly at us as we shuffled off, like we were getting blamed for Mrs. Wegliecki's acid reflux. It wasn't my fault. She didn't have to eat the whole damn pie.

Chapter Ten

We got home at 5:14. I started thinking about dinner and found the refrigerator empty. Not even ketchup. How could one guy eat and drink so much? I wondered.

I shouted up the stairs to Bosco who was in his room, no doubt admiring himself in the mirror. "I'm going to the grocery store."

He didn't respond, but as I was pulling out of the driveway, he came running out, waving something in the air. "Mind returning this?"

"*Raiders of the Lost Ark.* You rented this? How many times have you seen it?"

"Seven. Can you return it?"

I took it from his hand, stuck it into my purse, and headed for the new upscale grocery store in Silverlake, with the gourmet deli, organic produce, and attached Starbucks franchise. I couldn't afford it, but I have a weakness for overpriced, low-fat snack foods.

* * *

I filled the cart with several boxes of whole wheat macaroni and cheese, a bag of air-popped cheese doodles, granola, and plain yogurt. I was hungrily eyeing the pre-made dinners when I felt a sharp push in my back, hard enough to stagger me.

As I stumbled awkwardly away from the grocery

cart, a dark man in darker sweats grabbed my hot-pink purse right out of the kiddy seat and shoved me again, knocking me to the ground. Stunned, I knelt there on all fours as elderly hippie housewives started yelling. Not really that loud, though. I struggled up, using the shopping cart for leverage, and showed them what a real scream sounded like.

"Get that asshole, he stole my purse. Don't let him get away!"

I started to give chase, noting that the shoppers obediently parted for him, like the Red Sea before Moses.

"Why don't you just roll out the freaking red carpet for the son of a bitch, you useless cretin," I snarled at the bewildered security cop. He stood at the front door, watching, slack-jawed, as the sweatsuit streamed by him, jumped into a red BMW Z4, and peeled out.

Too late to be of any real use, the patrons of this palace of holistic dry goods sprang into action. They sat me down, offering me St. John's Wort and calming elixirs.

"You've had a terrible shock to your system," a woman with grey hair to her waist solemnly informed me. "You need to restore your chi."

"I don't need to restore my chi," I replied with an edge. "I need to restore my purse."

But my heart wasn't in it. I was totally effed. Shoppers and sales clerks hovered around until I accepted the calming elixir. I sat there and fumed for several minutes, remembering that my car keys were in my purse, which meant I would have to call AAA. But my membership card was in my purse. I could probably borrow someone's cell phone to call Bosco, but what good would it do? He didn't have a valid driver's license or a car. VJ would be out of court on her way back to the office.

As I reviewed my dismal options, a new commotion started at the front of the store. In fact, a cheer went up. I raised my head to see the cretinous security cop proudly raising the pink purse aloft. My heart soared. Okay, the wallet was probably gone, but maybe the keys were still in there.

I awkwardly thanked the nice man and apologized.

"Heat of the moment," I excused myself. "Really, I can't thank you enough."

"I didn't do nothin'," he mumbled. "The guy threw it out the window as he was turning the corner."

I looked inside. To my amazement, not only was the wallet there, but the keys, all the cards and the thirty-six bucks in cash were untouched. I glanced at the anxious faces around me.

"Why would he steal my purse and just throw it away?" I asked. No one knew, but they all had theories.

"Maybe he thought you were rich," said one woman who would obviously never make the same mistake.

Another woman disagreed. "No, it was probably just a manifestation of the randomness of the universe."

"I thought he was, like, your ex-husband," said a thin brunette with a gamine cut. "Or ex-boyfriend. Or something. My ex used to do stuff like this, all the time. I hadda get a restraining order."

"No," I shook my head. "I don't have anybody like that screwing up my life. I didn't recognize him. Of course, I didn't really see what he looked like. Did anyone see what he looked like?"

The descriptions offered were no help. It was generally agreed that he had been larger than average, but not by much, and he was wearing a hat, either an old-fashioned fedora or an Australian bush hat or a deerstalker (this last according to wide-eyed teenager). He was Mexican, by consensus.

Everyone lost interest. I finished shopping, paid for my purchases with my blessedly intact credit card, and drove out of the parking lot. When I got to the movie rental place,

I realized the one thing that had been taken. *Raiders of the Lost Ark.* Damn.

* * *

I was heating up a can of hard-won organic cream of potato soup that evening when I heard a knock at the door. I was only sort of surprised to see Violet standing there, dressed in a lightweight gray dress with asymmetrical closures. Looking gorgeous. She glanced disdainfully at my stained sweats and faded Bennington College T-shirt. I hate being caught in my spinster rags.

"Hi, Fifi, good to see you."

She didn't mean it, so I didn't respond.

"Bosco invited me over for dinner," she announced. "I brought the pizzas." She thrust them into my arms and gave her unbelievably lustrous hair a little shake.

Don't waste it on me, I thought, but she hadn't been. Bosco was right behind me.

"Interesting place you got here," she said to him, looking around at the black-beamed ceilings and bare, hardwood floors. "I guess you're planning on doing a lot of remodeling, huh?"

"Oh, absolutely." He has no shame. "I just moved in. You caught me in the midst of redecorating. New furniture hasn't been delivered yet."

As I followed them to the kitchen, where my soup was bubbling over, I heard Violet whisper to Bosco "Your sister doesn't live with you, does she?"

And Bosco's whispered response, "No, no, she's just staying here until she finds a place."

I jammed the pizza boxes into Bosco's hands and shoved open the pocket door to the laundry room where Sketch had been held captive all day. Smelling the pepperoni, the big dog lurched into the kitchen and went skidding toward the pizza. Bosco lifted the boxes over his head and dodged just as Sketch made his leap. Violet took the brunt of it. She tried to be a good sport about the paw prints on the light-gray fabric, but she was not really feeling it. I could tell.

I calmly ladled my soup into a bowl and sat down at the table. Bosco tried to signal me to get lost, but I ignored him. There isn't any other place in the house to eat, except the card table I use as a desk. And if I eat at my desk, it's exactly like working.

Violet sat down on the opposite side of the table, and crossed her arms. "You know, Fifi, Norman Chu is a real estate lawyer and he knows lots of people that own apartment buildings. Affordable housing. He could help you find something. I mean, don't you think it's time for you to find your own place?"

I smiled. "Don't be silly, Violet. I enjoy staying here and getting to know all of Bosco's girlfriends."

Violet turned back to Bosco as if I hadn't spoken. "You know what I'd do with this kitchen: I'd open up that pantry area. Think about French doors—you know, to let in the light. You want light wood cabinets, a Viking stove. And a Sub-Zero; you really need that."

Violet went on and on about her plans for my house as I sipped my soup. I was an inch from ratting Bosco out when he sent me a pleading glance.

I flapped my hand, letting him know he was safe. Sticks and stones, blah blah. I was stuck anyway, since we were working for Wong, Wu & Chu, and Violet was the big client in the big case. If I told her the truth now, she'd take it out on us by running to Reg Wong. Old Man Wong would kick us to the curb in a heartbeat. I had, after all, promised VJ not to piss him off, and that meant not pissing off Violet. I would keep that promise, I told myself, if it killed me.

Chapter Eleven

Wong had commanded me to court again on Thursday, to report on my visit to Grandma and to help with the exhibits he planned to use with his expert witness—about a gazillion exhibits, if my math was right.

I got to the courthouse early, in time for a leisurely latte and bagel. I made my way to the Starbuck's kiosk in the plaza. The morning air was clear and warm under a baby blue sky.

Like everything else, the perfect weather had a downside. Everybody and their associate had the same idea, and the line for coffee was out the door. I hate waiting. But, I reminded myself, if I went to sit upstairs outside the courtroom I'd be waiting anyway.

I filed in behind a wide-body in charcoal tweed. I noticed he had dandruff and took an involuntary half step back. Jostled from behind, I turned and found myself face to face with Janet Porter. She was impeccably groomed as always, in a green gold gabardine suit, matching spectator pumps, and her signature silk scarf trailing temptingly behind her. Reminded me of this old movie about some dancer chick who always wore long scarves. So where's a convertible Bugatti when you need it? I thought.

Porter looked just as pleased to see me but she had better manners. Or maybe, as a lawyer, she just had more practice at fake cordiality. "You work for Wong don't you?" she said.

On up-close examination, I saw she was nearer to the mid-century mark than I had originally thought. The strong planes of her face were too evident and even the careful application of foundation didn't conceal the bags under her eyes.

"Yup," I replied.

Porter set down her briefcase and adjusted her Coach bag. "That must be a treat."

Wary of candor, I flicked a glance her way. "I've had worse jobs."

"You're new. He probably hasn't exposed you to the full force of Wong Power."

Despite myself I had to ask, "What's Wong Power?"

"It's the black hole created by the all-consuming ego of the greediest, most arrogant old shit ever to walk these halls." Porter swept her arm to include the crowd of caffeine-seeking lawyers around us. "Do you have any idea just how greedy and arrogant you have to be to earn that title around here?"

I shrugged. "I don't have that much to do with him. I work more with Chu and VJ."

"Chu's a stiff." She patted a sproinged auburn lock back into place. "Smith's okay. Wong treats her like crap, you know. Condescending prick."

"Wow, I guess honesty really is the best policy."

Janet gave me a weary smile "What do I care? He's retiring on this case, isn't he? That's what he says, anyway. Listen, Reg Wong and I, we've known each other for twenty years and hated each other for nineteen years and eleven months. We've tried three cases against each other before. I won two of them and the third was a draw. You mention that to him."

"Yeah, I probably won't," I said as we got in the door.

We each got our orders without further conversation and I was hoping the encounter was over but as we exited and I looked for a seat, there were none. My eye was drawn by a round faced woman waving at me from a primo table near the flower bed. Uncertainly, I smiled back at her and then realized she wasn't waving at me, she was waving at Porter behind me. The woman saved me by pretending she was waving to both of us.

"Hi, I'm Cissie McMull. From ICARUS. You're from the trial, too, aren't you? Come on sit with us."

Cissie was of indeterminate age, all big nose and gap-toothed smile. And awful clothes. Her navy pants were pilled and the acrylic sweater she had paired them with was such an odd shade of beige. Which would have been just an eye roll if it wasn't for the large awkwardly placed brooch—a rhinestone cat with a curlicue tail. It was obviously hiding a stain and tugged at the fabric. That turned the ensemble from an eye roll to an "Are you kidding me?" Which I didn't actually say. A voice inside my head told me to stop it. She was being nice.

Porter wasn't pleased at Cissie's generosity, but before she could say anything to dissuade me from sitting down, she got pulled aside by a stout man in regulation navy blue who apparently remembered her from some trial they'd had together years ago.

"Janet, haven't seen you since that little encounter in Judge Holliway's courtroom. How have you been?"

Porter nodded a reluctant okay in my direction before replying, "I'm good, Jim, how are you?"

With mixed feelings, I plopped myself down. "Hi, I'm Fifi Cutter. I work for Reg Wong. Document clerk. Just happened to be standing next to Janet in line," I explained.

"It's good to meet you, Fifi. Isn't it a beautiful day?"

I agreed it was, concentrating on sipping the latte and nibbling the biscotti. I had a feeling that not much would be required of me to keep the conversation going and I was right.

"I just love LA. I'm originally from Tulsa. You know, Oklahoma. It's nice there but I wasn't sorry when I got transferred here. It was a promotion, for one thing. But also the cases I get here are much more interesting. And you never know with the juries, either. The land of OJ." She met my eye, and was momentarily abashed as if it was a social solecism to mention the OJ verdict to any black person.

And maybe it is, at that. I mean, okay he did do it but it's not like some white cops don't throw down and lie, so blame all around, am I right?

In any event, it only slowed her for a second. A nano-second. "This case is really fascinating to me. I'm new to product liability cases, really. But I've learned so much. Janet Porter is one of the most experienced trial lawyers in LA. In Southern California really. Grund has been insured by ICARUS for a long time, a very important account. We wouldn't have just anybody try this case, I can tell you." She lowered her voice like a naughty girl. "I have to admit that Janet can be a little caustic. But I think that's what gives her the edge."

"She does have an edge," I agreed. Porter chose that moment to join us and Cissie turned the conversation as nimbly as a snowboarder hurtling down hill. After that, I paid just enough attention to be polite, and excused myself as quickly as I could.

* * *

We were all in our places by 9:12, but Judge Stein still hadn't made his appearance. As we waited for him, Wong whispered out of the side of his mouth, "We're going to put my widows and Violet on this morning. We'll start with the expert testimony after lunch." He nervously smoothed his hair. "I hope Judge Stein's going to pay more attention today than he did yesterday. He acted like he never heard of the Rules of Evidence."

VJ whispered back, "Well, if he's drinking to forget, then his mission has certainly been accomplished."

Wong looked over at the jury. "That Jap accountant looks upset. I think she's turning against us."

"Probably just having a fight with her husband," VJ replied.

Judge Stein took the bench twenty minutes late, red-eyed and sallow. VJ caught my eye. Hangover headache, we silently agreed. "Let's get started. We're wasting time here."

Man, I tried to be a good team player and look interested as Mrs. Fang and Mrs. Han testified, stifling a yawn and covering it up with a cough. But it was hard. They loved and respected their husbands, and had been looking forward to spending their golden years with the one that had been meant for them (or, more accurately, the one that had been arranged for them by ambitious parents). Mrs. Fang had two children, including the lovely Violet, who had been born in the United States, and was, Mrs. Fang assured the jury, "a real citizen." Mrs. Han had adhered more faithfully to the One Child Policy.

When Violet took the stand, I was amused to see that her usual cutting-edge, Rodeo Drive, designer-label ensembles had been replaced by a winter white, preppie twin set, a choker of pearls, and a pleated skirt, short enough to be cute; not quite short enough to be slutty. Her black mane was restrained by a hair band. Born in Orange County, Violet made sure that everyone understood right away that she was a US citizen.

"My dad was such a great guy. A sort of Chinese Ward Cleaver." She spoke directly into the microphone, allowing a hint of wistful humor to creep into her voice. "He was loving and wise. Strict with us, but never mean. Caring, you know? He came to every recital, every school play."

She kept this up for an hour and forty-five minutes and finished with tears. She was, I reflected, a much better actor than Bosco would ever be. I saw Wong glance over to the defense table. I knew he was expecting Boatwright and Porter to waive cross-examination. He under-estimated them, or at least Boatwright, who rose and swanned to the lectern. He beamed pleasantly at Violet.

"Just a few questions if you don't mind, Ms. Fang. You have a brother, do you not?"

Violet smiled lightly. I could tell there was something she was bracing herself for, but I didn't know what it was.

"Yes I do."

"And this brother of yours, is he here in the courtroom today?"

Wong bounced up. "Objection. May we approach the bench?"

Judge Stein cast his cold eye over our table. "No."

"But your honor—"

"I said no. The brother is a party to this lawsuit, isn't he? This is fair game."

"With all due respect, your honor, Ms. Fang's brother is not a party. Mr. Fang filed a waiver of any rights he may have as an heir, when he decided to join the armed forces. He said he wasn't interested in—"

"Your honor, I would appreciate it if counsel did not testify."

Boatwright kept his cool, but he was annoyed.

"May I have an answer to my question?"

Even if he didn't get an answer, Boatwright was going to make it look like the darling of the courtroom had something to hide. But little Violet was a match for him.

Before Judge Stein could rule, she blurted out. "He isn't here. He couldn't be here."

Nice answer. Implying that poor brother Fang was slogging it out in the slums of Tikrit or Islamabad or some such place. Of course, he could just as easily have been holed up in a residential apartment complex in Pacoima, addicted to meth and online poker, but that wasn't the impression the jury was left with.

Boatwright's eyes sparked with frustration. "Perhaps you could tell the jury why he couldn't be here?"

"This is an irrelevant waste of time," the judge rasped, as convinced of Wong's position now as he had been of Boatwright's position a moment ago. "If he's not a party, and you don't have him on your witness list, then I don't care where he is. And neither should the jury."

Momentarily defeated, Boatwright resumed his seat as if it had all gone exactly as planned. I had to admire his poise. And I had to admire his ass.

Just before the lunch break, Boatwright half turned in his seat at counsel table. He briefly met my eye, giving me that little lip curl of a smile. He was good looking, I confirmed to myself, surprised by an unaccustomed stomach flutter. Damn, why did he have to be VJ's enemy?

When we all settled back into places after lunch, Judge Stein looked over at Porter. "Don't bring the jury in yet." Judge Stein glowered at his clerk. "Defendants have brought a motion to exclude Mr. Wong's expert witness on economic loss."

I could see Wong tense.

The insurance adjustors, sitting in the row across from me, suddenly sat up straighter, as if pulled by a string attached to their heads. The big bald guy from Brunswick, Yarborough, was looking pompous in Glen plaid. "VJ, I think I'm going to be ill," I whispered. "Cissie McMull is wearing navy tights with tan sling-backs."

"You should talk," VJ whispered back. "You own a pair of zebra-striped capris." Wong motioned impatiently for us to be quiet.

"Mr. Boatwright, you want to be heard?" Judge Stein flicked his hand toward the defense table.

Boatwright stood up. "Plaintiffs propose to present the testimony of expert witness Hon Chung. Mr. Chung is apparently prepared to testify that lost earnings occasioned by the death of Mr. Fang and Mr. Han amount to over $60 million. But the model on which Mr. Chung bases his calculations is wholly speculative."

"I read all that in the brief you filed," said the judge. "If it's so speculative, you should be able to prove that to the jury, right?"

Boatwright shook his head. "Juries, your honor, can be confused, which is why trial courts have the discretion to exclude evidence. In this case, the jury might not have the background in accounting to appreciate the obvious flaws in Mr. Chung's analysis. Expert testimony has to be based on something more than mere guesswork and wishful thinking."

"You're just saying that juries are arbitrary and unpredictable."

"Of course not. I have the highest regard for the jury system."

Judge Stein interrupted again, and Wong relaxed. It looked like the motion would be denied.

"Maybe we'd better hear from Mr. Wong. Mr. Wong, there is absolutely no basis for the numbers in Mr. Chung's so-called opinion."

Wong jumped to his feet. "Your hon—"

But Judge Stein didn't really want to hear from Wong. Not at all. "You can get an expert to say anything, pay him enough money. I'm going to exclude this testimony."

"But your honor—" Wong was spluttering.

"Sit down. I've heard enough."

Wong sat down. He looked dazed and suddenly older. He could never convince the jury to award big, juicy, headline-grabbing numbers without an expert witness to testify about huge lost earnings. Wong's dreams of an eight-figure verdict, the crowning achievement of his career, financial security for retirement, a Lamborghini, a swimsuit model—it had all dissipated in an instant, on the words of a cranky drunk.

"Who's your next witness?"

Wong didn't move.

VJ spoke up. "Ms. Kimberly Johnson, your honor. She is our liability expert with regard to the standard of care in not outfitting the jet with a locking cabin door."

Judge Stein wheeled on his clerk. "What are you waiting for? Get the jury in here. Let's get this show on the road, people."

Ms. Johnson was a good-looking woman, with a strong chin and short, brown hair. She had an authoritative air and she certainly knew a lot of statistics about how much it cost to install locking cabin doors. I fell asleep with my eyes partly open, woken only by the tap of the gavel, when Judge Stein called it a day.

"Tell us what happened with the grandmother," Wong commanded as we congregated in the hall outside the courtroom. He seemed agitated. I cast a glance at VJ as she and Violet joined us.

I gave my disappointing report on the pie-eating granny. "She supports the argument that all was well in the brain of Jimmy Farnswell. Nice normal guy in every way."

"That doesn't make any sense," Wong growled. "The testimony of this grandmother—this is the woman who lived with Jim Farnswell and knew him better than any one—would have been great for Boatwright. You said he interviewed her and then decided not to put her on? Christ, he not only decided not to put her on himself, he hid her from us." Wong shook his head. "I'm an old dog and I know all the tricks. I think there was something else there and I think you gave up before you got it out of her." I had a sharp and uncomfortable memory of Edna Wegliecki pursing up her lips, letting her gaze slide away. What was it she had said? "That cat, that wasn't Jimmy's fault."

Wong saw the look on my face. "Go back. Get it out of her."

VJ gave me a sympathetic head tilt, but then nodded in agreement. Aw, shit.

My house, on the end of a cul-de-sac overlooking Sofia Canyon, made a pretty sight in the evening sun, the dilapidated shingles and peeling paint camouflaged by the overflowing tufts of light purple wisteria. The air was warm and fragrant, and I didn't feel totally pissed off as I unlocked the door and headed to check my messages.

"Hi Fifi, this is Carlotta Anelli, when can I expect that report? I need to get this file closed, OK?"

Bitch.

"Hey Feef, this is D'Metree. How's Bosco coming with that car repair? You know, he said it wouldn't be any problem, and I'm getting some pressure from my friend to get the car back. Call me, okay?"

Jerk.

"This is Dolores from Villa Flora Assisted Living calling for Bosco Dorff. Oh, Mr. Dorff, we're so sorry to have to call you with this news, but Mrs. Wegliecki passed away last night. We thought you'd like to know, Mr. Dorff, since you were just here visiting her. Call me."

Slut.

Slut, with very bad news. I winced. Wong wasn't going to like this. How come everybody he sent me after died?

I glanced up and saw Bosco approaching from the kitchen, beer in hand. He had heard the answer machine.

"Mrs. Wegliecki is dead?"

"Yeah, well, apparently so."

"God, Fifi, you see what this means, don't you?"

"Yeah, it probably means I'm out of another job."

"It means that something bad is happening here."

"That's what I said. I'm probably out of another job."

"No, I mean really bad," said Bosco. "Like maybe something happened to her."

"Something did happen to her. She died."

"Not naturally. It's too much of a coincidence."

I gave Bosco my serious attention. "You could be right, bro. Someone kills Burton. Who was the document clerk who worked on this case, if you remember. A Mexican guy snatches my purse."

"And what about the trucks that tried to kill us? On our way to go see her."

Hmm. Well, the trucks could have been typical LA road rage. You drive a dinky little foreign-looking car, you're going to get some long-haul attitude. But Burton dying. And Mrs. Wegliecki dying. And the purse. Let's face it, Bosco's suspicions weren't totally insane. At least not butt-probe-by-Martians-in-an–unidentified-flying-object insane. What if he was right?

"Maybe we can go talk to Burton's girlfriend," I suggested. "She's the one who found the body and she lived with him, after all."

"I'll talk to Violet, maybe she can get Wong to agree to pay for us to go over there."

"No, don't bother. We'll go on our own time. Wong doesn't give a crap who killed Burton. The dude was trying to con money out of the firm. The only reason Wong would want to find out who killed Burton would be to plant a big wet kiss right on his cheek."

✻ ✻ ✻

I walked out of the house Friday morning and realized I didn't have the mental energy to fight with the Squire in downtown traffic. I walked down the hill to the Gold Line station. Walking down was pleasant. Walking up would be impossible. I decided VJ could give me a ride home.

I got off at the last stop, Union Station. The morning was cool, and I stopped for coffee at a Cambodian doughnut shop. I approached the white industrial-strength box that was the Los Angeles County Superior Court from the back. It was a typical urban scene. The homeless beggars gave way to the AM parade of bustling suits funneling through the security checkpoint in front of the courthouse.

The door to Department 37 was still locked when I got

there, so I sat down on the hallway bench and rated the fashion sense of the lawyers who passed by. Short guy shouldn't wear his pants so long. Tall guy shouldn't ruin the line of his suit with a shoulder bag. And that hot brother in the nipped-waist four-button navy blue silk-blend should come right over here and sit next to me. He didn't, but there was no time to be disappointed, as I spied Dan Boatwright wheeling his trial boxes down the hall. He hesitated for a moment and then sat down next to me.

"Hi, I've seen you in the courtroom. Are you with Wong's firm?" he asked.

"No, I'm just temporary help," I smiled.

"Well, I'm Dan Boatwright." He stuck his hand out. "Pleased to meet you."

"I'm Fifi Cutter." I took the proffered hand. We held on a little longer than the usual press-and-release. We both noticed.

"You do a lot of trial work?"

"Not really, I'm actually an independent insurance adjuster. I have my own business. I'm just helping out with this case as a favor to Victoria. We went to school together."

"Oh, I see." Dan considered my answer, which I hoped conveyed the proper amount of disassociation from the plaintiff's team without being overtly disloyal.

The court clerk came up, keys jangling, and unlocked the door.

Dan looked over at me. "I gotta go in and start preparing. My expert's on today."

Yeah, I thought to myself, the guy who was going to say that Skyblu had met the standard of care in conducting background checks, even though it had failed to uncover the fact that Jim Farnswell was a whacko nut ball.

But I refrained from comment and stuck to a noncommittal, "Nice to meet you."

"Very nice to meet you." He gave me a killer smile,

and maneuvered his boxes through the heavy double doors.

I wondered if that rather tepid exchange qualified as flirting. Was it wrong to flirt with opposing counsel?

"Jesus, Fifi." VJ came up behind me. "Put some hip-hop music in the background and you'd have been pole dancing with that jerk."

"I wasn't—"

"Never mind. Concentrate. I need you to keep track of this expert's deposition testimony and compare it to his trial testimony. We can catch him on inconsistencies."

"You're doing the cross-examination?"

VJ snorted. "No, Reg is insisting that he has to be the one to question all the experts. Reg wouldn't let me ask the man for a glass of water."

"Sucks."

Skyblu's expert was a tubby man with a Yoda-shaped head, an unexpected baritone, and a slight New York accent. It gave him presence. People always say how much they hate New Yorkers, but the truth is, they're also intimidated by them.

He took the stand. "My name is Mordecai Baumgartner. I am the owner and operator of National Aviation Security Company. It's a consulting firm."

"Can you give the jury some idea of what you did before you went into consulting?"

"Yes." I saw Mordecai glance over at the jury, making sure he had their attention. "Before I opened up my own shop—I guess that was some ten years ago now—I worked for the National Transportation Safety Board, crash investigation, and I was with the FBI for five years before that."

Wong stood up and announced, "Your honor, plaintiffs stipulate to Mr. Baumgartner's credentials as an expert." This cut off any more self-aggrandizement that might be coming.

Judge Stein nodded, and Mordecai found twenty-eight ways to say it wasn't Skyblu's fault that Farnswell ended up on the plane with a small-caliber handgun and a grudge. He emphasized that security systems were in place to screen for political terrorists, not for the mentally ill. I wrote that part down. VJ might be able to use it later.

When we broke for lunch, VJ nodded me over and we rode up the escalators together. I was beginning to feel like I had spent the better part of my youth on those escalators. I tried to talk to her about Bosco and Violet, but she shut me down.

"Bosco's an adult, Fifi. I'm pretty sure he can take care of himself. And it's none of your business, anyway, who he's dating."

"It's my business when she comes over and I have to see her and talk to her."

"That's the way it is with roommates. You don't get a say in who they date."

"He's not my roommate. He's my half-brother."

"Same principle. You don't get a say. People get to date whoever they want to. That's it. Anyway, I've gotten to know Violet. She isn't that bad. She's had a hard life, really, in spite of the looks and the money. Her parents had to keep her with relatives here in the States because they already had a child when she was born. You know the One Child policy. Her mother didn't move back here permanently until she was in high school."

"Oh great, now she's your BFF? Look, we all have our baggage. My mother and father were divorced, and, as you well know, my mother is an emotionally unavailable, self-centered narcissist."

VJ was unmoved. "You're just jealous because she's an LA Asian ten, which is the highest level of LA tens that a girl can be."

"Of course I'm jealous. That goes without saying. I'm jealous of a lot of people and I still like them."

"You don't like a lot of people. I'm not sure you like five people in the whole world."

I stopped to count. "Okay, true, but that's only because my standards are high. And my point is that jealousy has nothing to do with it. I don't like Violet because—she's shallow."

VJ silently chuckled as we reached the top floor. "And Bosco isn't?"

"Bosco is appealingly shallow. Violet is just shallow."

"Face it, Fifi. Bosco may just have met his soul mate."

Wong joined up with us in the cafeteria line. The large space was crowded with grey-clad attorneys, men and women, balancing trays of the meatloaf special while trying to hold on to their briefcases and file folders. As soon as we had gotten our food (grilled cheese for me and VJ, yogurt for Violet, and the full meatloaf special for Wong), Wong started in.

"That little toad made a great impression. God-damn Boatwright, he handled him beautifully. We've got our work cut out for us, I could see the jury nodding at everything Baumgartner said."

VJ dismally concurred. "And Porter isn't helping. Grund should be on our side in trying to convince the jury that Skyblu's at fault. But she's just sitting there. She didn't object or say anything, not one word. Good lord, doesn't she realize that if Skyblu gets off, Grund's going to be paying the whole enchilada?"

"Maybe she's thinking there won't be an enchilada," I commented.

"She can't be that optimistic," VJ replied. "The jury has to find that one of those two defendants is responsible. I mean, this is exactly the sort of thing that just shouldn't happen."

Wong shook his head. "I've known Porter for years. I hate her guts, but she's a good lawyer. I don't know what it is. She seems distracted on this one. Like she isn't even trying."

"Maybe she just thinks this case is a slam dunk for her." I ate my chips. Wong and VJ glared. "I'm just saying, it's kind of a hard theory to sell. That a private jet should have locking cabin doors."

Wong and VJ ignored me and dove into a discussion of how to best cross-examine Mordecai.

I happily finished my grilled cheese sandwich, and was reaching for the remaining half of VJ's—she didn't seem hungry—when Wong gave me a head bob.

"So when are you going to re-interview Mrs. Wegliecki?"

* * *

I got reamed out by Wong for five minutes before he had to go make a phone call. VJ shook her head. She had put herself out there by recommending me and, so far, I'd bombed.

That afternoon Wong crossed Mordecai and did an excellent job of it. His tone wasn't exactly sarcastic, but sort of bordering on condescending. Subtle intonation. Very effective.

The day ended late because the witness couldn't come back the next day. And because Judge Stein wasted about twenty-seven minutes castigating the witness for having the temerity to schedule elective surgery while the trial was in session. If Judge Stein's nose had glowed any redder, we'd be wondering about why he didn't have any reindeer friends.

At six o'clock we finally shuffled out. The jury looked like they'd spent the whole day locked in a room with a time-share salesman. Boatwright had dark circles under his eyes, which only added to his appeal. Porter's linen skirt was corrugated and her face was shiny. Wong slumped. VJ didn't, but I could tell she wanted to. Violet looked as fresh as a lotus blossom floating on Echo Park Lake at dawn. I had to remind myself that jealousy had nothing to do with it.

"Can you take a look at these this weekend?" VJ indicated a stack of documents at her feet. "They're the exhibits we're going to use to cross-examine Grund's expert witness on Monday."

I looked at the box without enthusiasm, but "sure" seemed to be the only possible answer. VJ waved and walked off.

It wasn't until five minutes later, as I was backing out of the courtroom with an overstuffed, really heavy briefcase in my hand, that I remembered I didn't have a car. What had been a delightful downhill stroll from my house to the Gold Line this morning, was going to be a grueling feat of endurance going uphill. I'd have to be a freaking triathlete to do it with this load.

"Crap!"

"What's the matter?"

I wheeled around to find Dan Boatwright seated on the bench, packing his own overstuffed briefcase.

"Oh sorry. It's just—nothing."

"Well, it's obviously something." He smiled.

"I just, well, I forgot I took the Gold Line in this morning. I live in Mt. Washington, you know, at the top of the hill. And now I've got all this stuff, and, really, it's nothing. I'm stupid." I mentally winced at how lame I sounded.

Dan looked at me for a long second. Then he smiled again. "That's not so far. I'll take you home. I'm parked right in the Music Center across the street."

For a second I was embarrassed. But only for a second. Then I was elated. You would have thought I planned this, as he gallantly took my briefcase as well as his own. A Southern gentleman.

We made our way through the urine-soaked underground tunnel that connected the courthouse to the parking lot, pretending not to notice the smell. When he suggested dinner I purred like a kitten on a fat woman's lap.

We stopped at an inexpensive little Cali-French bistro in South Pasadena; brick walls, exposed ceilings, lots of windows, starlights on the trees in front.

He ordered the cassoulet for both of us, and a half carafe of the white burgundy.

"You're not from around here," I said as we waited for the food to arrive.

His eyes crinkled. "Not exactly. I was raised in Virginia, near the North Carolina line."

"What brings you to California?" Everyone in LA asks everyone else that question. The answers are "I want to be in movies" and "the weather."

"I interviewed with a lot of the big law firms, but didn't want to go to New York or Chicago. Got an offer with a good firm here in Los Angeles and thought why not? Sun shining all the time."

Ahh, the weather.

"I love it here," he continued. "Miss my mom and dad though."

"You close to your mom and dad?" I asked cautiously. Stable family, good. Possessive parents, not good.

"Of course." He answered with a simplicity I found heartbreaking. I took a drink of water and dabbed my lips with my napkin to hide that thought.

"So are you close to your parents?" he asked.

I glanced at my watch. There wasn't enough time left in the evening to answer that one. Shit, there wasn't enough time left in the year to answer that one. "My mom and dad divorced and then my dad died last year," I said instead.

"I'm sorry, Fifi," he patted my hand and then his eyes widened. "Wait a minute. I just put it together. Was your dad Joseph Cutter?"

I nodded.

"So Victoria's at your dad's old firm. How come you didn't follow in his footsteps? Man, your daddy was the best. I saw him at trial once; I was second-chairing. He kicked old Stellhoffer's butt, he really did."

"The bad tire case? I remember that. I think Mother got a new car out of that verdict." I took a sip of wine. "You an only child?"

"Yeah. What about you?"

"I'm kind of an only child. I have two older half-brothers, unrelated to each other."

It took him a second to work that out but then he nodded. "That doesn't sound like an only child to me. You've got to be close to your brothers?"

I pondered. Living with somebody was pretty damn close. On the other hand, before he moved in with me, I hadn't seen Bosco in years. And I was barely speaking to the other brother.

"Yes and no." I shrugged.

"I guess like most of us and our families."

I let him think that.

The dinner came. It was delicious. Dan was interrupted once by a cell phone call, but managed to keep it brief.

"Work. Sorry," he clicked the phone closed. "You know how it is when you work for yourself, you have to do everything."

"True. It can be a real hassle. But I doubt I could go back to working at an office. Or at least not an insurance office."

His eyes inquired.

"I used to work at Colchester Casualty. My first job out of college. I got fired. They said I was insubordinate. I guess I was. The only other choice was to be subordinate."

"You spoke Truth to Power?"

"It was more like speaking Truth to Aggravation," I confessed.

Dan laughed, a great, head back, full-throated laugh that was neither a bray nor a honk. It was good laugh.

I offered to split the check but he waved my offer away. He even took me home and I never thought that it might not be a great idea for him to know where I lived.

Chapter Twelve

Saturday afternoon I spent working up Carlotta Anelli's report, reminding me yet again how much I hated working on the weekend. I typed up the facts I knew about the accident, which had taken place on a rainy day in March, and I looked at the pictures Wade had taken of the underside of the Cadillac. Clearly the car was totaled. The axle was bent, and there is no way to straighten that out.

As I went through the photos, I carefully reviewed the damage, numbering each print and jotting down a description. And then I got to the photograph of Wade sitting on the john and grinning at the camera. I really, really wish I was kidding about that.

At least now I understood why Carlotta had called me up and unloaded Wade Brockett on me. She must have dealt with him before.

I was sorely tempted to go ahead and send Wade's photo to her along with the rest. It would serve her right for landing me with Wade in the first place. But that would only come back on me, I realized, as she would certainly squeal to management. I couldn't jeopardize my relationship with Colchester Casualty. I clipped the damage pictures to my report, threw the portrait of Wade in my desk drawer, then took the dog for a walk.

* * *

"Some guy called for you," Bosco mentioned, an hour after my return.

"What kind of guy?" I asked sweetly. "A guy with a name?"

"Yeah, he had a name," Bosco conceded, as pulled out the ironing board. "I just don't remember it. Number's next to the phone."

"What's with the ironing board? You going somewhere tonight?"

"Violet's taking me to a blues club."

"You hate blues. Why do you let her boss you around?"

Bosco squirmed. "I don't hate blues."

"You do so. I've heard you say so a hundred times. I think it's pathetic to pretend to like something you don't just to impress a date. You're letting her get the upper hand in this relationship, Bosco. If she only knew—"

"Fifi, you're not going to tell her," Bosco actually looked worried, which made me even madder.

"No, I'm not going to tell her. But I'll tell you something. This girl's pushing you around like a drill sergeant. You need to establish yourself in this relationship. Be the man."

"What do you expect me to do? She already knows that I'm just an insurance adjustor."

I stifled the impulse to point out that he was not even an insurance adjustor; he was merely pretending to be an insurance adjustor, while living off an insurance adjustor. After all, I was trying to build him up. I knew Bosco. Once the chase was over, he'd start treating her like all his other women, which meant he'd put her in the rotation and dump her if she didn't like it.

"You have to do something to impress her."

Bosco looked affronted.

"Outside the bedroom," I clarified.

Bosco looked confused.

"Hey, I know," I said. "Why don't you tell her that you're

a poet or an artist or something romantic and this is just your day job? I mean since it's all fantasy, you may as well go with the fantasy that gives you some juice."

Bosco glared. "You're telling me how to make it with women?"

I had to agree that ordinarily the idea that Bosco needed any help in that direction was absurd. But in Violet he had more than met his match. I heard VJ in my head telling me to butt out. I knew she was right. Then I heard myself in my head telling me that the situation needed me to take control. It was inevitable; I would listen to me.

I expounded on my theory. "You could pretend you have some creative interests."

"So it's okay to pretend to have a job and okay to pretend to have some creative interests, but not okay to pretend I like the blues?"

A car horn honked, and Bosco rushed out the door. A dog responding to his master's whistle. Even Sketch looked disgusted.

I waited until I heard Violet's Lexus back out of the driveway and start up Sofia Drive, then raced to the kitchen to find the phone number. A 310 area code. West Side. Dan said he lived on the West Side.

Dan answered the phone. I grinned. I knew it would be him.

"Hey, I was starting to think you weren't going to call back."

"Sorry, my brother just gave me the message."

"Oh. One of the unrelated half-brothers." Did I imagine a little relief in his voice? "He doesn't, like, live with you, does he?"

"No, no, he's just staying here until he finds a place."

That wasn't a lie. It was a hope.

"Maybe this is too late or you probably already have plans, but if not, I was thinking maybe we could see a movie. I don't know if you like foreign films?"

I totally hate foreign films.

"Oh yeah, sure, who doesn't like a good foreign film?" I heard myself say.

"Well, *The Queen of Minsk* is playing at the Laemmle Grand downtown. It's gotten good reviews. Starts at eight. We could meet there."

I wondered briefly why he didn't want to pick me up, but figured it was just the usual first date caution. Except that—technically—this was our second date.

"Sure, great, I'll meet you at the window," I countered. Meeting at the window, instead of the lobby, would force the issue of whether he was going to pay for my ticket. It's not about the price the ticket. It's about the message being sent.

Okay, in my case, it was about the price of the ticket.

I figured I had twenty-seven minutes to do something about my hair, decide what to wear and put on some makeup. Tight, but possible, since there really wasn't very much I could do about the storm cloud sticking out all over my head. I stuck on a hair band, swiped on plum eyeshadow, and slipped into a black spandex dress. I could be an LA seven. Maybe an eight.

Dan paid for the ticket, which was especially good because the movie was awful. The subtitles were printed in white, and most of the conversations occurred outside during a snow storm. I had eyestrain fifteen minutes in. About twenty minutes in, I felt Dan's phone vibrating in his jacket pocket. He excused himself and didn't get back until after two minor characters had sex and an important character died.

"Sorry, that was about a witness; guy I needed to get a hold of," he whispered to me upon his return. "What's happened?"

"That big bearded guy just fell under a snow plow."

"Ivan? The head of the secret police?"

"Right. See he—" I was just about to make something up when the screen went black.

"Interesting technique," I whispered. But when the screen stayed black and people started to grumble, it became apparent that something had gone wrong. The final clue was when the weedy little high-school junior in the badly fitting jacket came to the front, nervously apologized for the technical difficulty, and offered everyone their money back.

Man, this date had just been jinxed from the beginning, I thought as we each headed toward our cars. Maybe he could ask me for a drink? I wondered.

"I guess I'd have to say I wasn't loving that movie. In fact," Dan looked sheepish, "I'm not too wild about foreign films."

I glowed.

"All in all, this date wasn't meant to be," Dan said as we stopped by the Squire and I fumbled in my purse for the key. "That phone call was a witness I need to talk to. He just got off the late shift. I could go talk to him now—I mean, unless you want to go get a drink or something—I told him I'd catch him in the morning—"

He so obviously wanted to go talk to his witness that I didn't really have the choice. If I'd been Violet, I would have been able to ignore completely what Dan wanted and insist on drinks and dinner. But, all my faults acknowledged, I'm still not Violet.

"Tell you what," I said. "How about you let me make you dinner tomorrow night?" This, I thought, would be a good test of whether he considered me a lesser someone he just could see whenever he wanted to see, or if he considered me someone for whom he would change his plans.

"Well, I usually work on Sundays, you know, when I'm in trial."

Wrong answer.

"But, well, I guess I gotta eat. What time should I be there?"

Right answer. I told him to be there at seven.

As I pulled out of the parking lot, I saw Dan standing next to his car, punching in numbers on his cell phone and looking very frustrated, obviously not getting through. I knew how he felt; we get terrible cell reception up on Mt. Washington.

It was with a mingled sense of anticipation and disappointment that I arrived home. Dan obviously was a workaholic, somewhat pretentious in his taste in movies, and not particularly considerate. But it's not like I was perfect. I was mentally cataloging the list of characteristics that made me less than perfect as I unlocked the front door. I was totally unprepared for what happened next.

* * *

An arm like an iron bar smashed against my throat. I gagged and kicked out as I was lifted off the ground by my neck. I couldn't see well in the dark, but I could smell aftershave and sweat. When the spiked heel of my Ferragamo knockoffs connected with shin, I heard a soft "Fuck!"

The arm tightened and I couldn't breath. My lungs began to hurt. I was dragged over to the hall closet which, I noticed through a rapidly darkening field of vision, was open, the light on. My attacker had been in there, searching for something.

"Where is it?" he hissed, dropping me on the floor, adding a vicious kick to the kidney. I gasped for air and curled up in fetal position. Out of the corner of my eye I saw the dim shape of Sketch stretched out on the floor in the living room, not moving.

Oh God, he's killed the dog, I thought with a pang. Poor

dumb dog. I grieved momentarily, but right then I needed to be concerned about me.

"Where is it, bitch?" the voice was louder now, but still hoarse and whispery. I felt another kick, and then another. I looked up and saw a largish man, dressed in black with the de rigueur ski mask covering his face. This mask, ludicrously, was topped with an orange pom-pom that bounced with each kick.

I scrambled behind the vacuum cleaner. I tried to scream, but my throat was sore and I had no air in my lungs. A box of old reports fell on my head.

"Where—is—it?" he asked again, punctuating each word with a vicious jab of the boot, shoving the vacuum cleaner into my arms and legs. I risked another look in time to see him take an object from inside his coat jacket. Nunchucks, and he twirled them like he knew how to use them. The vacuum cleaner shell shattered at the first blow. I finally screamed.

Sketch, who wasn't dead, just totally unconcerned about his temporary owner getting the crap beaten out of her, finally woke up and saw what must have looked to him like a man having fun with a stick. In a single graceful lunge, one end of the nunchuck was in the big dog's mouth, and he was pulling like a tractor.

The asshole in the pom-pom hat was strong and pulled back, dragging Sketch with him. Until the dog let go and the big man crashed to the floor. I scrambled up and ran out through the kitchen to the back door, but there was no pursuit, except by Sketch, who was overjoyed that people were finally playing proper doggie games.

I made for the rickety old fence in the back yard, ready to fling myself over it into the neighbor's yard, but stopped when I heard a car start up and peel out, zooming down Sofia at a very unsafe speed. I couldn't have pursued in the Squire even if I wanted to, which I very much didn't want to.

I walked slowly back to the house, and, holding Sketch by the collar, went around in front to make a hundred percent sure that the pom-pom man had truly departed before I went back in.

A portly neighbor in a tangerine sweatsuit taking her shitzu for a late night walk sauntered by.

"You should tell your friends to drive more carefully around here," she scolded me. "That guy in the red car, he could have run right over little Sheba's Dream." She indicated the fur ball at the end of the leash.

Sketch saw the fur ball and lunged, practically dislocating my shoulder.

"You'd better get little Wet Dream out of here," I advised the neighbor. Since the big goof had, technically, if not by intention, saved my skinny ass from a bad beating, it didn't feel right reprimanding him. Especially not in front of his new girlfriend.

Red car, I thought, as I turned to go back in.

Chapter Thirteen

Bosco showed up with Violet the next morning. She was fabulous in a black-belted top and red satin pants. I told them what had happened. Violet looked skeptical, like I'm some neurotic attention whore just making shit up. As if.

Bosco's reaction was pretty much focused on Sketch and how heroic he was, but at least he believed me.

"If it weren't for Sketch, you'd be history," Bosco exclaimed. "Man, it's a good thing I have a dog. See, that's why I thought it would be good to get a dog. Protection."

"I thought you got the dog so you could—" I began.

"Yeah, that's right. I also needed him for my show with Wildman," Bosco cut me off, glancing at Violet.

"Your show with Wildman?" I wasn't catching on.

"Yeah, Dante Wildman. You know that Gallery, the Tomlinson-Teague. They proposed a joint show, Wildman will get top billing of course," Bosco made a self deprecating moue. "But it would be a big step in my career."

"Your career as an insurance adjustor?" I asked, still slow on the uptake.

"My career as a photographer," Bosco corrected me.

"Oh," I said, finally catching on. "That other career."

"I've told all my friends that Bosco's kind of a Renaissance man," Violet cooed. "I mean, he owns his own business, and he's writing a book, and his photography. There aren't too many guys who are so successful and also have a wonderfully developed artistic side."

I glanced over at her perfect face. Looked as if my little plot was working. Or had I just shot myself in the foot?

He beamed. "Violet and I were talking last evening about my next project. Kind of an industrial take on the Wildman themes. Placing the iconic dog against the gritty urban background of modern man."

I glanced over at Sketch, lying on the floor. He twitched and passed gas. Iconic.

"I know just the place!" Violet exclaimed. "One of Chu's clients owns a warehouse in an industrial complex. I've offered to get Bosco into the lot. I think it would be marvelous."

I mentally grumbled. She was still taking charge.

"Can't you just see the aesthetic potential?" Bosco enthused. "Rows and rows of nearly identical trucks lined up, gleaming in the bright sunlight." Bosco stared off into the middle distance as if he was visualizing the artistic possibility of trucks and dogs.

Violet flashed a big smile, or big for her. "We're going to get some great shots. Wildman is going to flip out. I'll bet we get some really big names at the opening. It's going to be so hot."

"Oh, yeah," Bosco nodded. "DeNiro came to the last one I did with Wildman, and Robin Williams too—you know he does some pieces for that gallery. It's going to be incredible."

Violet's eyes lit up in anticipation of impressing all the celebrities. She was wriggling as she pecked Bosco's cheek. "Gotta run, babe." Babe? I snorted, as she sashayed out the front door.

* * *

"Say, that bruise on your neck is turning purple, maybe we should have a doctor look at it," Bosco said. He reached out to give me a poke, and I slapped his hand away.

"Listen, I've been thinking, you know, since I almost got killed last night."

"Yeah," said Bosco dreamily, "Isn't Sketch great?" He looked fondly at the still inert form on the floor beside him.

"What I've been thinking is, that guy was looking for something, Bosco, and I don't know what it is. I don't even have any idea."

"So we should investigate?" Bosco perked up.

"Uh, no. I was thinking of going to Joe. Telling him about it," I said.

Joe was my other half-brother, the black one. An LAPD officer, he had been in vice for years. Thanks to me, and a serendipitous event, he had recently been promoted.

"What, are you crazy? He won't be able to help you. It's not like the members of the LAPD are his own personal assistants. We have to do this ourselves."

Bosco and Joe didn't get along. Not that they saw much of each other as adults, but even as kids, there had been a deep-seated antagonism. When Half-Brother Joe went into law enforcement and Half-Brother Bosco went to law ignoring, the antipathy grew deeper.

"I've got a plan of action," he urged. "Violet and I went to the Back Room last night"

I was impressed, in spite of myself. "How on earth did you get in there? You're telling me somebody actually remembered that stupid sitcom you were on?"

"No, Violet got me in. Burton's girlfriend works there."

"Oh yeah, Wong told me that."

"You know, Burton was the document clerk on the Skyblu case. He knew Violet, of course, and took her there one night with a bunch of people from Wong's office."

"Like Norman Chu? I have a hard time picturing that geeky dude being let in at the Back Room."

"I don't know about Norman Chu, but Burton's girlfriend got Violet in. She's a total regular there now."

She would be, I thought. "Did you meet the girlfriend last night?"

"Just briefly, but I got her number. I thought we'd call her up now, and see if she'll talk to us."

I sighed and reached for the phone.

"Let me do it," Bosco forestalled me. "We're going to have to convince her to talk to us. You piss people off."

The yin and yang of my existence. I piss people off. People piss me off. I ceded the phone.

Nadia was home, and willing to talk. We got the Squire fired up and drove over to the apartment complex where she had lived with Burton. The 2 to the 134 to the 210 would have taken no more than eighteen minutes with a normal car, but in the Squire it was a solid thirty-three minutes.

I recognized the building from the newscast. The Altadena Arms was well protected. Every window had bars, and the front door was heavy glass. There was no buzzer to connect to the occupant. Presumably you were supposed to call your party on a cell phone, but I didn't have one. Bosco used to have one, but he stole it off a dead guy and eventually the calling plan ran out.

So we yelled up until somebody heard us and yelled back.

"Shut the fuck up!"

Not a promising opening line but it was the only response we had gotten.

"Hey, wait, wait, we need a little help here." I tried to sound pleasant, but it's hard when you're royally aggravated and having to scream at the top of your lungs to be heard. Still, it worked. Mr. "Shutthefuckup" did, in fact, know Nadia, called her up for us, and she came down and let us in.

"Hard as hell to get in here," I complained. Nadia was a thin woman, hard-looking but in an intriguing way. Her black hair was cut short and shaggy, and her face was sharp—chin, cheekbones, and nose. She smoked, the way people used to smoke, the cigarette as a prop. We followed her into the elevator where she punched 4, leaned against the No Smoking sign on the back wall, and inhaled deeply.

"If it was that hard to get in here," Nadia said, picking up on my last comment, "then you tell me how some brain-fried druggie figured it out and shot the shit out of my boyfriend."

"Sorry," I muttered.

"Why are you sorry? You didn't shoot him, did you?" Nadia asked as she sauntered off the elevator.

I gave Bosco a look that said, "She's all yours."

The apartment was at the end of the hall, I noted. The druggie-burglar home invader would have had to skip seven other apartments to light upon Burton and Nadia's.

Inside, the apartment was much nicer, if somewhat bare. A couch of rich, oxblood leather dominated the space. A complicated-looking entertainment center sat half in and half out of boxes, as if someone had been interrupted setting it up.

"Nice place. Are you going to stay here?" I asked, sinking down into a ratty, tan butterfly chair that clashed with the new leather couch.

"Hardly." Nadia injected more scorn into that one word than I thought possible. She sat down on the couch and patted the cushion next to her for Bosco. "It was Steve's place. I think he, like, knew the owner or something, got a great deal on the rent when he moved in. But it's nowhere near the Back Room. It took me like fifty minutes to get home last night. Anyway, they'll probably raise the rent on me. And I'll never be able to afford the payments on that stuff." She indicated the wide screen, DVD player, and speakers. "Steve bought all this the day before he died, you know. He never even got to see it delivered. Nice bruise, by the way." She indicated my neck, and cut her eyes to Bosco. "Did you throttle her?"

Bosco smiled, even though I didn't find it the least bit funny. "No I didn't, Nadia. I'm not that kind of guy."

"In fact, if I could interrupt here, that's why we wanted to talk to you," I swallowed my irritation. "I think that whoever did this to me might have shot Steve."

Nadia stared. "What are you talking about?"

"It's like this, Nadia," Bosco interjected. "Fifi here was hired by Wong, Wu & Chu to help out on that airplane case, you know? Steve worked on it too."

"I know. He talked about it some."

"So right after your boyfriend got shot, someone tried to steal Fifi's purse, and we were almost run over by a couple of big rigs. And then somebody came into the house and did that to Fifi last night. They were looking for something."

"Something connected to the airplane case?"

"Well, that's what we don't know," Bosco admitted. "But did Steve say anything to you? Anything that might lead you to believe that he had something in his possession that other people might want?"

"What kind of thing did you have in mind?" she asked.

I thought I sensed nervousness. After all, the universe of things that other people might want was a broad field. For example, it was possible that a fairly brisk business in weed, meth, and Ecstasy was done out of the Back Room, which might have made a perfectly good sideline for Burton. But this chick certainly wasn't going to admit that to a couple of strangers, especially if she was complicit in it.

"Something that could be hidden in a hall closet," I offered. "In fact, something that could be in somebody's purse."

That let out a huge stash of marijuana, I thought. Nadia must have thought so, too, because she warmed to the idea.

"So it would be something like a document or

photograph or something like that?" she mused, and glanced around the apartment.

I shrugged. "Sure."

"The cops searched, you know, the night it happened. They didn't find anything."

"Yeah, but they wouldn't necessarily know what they saw was connected to what they thought was a random breaking and entering."

Nadia looked speculatively at us for a moment. "I went through Steve's things, too. Afterwards. There wasn't anything connected to work at all. He'd been on disability, you know, for a long time."

"Can we take a look?" Bosco asked.

Nadia crossed her arms. "No, pretty boy, you can't. I wouldn't let you anyway, but I already gave most of his personal stuff to his mom and dad when they came out. It was just like his clothes and books, his wrestling trophy from high school, stuff like that." She considered. "I'm not sure I see how the shooting could have anything to do with the airplane case. Steve was basically a document clerk at Wong, Wu & Chu. It was just a temporary job until he finished his degree. He was going to go back to school." She seemed defensive on behalf of her dead lover. I nodded to show that I understood Steve was so much more than just a document clerk, which irked me since, at the moment, I was just a document clerk.

"But," she added grudgingly, "now that you mention it, he did say something the day before—you know, the day before it happened. Something about the airplane case and strange bedfellows."

"Strange bedfellows?" Bosco repeated. "Did he say anything else?"

"No, but he seemed pretty amused by it."

"Like it was a joke?" I asked.

"No, not like a joke. Like something good was going to come of it."

"Good in what way?" I pressed.

But Nadia shook her head. "I have no idea."

That's what we were left with, no ideas.

* * *

Leaving the apartment building, Bosco pointed out the thickness of the front door. It wasn't a bank vault or anything, but it was certainly more than your average front door.

"Fifi, I don't think it could be a simple breaking and entering." Bosco voiced my thoughts as we got to the Squire. "The killer had to be let into the front door, and then he had to go to Burton's floor, and then he had to walk by all those other apartments. A random burglar would have tried one of the closer apartments. And why didn't anyone hear the shot?"

"I don't know. Maybe he used a silencer," I suggested, untroubled by assigning a male gender to the killer. That's not stereotyping; statistics bear me out.

"Exactly. What strung-out druggie do you know who bothers to use a silencer on a routine job?" Bosco countered.

"Let me be clear, Bosco. I don't know any strung-out druggies. But he could have just followed somebody in and happened, in his drug-induced state, to wander up to Burton's door and knocked, and the guy answered. People do. And maybe druggie had a silencer because he stole the gun from somebody who had a silencer. I don't even think they're hard to buy any more. You can probably find some website that takes PayPal." I climbed into the Squire and unlocked the door for Bosco.

"You know I'm right," Bosco said as he struggled with the flimsy aftermarket seatbelt. "You're just being an asshole."

Bosco had a point, I conceded to myself.

"I'm telling you, Fifi, it was someone Burton knew.

Here's another thing. That's a way nice apartment with some way nice furniture. He had a brand-new entertainment system and a brand-new leather couch. Burton was just a document clerk. He'd been on work comp for a while. How'd he afford all that stuff?"

"You're right about that," I said. "I happen to know exactly how much he was getting." I remembered this piece of information because it had rankled. Burton's monthly payments for doing nothing were roughly equal to my monthly take-home for busting my ass. "But Nadia explained the apartment. She said a friend got him a good deal on it. Of course, it's possible that Burton was supplementing his income with the sale of recreational pharmaceuticals. The kind of business that can lead to sudden, unexplained termination."

"You have no reason to believe that."

"Young guy, club connection, more money than he should have."

"Total speculation."

"Semi-total speculation." I pulled out of the parking lot onto the street.

"If we could have gone through his stuff, we might have been able to see something," Bosco fumed.

"Well, we can't. But maybe we can look through the stuff of another dead person. Let's go do that." I headed the little car to the 210 Freeway and we were rattling into the parking lot at Villa Flora thirty-seven minutes later.

Dolores lit up like the Vegas Strip when she saw Bosco walk in. She came out from behind the reception counter.

"How are you doing, Mr. Dorff; not too sad, I hope? I was so sorry to have to call you with the news. Poor Mrs. Wegliecki."

"Not too sad," Bosco replied, with a subtle emphasis on the too, implying that he was just the right amount of sad. "We didn't know if there would be a memorial service or anything."

Dolores shook her head regretfully. "We don't do that here, you know. If we did," she lowered her voice confidentially, "we'd be having them all the time and it would depress the other residents."

"Of course." Bosco patted her arm, and she practically squealed. "I understand. We're just here to pick up her things."

Dolores hesitated, and I moved in with the story Bosco and I had prepared on the way over. I'm not a very good liar, but she wasn't looking at me too closely.

"She left everything to Rudy Dunlap, didn't she?" I asked. This was a guess on our part, but it seemed like a good one. "For taking care of her little dog for her?"

Dolores relaxed. "Yes, that's right. He brings the little poodle. You know, she didn't leave much."

"He asked us to bring whatever there is to him," Bosco smiled. "He still drives, but not as much as before. And besides,"—the clincher—"I think he's really upset. You know, at one time he and Mrs. Wegliecki were—"

"Oh, I didn't know it was like that," she cried, her romantic heart was touched beneath her ample breast. "Poor man. And how sweet of you," she patted Bosco's hand, "to come all this way to help him."

Dolores turned to lead us back through the EMPLOYEES ONLY door into the receptionist's area and the inner office. The space was long and narrow; shelves filled with messy files, random office supplies, and dead plants were built into the walls on both sides.

"I'll call José and tell him to get the boxes," she said. "You just sit there." As we perched our bottoms on the two folding chairs indicated, she turned to make the telephone call. Maria, the shorter and stouter nurse, observed the proceedings and looked sourly at us.

"They have to sign for anything they take," she announced officiously. "And it needs to go in the file."

"I know." Dolores tossed her head. "They said they would."

We hadn't, of course, but Dolores was right in concept. We would be pleased to sign anything they put in front of us.

Dolores flounced over to a low shelf and, after some pointed riffling, withdrew a file. She waved it like a flag in front of her co-worker's face. Edna Wegliecki's file, I surmised.

We waited for José in strained silence until the phone rang. There was something I really didn't like about the way that phone rang.

"Villa Flora." Maria paused. "What do you mean?"

She looked at us and my bad feeling increased.

"The man who is picking up her things is already here." Another pause.

"No, he's here. He's here now. I'm looking right at him." And she was. "I don't know what to tell you, sir, can you hold the line a minute?"

Maria's face betrayed signs of confusion. She covered the hand set and hissed at Dolores, "Some guy is calling. He says to hold Mrs. Wegliecki's things for him, he's on his way to pick them up."

"What's his name?" Dolores demanded. Maria put the phone back to her ear.

"Sir, what is your name?"

"He says his name is John Cartwright."

Dolores picked up the file and flipped though it. "I don't see any John Cartwright listed here. He never visited her. Unlike Mr. Dorff, who has visited several times." She smiled in our general direction.

"Find out what his connection is," I suggested, shifting nervously in the chair.

"Sir, can you please explain your connection to Mrs. Wegliecki? I'm not understanding who you are."

As the nurse listened, she became more agitated.

She bit her lip and shifted her weight from foot to foot, obviously feeling out of her depth as the person on the other line became more aggressive. The caller's voice rose loudly enough for the whole room to hear.

Bosco popped up and stretched out his hand. "Let me talk to him. I'll clear this right up."

Mesmerized by hazel eyes crinkling kindly at the corners, Maria gratefully relinquished the phone.

"Hello, sir, this is Mr. Dunlap's representative speaking. We have been authorized by the residuary legatee to take immediate possession of the remains of the estate. What, may I ask, is your authority?" Bosco strode around the office as he talked.

Both Maria and Dolores breathed sighs of admiration for the Masterful Man in Charge. I fought to keep my face expressionless.

"I see, I see. So essentially you are only interested in the return of library books? Hold on, I'll check." Bosco looked over to the admiring pair. "Mrs. Wegliecki didn't have any library books did she?"

Dolores and Maria both shook their heads.

"Sir, I'm not sure what information you had, but there were no library books. Yes, we're certain. No problem. Glad to be of help."

I was the only one who noticed that Bosco had rung off several seconds ago and that he had kicked the cord out of the jack on his third pass by the desk.

"Just a misunderstanding. Had to do with some library books they thought Mrs. Wegliecki still had."

"Well, he didn't have to be rude about it!" Maria exclaimed. "I mean, you expect better manners from a librarian."

At that moment José arrived with a dolly and four cardboard boxes. We signed the release and carried the boxes out to the Squire as quickly as we thought we could without arousing suspicion.

As we were backing out, the front door opened once again. I was surprised to see the figure of our old soldier girl come haltingly toward us, waving her stringy arms. I stopped the car.

"Fifi, get going," Bosco urged. "We don't have time to wait for her. That guy could show up any minute. He said he was on his way."

I raised my finger to punch the starter button again, but something about the look of purpose on the old bat's face stopped me.

"Just a sec," I said and ran over to her, to save her having to make her painful way to the car.

Dolores and Maria appeared at the door and yelled in unison. "Mrs. Henderson, you have to go back inside, it's time for *Jeopardy.*"

Mrs. Henderson tossed her head dismissively at them and grabbed my wrist. "She died right after you came here, you know. Right after."

"What are you saying?"

"I'm saying she died that afternoon."

I remembered, with a chill, the acid reflux episode. Mrs. Henderson read my eyes.

"That's right. Acid reflux. Acid reflux, my fanny. She was poisoned."

Chapter Fourteen

I saw spots. "No, no, you've got it wrong," I protested. "I wouldn't hurt Mrs. Wegliecki. I came to her to find out what she knew about something, something important, at least it could have been important, except I never found out. I wouldn't kill her. I wouldn't kill anyone."

This last was patently untrue; there were plenty of people I would kill, if I was a hundred percent sure I could get away with it and no blood was involved. And there was even one person—one—that I may have already helped kill, but that was in the past, and I had put it firmly behind me.

What I meant was, I wouldn't kill an innocent, helpless old woman. Mrs. Henderson, a soldier who had Done Her Share of socially sanctioned killing, or had, at least, requisitioned the correct forms for it, understood.

"I'm not accusing you. I'm giving you the proof." She thrust a pill bottle into my hand. "Maybe I'm wrong about you, but I've got to trust you. Nobody here will ever believe me, and if they did, they'd try to cover it up. Bad for business. You're the only chance I've got."

I really hate to be somebody's only chance, but before I could protest, Bosco yelled, "Move it!"

I looked up and saw a red car that could very well have been a BMW Z4, trailed by a cloud of dust, swing into the access road about a half-mile away.

"Thanks, I'll do what I can," I gasped. I slipped the

117

bottle into my jacket pocket and ran back to the Squire, pushed her button, and neatly reversed. In the rearview mirror, I saw Maria and Dolores converge on either side of Mrs. Henderson and lead her back through the front door.

"He's parking on the other side," Bosco advised me as I accelerated onto the main road. "It doesn't look like he's seen us yet. He's getting out, looks like he thinks he's still in time."

"Who is it?'

"I can't tell. I don't think it's anyone I know. He looks Mexican."

"Mexican? The guy from the grocery store was Mexican."

"Kind of a tall Mexican."

"Well, he'll find out we've split with the stuff as soon as he talks to your Not Very Secret Admirers," I muttered. "And then we'll be toast. I can't outrun him."

"Pull in here," Bosco commanded, pointing to a driveway, marked by a mailbox and bordered by overgrown hedges. I did as instructed and was relieved to find it was a rather long stretch, although uphill, bumpy, and, for the last forty meters, unpaved.

"What happens when we reach the house?"

"We'll just say we're lost."

"We can't say we're lost, that's so obvious," I complained.

"It's obvious because people get lost all the time," Bosco argued back.

"Can't you pretend you're selling something?"

"No. I am not going to be a door-to-door salesman, Fifi. Everybody hates a door-to-door salesman. We'd be back on the road in ten seconds. Just in time to meet up with the red-car guy."

"Yeah, but—" I started and then realized, as we reached the crest and a large ranch house came into view, that a cover story might not be necessary. It appeared, from the large collection of white pot-bellies and spindly legs, that there was a pool party going on. I gazed with satisfaction at the scattering of brightly colored lawn chairs and striped umbrellas.

"Hey, cool car," somebody yelled. "Park in back."

I was more than happy to oblige, especially as that is where the smell of barbeque was coming from.

We spent a companionable hour-and-a-half, sheepishly explaining that we had forgotten our swim suits to everyone we met, which of course was everyone, including our host and hostess, Gerry and Arleta. Nice people.

When we finally said our farewells, Bosco was seven beers and two burgers to the good and we were convinced the red car was long gone.

It was a pretty ugly surprise to see a guy on my porch and a red car parked in front of the house when we got home.

✳ ✳ ✳

"Oh shit!" I braked and started to reverse.

"Wait, wait, I don't think that's the same car." Bosco was looking more carefully. "That's an old piece of crap car. Look, it's all dented."

He was right. It was not a new BMW Z4. Not by any means. It was a 1980's vintage Corolla that probably belonged to a neighbor.

"And that's not some weirdo in a ski mask on my porch," I said, with a grin. "That's Dan."

Bosco shot me a quick look, but I didn't stay to wonder what it meant. I parked at the curb and hopped out. Dan was just coming down the steps. He had parked his Audi in the driveway, which is why I missed it.

"Hey, I thought maybe you were standing me up." He grinned like a Little Leaguer who'd just knocked the ball past the first baseman and hadn't yet remembered that he still had to run. "I mean, I know I'm a little early. I hope I'm not throwing you off."

"OK by me. It means you can help me cook."

"Well, I don't like to brag," Dan linked his arm though mine, "but I'm a great cook. In fact, I make Mario Batali look like the fry guy at Burger King."

"Wonder what you'd say if you did like to brag?"

I felt, not exactly happy, but sort of a pleasant anticipation, as if I could be happy, very soon. Dan helped me into the house with the boxes and I hardly heard Bosco's shouted advisement that he was taking the car, and didn't wonder where he was going.

By 8:30 I was ready to be happy right now. We'd spent a delightful fifty-eight minutes stirring a creamy, fragrant risotto, thirteen minutes washing and tossing the baby green salad, and twenty seconds taking the profiteroles out of the box. Dan had brought the wine, and after viewing the alternatives of the card table or the kitchen table, he decided we should eat outside. I got a blanket and some cushions. We carried our food out on plastic trays and pretended my overgrown lawn was a meadow.

"Reminds me of summer nights in Virginia, only without the humidity." Dan stretched out, propped up on one elbow. The sky was an inky haze, but there was enough illumination from the assorted security lights of my neighbors for me to see his face. "I grew up in an old house, older than this one. No air conditioning, you'd pretty much have to have supper on the porch, couldn't stand the heat. My momma and daddy and I would play cards until the sun went down and it was cool enough to eat."

I tried to picture that and all I saw was Bubba and Becky Sue with the chickens. Or what if Dan came from money? Then it wouldn't be Bubba. Maybe the Colonel in his white suit and Mrs. Colonel, in Laura Ashley prints and pearls? Her name would be Magnolia Belle, but everyone calls her Miss Dolly. I started to feel uneasy. After all, I haven't spent a lot of time in the South, but sometimes people named Colonel and Miss Dolly have strong opinions relating to the color of their children's friends. "You an only child?"

"Yeah. The Boatwright pride and joy." He grinned, and I tried hard not to let the bad thought slip into my head that the Colonel and Miss Dolly aren't going to be founding members of the Fifi Fan Club.

"What are your folks like?" I said, trying to make amends for my terribly unjust, but probably accurate, suspicions.

"Daddy's just a good ol' boy." See? "Likes to hunt and fish. Momma's sweet most of the time, but you don't want to cross her."

We talked a little more, and then a nice silence fell. We finished the wine and Dan got up. "It's getting chilly." We dragged the cushions back inside.

Dan did the dishes, and I had just gotten a fire going nicely in the old stone fireplace when he pulled out his cell phone and asked me if I minded if he just "checked for messages."

"I don't mind but you won't get reception up here."

"What do you mean? We're ten minutes from downtown Los Angeles."

"The way it is. It's why I don't bother having a cell phone."

Dan tried to smile and then asked if he could use my land line. I pointed him toward the kitchen. "It's just that the client asked me to check in every few hours."

I watched his receding back with some disbelief. Who requires their lawyer to check in every few hours?

I politely stayed where I was and didn't try to eavesdrop, praying that this wouldn't be a repeat of last night. But from what I could hear, it didn't sound good. The call lasted for eighteen minutes. When he finally came into the kitchen, I could tell that the night was done.

Dan looked angry and embarrassed.

"Fifi, I am so sorry," he began.

"No, it's okay, something to do with the trial, right? Or shouldn't I ask?"

"You can ask," Dan replied. "I just can't tell you. I really am sorry. When this is over, which will be very soon, as it turns out, I'm going to make it up to you."

"Hey, it was a great evening." I did my best to smile sincerely. "I can't complain. You did all the work. What could possibly be better?"

He lifted an eyebrow in answer.

"OK." I tried to sound perky and not sigh. "Whatever. See you tomorrow."

"See you tomorrow."

Tomorrow, however, turned out to be pretty crappy as well, because I found out what the phone call was about.

Chapter Fifteen

It had probably never even occurred to Dan that I hadn't mentioned our relationship to VJ. I mean, until Saturday it wasn't even a relationship. It was just a ride home. A ride home with dinner. Now, however, it was three dates. Or one quick date and two truncated dates. I could totally have justified not telling VJ until that morning, when I could have casually mentioned it, and made it sound not so bad. Didn't get the chance.

"Hey, sorry again about last night." Dan came behind me in the courtroom, as I was arranging the notebooks VJ would be using that day on counsel table. He nodded pleasantly to VJ, whose black eyes glittered dangerously.

"I told you it's—" my voice dried as I was pinned to the wall by a laser glare. "It's fine, really," I finished weakly.

"Well, I still feel bad, I'll call you tonight." Dan leaned in to say something else, but VJ slammed a stack of papers on the table.

"Do you mind?" she asked. "I believe your table is over there." When Dan had backed away, VJ turned to me. "Perhaps I could have a word with you outside?"

The big doors closed behind us, and VJ grabbed my arm, propelling me further down the hall.

"Have you been seeing him?" she demanded.

"Well, I don't know if you could say I've been seeing him," I stalled.

"Don't prevaricate. This is serious."

"Last night I invited him over to dinner," I admitted. "But he got there and he couldn't stay, that's what the apology was for. So that's not really seeing someone, is it?" I hoped she wouldn't probe further, but she was in trial mode and ready to deliver a blistering cross-examination.

"When was the first time you went out with him?" she demanded.

"Look, on Friday he drove me home." I gestured. "I didn't have a car here. And I had all your stuff. He was just being nice."

"He isn't nice," VJ told me. "He isn't nice at all. He is the enemy. I told you that. When was the next time you went out with him? Saturday? Did you go out with him on Saturday?"

"I tried to, but the movie we were going to was cancelled," I answered her, making it sound like we hadn't gotten out the door.

"Movies don't get cancelled."

"The film broke," I admitted.

"So you were already there in the movie theatre with him?"

I nodded.

"And last night?"

"I'm telling you it was just dinner. He left early. VJ, come on. What's all this? You're the one who gave me that big lecture about not interfering with other people's love lives."

"Bosco and Violet are a completely different situation. It isn't a question here of playing Dear Abby. This is a question of compromising my case. The most important case I've had in my career to date. And you didn't even tell me."

"Look I didn't have a chance—"

"Balls! You could have called me over the weekend. You knew where I was. I was working."

"Yeah, see, you were working, getting ahead, getting an

advantage, while I was distracting Dan so he couldn't work. So really I was doing you a favor."

"You are done," she said. "I've had it with you. I'm going to advise Reg Wong and you will be off this case. Get out."

She spun on her heel so fast I felt the breeze.

"Aw, come on, Veej, have a heart. I didn't say anything to him about the case." But I was talking to a quickly receding back.

Hurting more than I thought possible, I followed her back into the courtroom and took a seat in the row behind plaintiff's table. I'd talk to her at the break. I'd explain again. I'd fix this. Because I needed the job, I told myself. Wong, Norman Chu, and Violet came in. If I'd been more observant, I would have noticed that they weren't carrying anything—no transcript, no briefcases, no nothing.

At nine o'clock, Judge Stein took the bench. "Before we bring the jury in," he said, "I understand that there is a partial settlement to be put on the record?"

What the hell was going on? VJ glanced furiously back at me, but I gave her my patented don't-look-at-me-I-don't-know-what's-going-on shrug.

"That is correct, your Honor." Wong and Norman Chu stood up. "A settlement has been reached between Skyblu and Grund on the one hand, and the Wong, Wu & Chu plaintiffs on the other hand."

"Do you want to put the terms of the settlement on the record at this time?"

Boatwright and Porter stood up and began to speak simultaneously. Boatwright gestured for Porter to continue. She drew herself up to her full height and fussed importantly with the floral scarf draped around her neck. I realized then how much you could get to dislike a tall woman who wears scarves.

"Your honor, we can put all the terms on the record except for the amount, which is confidential."

The judge nodded and Porter proceeded to recite the

terms of the agreement, which was a complete and full release of both defendants from all liability in exchange for the payment of a sum agreed to by the parties last night, which was documented in e-mails by and between Mr. Walton Yarborough of White Plains Insurance Company by and on behalf of Skyblu, Ms. Cissie McMull on behalf of the insurance conglomerate known as Insurance Coverage for Aviation Risks (US), also known as ICARUS, and Mr. Norman Chu of the law firm of Wong, Wu & Chu, which are not to be made part of the record.

"Are Mr. Yarborough and Ms. McMull present?" the judge asked.

"Yes sir," Porter tilted her head at the two figures sitting in the back, inviting them to come forward.

"Mr. Yarborough, vice president of claims, Orange County," said the big bald guy, practically swallowing the microphone and wrestling down the lectern as he grabbed the sides with both hands. His suit was a grey cashmere tweed, beautifully tailored to his considerable girth, and his shoes looked handmade.

"Cissie McMull, for ICARUS, your honor." Ms. McMull was dressed in a polyester yellow and brown windowpane jacket, which didn't precisely match the tan pants.

"You agree to the terms of the settlement as Ms. Porter has recited them?" They both did. Then we had to have the entire contingent of the Wong plaintiffs come up and likewise give their consent. It was nearly ten before they were through, and the judge decided to take a fifteen minute recess before calling the jury in.

VJ had complained about not being able to do as much of the trial as she liked. Now she'd be doing the rest of it. Alone. She was good, I knew that. But she'd had what? Maybe three trials before this? Smaller cases.

As soon as the judge had disappeared into chambers, VJ buttonholed Wong. I maneuvered my way to within ear distance.

"Don't blame me," he was saying as he held up his hand."I didn't know a goddamn thing about it until late last night. Norman negotiated it."

"You're telling me your junior partner negotiated the biggest wrongful death settlement of your career. I'm expected to believe that?"

"It's true. These were Norman's clients to begin with. He did real estate work for Han and Fang for a few years before the accident. And anyway, the defendants are the ones who called us and made the offer. I would have done the same thing Norman did. Accepted."

VJ stared at him.

"Look, kid, if I'd had any inkling of this, I'd have warned you. But I didn't know. All I can do is tell you that I'll give you all the help I can. All of our files; we'll turn them over to you this afternoon. Even work product. I'll give you everything. I'll pay Fifi through the end of the month. How's that?"

I looked at VJ. I knew she was stuck. She looked at me and knew that I knew she was stuck. She shifted slightly to include me in the conversation, without exactly looking at me. "Can you be over there this afternoon to pick up the files? I'll need to prepare for the cross of Grund's expert witness tomorrow, which Reg was going to take."

"Apology accepted, VJ. The files won't fit in my car, but maybe I can borrow my cousin's catering truck. Lemme use your cell phone."

I went outside to call D'Metree. He agreed, but roped me into delivering party supplies for him in exchange.

As I walked back into the courthouse, I realized that according to Wong's account of how the settlement went down, the trial attorneys hadn't anything at all to say about it. No wonder Dan was so mad last night. Skyblu's insurance carrier must have settled the case right out from under him, without even asking him what he thought. And Wong apparently didn't have any more to say about it than

Dan did, except he didn't look angry. He looked dazed with joy.

When I returned, VJ was in a huddle with Yarborough and McMull, Dan and Porter hovering on the fringes.

"I'll communicate your offer to my client," I heard her saying icily as I approached.

She caught sight of me and ordered me to find Mrs. Rayburn, which I did. She was propped up against the wall, looking like she'd like a cigarette and surrounded by an excited chattering group of Wong, Wu & Chu plaintiffs.

"Ms. Smith wants to talk to you," I told her. She looked at me shrewdly. "They make me a settlement offer?"

"I think so, but we'd better let her explain."

VJ's face softened when she spoke to Mrs. Rayburn.

"They made an offer. You're not going to like it."

"Don't hurt me none to hear it," the older woman said.

"It's one hundred seventy-five thousand dollars. I feel it's too low, if you want my opinion. I think the trial is going well, but of course there are no guarantees. And like you just heard, all of Wong's clients have settled. Reg Wong won't be taking the laboring oar." VJ cleared her throat. "Reg Wong is a very good trial lawyer. He's done a great job. If you don't settle, we have to finish this trial with just me. I'll be flying solo. Pardon the pun."

Mrs. Rayburn's mouth thinned. "Bastards. Tell 'em to go stick it in their ear. How dare they offer me a hundred seventy-five thousand for my Earl, when they're paying sixty million dollars for those other guys. Do the math; the Chinamen are getting fifteen million a person. It's not right."

"Well, actually, Mrs. Rayburn, we don't know how much they are getting," VJ gently explained. "The settlement was confidential."

"I know exactly how much they're getting," stated the woman, jerking her thumb down the hall. "They were discussing it right in front of me. Probably thought I didn't understand."

I stared. "You speak Chinese?"

"Spent eight years in Beijing. Worked for a hotel. We catered to English-speaking tourists and businessmen, but I was in charge of the domestic staff and ordering supplies. I wasn't what you'd call real conversational or anything, and I never could write one letter, but I learned my numbers real good."

I recalled her testimony that she had done hotel work and was embarrassed to admit I had assumed she meant places like Barstow and Rancho Cucamonga.

But VJ was focused on a different line of thought. "That's incredible. At the last settlement conference we had, Reg's opening demand was sixty million. And they didn't offer anything. What the hell happened? I mean I know I said the trial was going well, but I can't honestly say it was going that well. Especially not for Reg. His damage expert wasn't allowed to testify. He couldn't put up the numbers to support his claim."

Mrs. Rayburn's forehead creased. "I can't be sure now, but I got the impression that Wong had found something out, had something on that big good-looking bald guy." She meant Yarborough, I realized. I guess you could call him good-looking if you like huge and hairless.

"What do you mean 'something'?"

"Don't know. Something that Wong agreed to give back to him. I couldn't understand that well."

"Wong found out something, and he's holding out on you," I said, mildly annoyed with Mrs. Rayburn. I mean, if you're going to bother to learn a language, learn the whole goddam language, right?

"Sodding bugger," VJ breathed. "What could it be? A sixty million dollar secret."

"Grund is paying most of it too, I did pick up that much."

"Grund? That doesn't make any sense at all. Yarborough doesn't have anything to do with Grund. Grund had responsibility, sure, but not as much as Skyblu. We've always said that. There has to be an explanation for this. I just can't imagine what it could be."

"I don't know, VJ, but I'll find out. I'll try to find out."

"What are you doing to do, Fifi? Ask your boyfriend?"

I shot a look at Mrs. Rayburn who was following the conversation with interest.

"I don't think Dan knows, if that helps. This settlement came as a total surprise to him."

VJ turned pointedly to her client. "Well, if we don't find out what it is, then I'll just have to win this thing straight up."

She looked at Mrs. Rayburn. "Are you ready?" she asked.

"I'm ready, dear."

They turned resolutely back toward the courtroom.

✳ ✳ ✳

As I walked down the hall, leaving VJ and Mrs. Rayburn to do battle, I heard what passes for a commotion in those quiet halls.

Up ahead, huddled next to the door of a courtroom not in use, What's-his-name Grund had Cissie McMull by the arm. Their eyes were blazing, but his eyes were blazing more.

"You let me down." Grund's voice rose, and several people ambling down the hall glanced over. He glared furiously around and lowered his tone. I slowed down as I approached, hoping to hear something.

"Get your hand off my arm." McMull was trying to wrench away from his grip, while not drawing any more attention.

"You let me down," Grund repeated. I stopped fifteen feet away, pretending to check something in my purse. Like

I was looking for my keys. I shouldn't have bothered. Grund and McMull weren't paying any attention to me.

"It wasn't my decision," I heard her say. "I was as surprised as you are."

"Yeah, but you're not as screwed as I am. You go on to the next case, like nothing happened." Grund gestured wide. "We ended up paying most of the settlement." He paused for breath. "And—We—Didn't—Do—Anything—Wrong!"

"I know that."

"Then what the hell did you settle for?" Grund's voice again grew loud.

"I told you, it wasn't my decision." McMull looked like she was going to say more, but the clerk assigned to that courtroom came out with her hands on her hips. "You two are going to have to take that someplace else," she informed them. "We're about to start a hearing in this department. You can't be making noise here."

Grund and McMull fell silent. I turned around so I wouldn't have to pass them, and went out the back exit.

I puzzled all the way home. If it hadn't been Cissie McMull's decision to settle, then whose?

* * *

"What could have made them settle?" I had delivered the Wong, Wu files to VJ's firm, and D'Metree's party supplies to an anxious mother of the bride, and was home by 9:31 that evening. I sat at my card table and gave Sketch a scratch on the head. He looked up and drooled a little. I pulled up Google and typed ICARUS. Five thousand plus hits, some referencing the myth of Icarus and Daedalus, a few salacious hits, and one site that will probably get me prominently featured in the Homeland Security data base. None had anything to do with insurance. I started over. What was the name again? Insurance Coverage Aviation Risks United States. It popped up.

I read through the site, as ICARUS detailed the corporate

hierarchy, the fabulous claims service, excellent financial stability, "drawing on the strength of twelve A-rated insurance carriers." Nothing in there about tossing away some large portion of sixty million dollars for no good reason. I was about to exit the site when my eye was caught by the list of members of the consortium. I skimmed through the list of participating insurers, some large, some small, none with aviation departments of their own. Brunswick Insurance was listed, for a two percent share. So Brunswick, the insurance carrier for Skyblu, also insured two percent of Grund's liability. What did that mean? Probably nothing. These companies just put up the money. They probably hired an independent adjusting company to handle the claims.

I hit the claims-handling link. "We offer the finest claims-handling services, designed to provide the most efficient claims-handling for our participating carriers and insureds. All of the claims personnel of Heartland Adjusting Services are licensed pilots blah blah blah."

I hyperlinked Heartland Adjusting. And found myself at the website for Brunswick Insurance.

Heartland, the claims-handling company responsible for adjusting the claim against Grund, was actually owned by Brunswick.

I blinked. That meant Brunswick controlled the settlement for both parties. And Brunswick was really in a tight place, having one hundred percent of the Skyblu loss, and two percent of the Grund loss and, according to the newscast I had heard, not doing so well.

Another thought occurred to me. If Brunswick insured one hundred percent of Skyblu and two percent of Grund, Brunswick would be much better off if Grund got hit for most of the liability. Of course, all of the insurance carriers would be better off if there was no verdict at all, but that wasn't going to happen. Skyblu was going to get hit for something. Maybe the defendants refused to settle before because Yarborough figured that by trying the case, there was at least a possibility that the jury would see it all through jury-colored lenses and find a large percentage of liability on Grund.

Once they decided to settle, Yarborough, through Heartland, could force Cissie McMull to pay out a larger part of the settlement share. But if he could do that, then why didn't he just do that a long time ago? I stared at the screen for eleven minutes, working out the permutations in my mind, when I almost heard my Pop's voice, *Fifi, you're stranded in nowhere with a bag full of nothing, and you were late getting here.*

Chapter Sixteen

"A great big party!" Violet's arrival interrupted my research. I came out of the dining room to find her beaming at Bosco. "To celebrate the settlement! Reg wants to have the party right away, like tomorrow, before my mother and Mrs. Han go back to China. We are having it at Reg's house, which is a truly fabulous property in the Hollywood Hills, ohmigod the view, but there is no way he can book a caterer by then. I mean, you would want to use Lucky Dragon or the Empress, but they are, like, so booked right now."

Violet nattered on for a while about party details, circling back to the catering dilemma. There were going to be over a hundred people, she said, including the entire office of Wong, Wu & Chu and their families. What could they do?

"I have a great idea," I heard myself say.

Violet opened her mouth, glanced at Bosco, reconsidered her sarcastic comment and cocked her head, as if ready to listen.

"Any kind of Chinese food you can serve here, they can get in China, right?"

Violet nodded.

"And probably better, right?"

Another nod.

"What would be super cool is if you served them something that they can't get in China. Something totally different."

"You obviously have never been to Beijing, Hong Kong, or Singapore, Fifi. We have the best of every cuisine in the world."

"Not every cuisine," I stated positively.

"Like what don't they have?"

"Like soul food, girl. Real soul food."

Violet was momentarily baffled. She wanted to insult me, and she wanted to dismiss soul food as a world-class cuisine, but anything she said along those lines would come out racist and she knew it. Racist would not look good in front of Bosco. I took advantage of her temporary silence.

"I know a caterer I can get there by tomorrow. D'Metree does killer barbecue ribs, honey chicken, sweet potato flake, spicy cornbread. Maybe start with some fried turkey wings, finish off with buttermilk pie. It'll be the best food those noodle chewers ever had, I guarantee it." See, I don't have a problem with coming off as racist.

Bosco picked up where I was going. "I know the caterer Fifi's talking about, does a lot of gigs for Oprah. Dante Wildman uses him, as a matter of fact. You should have seen DeNiro scarfing up the jerk pork at his last show. They were talking about it for days. If you were able to line up D'Metree, you'd be a hero, Violet."

"Oprah? DeNiro? Top end? Really? You think? And you could get him for me?"

"Absolutely," I promised. "We're like this." I crossed my fingers to show her.

As soon as Violet left, I got on the phone to D'Metree. He was so tickled, I hated to bring him down. But I had to.

"Just one tiny little thing I need you to do for me in return."

"What's that, Fifi?"

"I need you to hire me on as a helper for the evening."

"What, are you crazy? You don't know anything about cooking. Or serving either. I'm not going to blow our first big chance to break into the crossover market."

"Hey, I'm the one who gave you your first big chance to break into the crossover market."

"Maybe so, but I'm not going to let you blow it."

"You don't even have to pay me."

"No way. Sharlene," I heard him calling out to his wife. "Fifi wants us to give her a job." I heard Sharlene yell back. "Tell her to forget it. I'd sooner hire that half brain Bosco."

"Sharlene says forget it."

"Listen, D'Metree, I'm with the deal, or there is no deal," I said firmly. Several seconds passed as D'Metree steamed.

"Okay," he finally caved. "But you stay in the kitchen, hear? You stay out of sight."

After a show of hurt feelings and reluctance, I promised to stay out of sight. Didn't promise to stay in the kitchen though.

✳ ✳ ✳

"I caught you hiding behind the sofa! Fifi Cutter, do you want to explain what in the name of God you were doing hiding behind the sofa?"

It was twenty-nine and a half hours later. Sharlene had caught me.

"I asked you a question, Fifi, and you goddamn well better answer it and answer it now!"

I opened my mouth to oblige but no sound came out.

"This is bad and this is serious. Do you hear what I'm saying, Fifi?" Sharlene's eyes blazed. "And you better be glad it was me caught you, not Mr. Wong. He woulda called the police. We'd have been ruined, Fifi. You woulda been arrested."

"But none of that happened," I managed to squeak, as I tried to struggle out from my slot between the back of the sofa and the wall. Sharlene was a formidable woman even when she was happy, and she was not happy right now. It was two o'clock in the morning. She and D'Metree had been trying to pack up since midnight, with the help of the Samoan woman who had viewed me with suspicion all evening, as if I was going come in and take her job. Right. In point of fact, I had been trapped behind the sofa in Wong's home office since nearly eleven 'clock, when Sharlene had tactfully chased out the revelers who had disturbed me mid-snoop and effectuated my entrapment. But it didn't feel like a rescue. It felt like a bad whipping and it lasted several minutes, culminating with a wholesale character attack.

"You are irresponsible and thoughtless, and you make everything worse, Fifi. You should be put down, in my opinion. You begged us to let you help tonight and you didn't help. You didn't lift one finger. And that's because you're a no-good, lazy ass, worthless piece of slightly dark flesh."

"Well, I couldn't help, could I?" I protested, finally shoving a word in. "I was stuck hiding behind the sofa for three hours, wasn't I?" I wished she would quit calling me out by name.

"Yeah, about that. You never answered my question, did you Fifi? What the goddamn hell were you doing hiding behind the goddamn sofa?"

"Look, I can't explain."

"You can't? Is that because an unexplainable, universal life force mysteriously took hold of your physical body and shoved you down behind the sofa and in some way unknown to man kept you there by telepathic force? Is that what you mean by you can't explain? Because if that's not what you mean, then I'm gonna think that maybe you can explain, you just don't wanna explain!"

"I mean, it's confidential, it's this job I'm working on—"

"No, no, no, stop right there. This here is the job you're supposed to be working on." She gestured at the ashtrays, glasses, and dirty plates that littered the study. "I was looking for you all evening to help out a little, and here

I find you, laying down on the job. Literally laying right down on the job."

"Fine," I huffed, "I'll pick up the glasses and plates." I worked my way to my feet from my uncomfortable posture.

"Don't you touch those glasses. Those are our good glasses. I am not gonna have you breaking all my glasses and plates." Sharlene paused for breath when D'Metree walked in and I had to hear it all again for his benefit.

"You want to know about your cousin, D'Metree? You listen up. Let me tell you where I found that girl. I come in here and finally shoosh all those drunk kids out so I can start picking up like I've been doing since midnight, and wondering where Fifi is. So I flip on all the lights and what do I see? I'll tell you what I saw, D'Metree. I saw a pair of little-bitty feet in nasty white Vans peeping out from behind that sofa against the wall. That is what I see. I like to have had a heart attack. Thought for a minute it was a dead body. But no, no dead body, just the laziest ass body in the whole wide world. Hiding behind the sofa to get out of work. Did you ever hear such a thing?"

"No baby doll, I sure didn't." D'Metree was staring at me.

"It's not like we twisted her scrawny little arm to make her come here. Oh no, she begged for us to take her on tonight. No, not begged, she blackmailed us to take her on and then what? Hiding behind the sofa."

I plopped down on my erstwhile refuge and hid my face in my hands. There was a lot more to say on the subject, apparently. Didn't get home until 4:12 AM.

✳ ✳ ✳

"Replay the scene, the whole scene," VJ demanded when I got her on the phone at 11:24 Sunday morning.

"OK, when we first get there, Mrs. Wong takes us on a tour, to show us the living room, dining room, where all the bathrooms are, stuff like that. Reg Wong has a study at the far end of the house, down a long hall. We don't go in, but she points it out to us, you know? All night, I'm working in the kitchen, right? Sharlene and D'Metree got this Samoan woman working for them; she's the one who hands stuff around, so I don't have to go out with the guests. Everything is great, nobody sees me. Then I scope the place out. At first, everybody is mostly outside, on the patio, hanging around the pool, drifting in to get some food, which we have all laid out in the dining room. You got some older people sitting down in the living room, but most people are milling around, getting pretty tanked. There's a lot of booze flowing—I mean a lot. Around eleven I'm pretty much done in the kitchen, food's all been served, we're just waiting to clean up, you know, and the crowd is all outside, listening to a bunch of speeches and stuff, congratulating themselves, remembering the dead guys, some in English, some in Chinese, the widows are crying, got the picture?"

"Yes, thank you."

"A pretty reasonable assumption is that this part of the evening is going to take some time. I slip out of the kitchen, real stealthy, and tiptoe down the hallway. The door to Reg's study is closed, but it isn't locked, so I sneak in. No lights, but I see there is a desk facing the door and a file cabinet to the right. I start looking around, you know. The desk is covered with papers; you got maybe five piles, all stuff about various real-estate deals. They must be the lawyers for every goddamn apartment building in Southern California. Then I thought I'd just look in the drawers—"

"I don't want to hear this, I'm going to put down the phone now."

"VJ, don't put down the phone. Don't. Listen to me. I got away with it. Well, almost, but Sharlene and D'Metree aren't going to rat me out. It would screw them, too."

"That is not the point. The point is my ethical obligations," VJ was sputtering.

"Ethical obligations, right. I know. Let's just say you're my lawyer, right? And I'm confessing to you, right? It's a lawyer-client communication, privileged. Anyway, I had a right to be in the house, and nobody said don't look at the papers on the desk, did they?"

"Bollocks and blast."

"Yeah, yeah, whatever that means. I'm in the study. I try the desk drawers, but they're locked. I start going through the file cabinet. While I'm doing that, I notice there's a seating area on the other side of the room; it's a pretty big room, with a loveseat and two armchairs, coffee table, like that. And then I hear steps coming down the hall, and there isn't any other room down at that end of the hall, and there isn't any other way out the room."

"Keen of you to have thought of that, if a bit late."

"Risks have to be taken, VJ," I reminded her. "I had no time to do anything but jump behind the sofa. What else could I do?"

"Sure, sure, you did exactly the right thing, I see that. The sensible course. Did I say sensible? I meant brilliant, actually."

"That's what I'm saying!"

"Go on."

"I'm behind the sofa. They come in. My heart is beating so bad, it was like a whole drum line. I think they gotta hear me. But they don't. They turn on a light, but just a standing lamp, not the overhead, so my part of the room is still dark. So I'm safe for a while. And then they start talking."

"They?"

"Wong and Norman Chu. I hear Wong unlock his desk drawer. He takes something out and gives it to Norman."

"What was it? Did you see it?"

"Are you kidding? I had my face mashed down in two inches of silk pile."

"Then how do you know—"

"I heard him, VJ, I heard Wong say, 'Here it is, Norman.

Take good care of it.' And Norman says, 'They want assurances that there aren't any copies.' And Wong says, 'They have my word.' Then they start to leave. But just as they open the door, a whole bunch of people come in and I heard Wong's son ask if it's okay if they sit in the study and listen to music, and they did. I was stuck behind the sofa for three hours, man, three hours. And their music was the worst. It was like 80's punk or something."

"Oh great," said VJ. "All to find out that Wong has something he's trading for the settlement of sixty million. Something we already knew. Perfect."

"We know something else, too."

"What?"

"We know that whatever it is, it's something we could theoretically have a copy of." I smiled.

Chapter Seventeen

Coming down for my coffee on Monday morning, at 6:50, I found Bosco staring blankly into space.

"What are you doing up so early?" I asked.

He looked at me with mournful eyes.

"Violet got you up?" I guessed.

He ducked his head in acknowledgment.

"She got some plans for the day?"

Another silent assent.

"What kind of plans? That photography thing?"

Bosco took another sip. "She said the light's better earlier."

"That is so funny. Like the light's gonna make a difference," I chuckled.

"Hey, all of this was your idea."

"What are you going to do for a camera anyway? I know you don't have a camera." I knew this because, if he'd had a camera, he would have sold it on e-Bay a long time ago.

"Girl I know let me borrow hers," Bosco gestured toward a black bag on the floor.

"Lindsey? Monica? Oh, no, it has to be Chelsea, the artist one, right?"

Bosco nodded. "I like Chelsea. She's very generous."

"I'll bet she is," I poured myself a cup of coffee. "But you'd better take her name tag off the bag. Probably want to try it out a few times, as well."

Bosco slipped off the heart-shaped leather name tag and

pointed the camera in my general direction. I scowled as he snapped the shot. "I don't like people taking my picture. Especially when I'm in my bathrobe. It's not even my good bathrobe."

"Ease up, it's just for practice. Anyway, it's not like I never took a picture before. What do you think this dealie is here?" he asked, fiddling with a little black dial.

"Ejector button," I replied. "And just in time. Your girlfriend's here." Sketch had alerted us to the car pulling in the driveway by barking manically and catapulting himself at the kitchen window.

After they left, I took my time, drinking coffee, munching toast. At 8:10 I reluctantly made for the dining room to finally go through the box of stuff we had picked up at Villa Flora Assisted Living.

The first two items were photograph albums; the usual bad photos of graduations, Christmas, birthday parties, vacations to Disneyland and the San Diego Zoo. They were ordinary pictures but they had an emotional edge—because I knew that the only person who cared about these photos was dead. There was one of a bride, taken in the seventies. Her hair was gi-normous and the lens angle emphasized a nose that didn't need emphasizing. It was probably little Jimmy's mom, I realized, the one who got hooked on coke and disappeared during Jimmy's formative years. She looked happy in the picture, though. I guess none of the bad things had happened yet.

The important pictures were all of little Jimmy. There were a ton of them. I cackled in glee as I pulled out one of him from what had obviously been his interminable awkward stage. He was dressed up for Halloween as the Son of Sam. Perfect! Blow that one up and it could be very useful in the closing argument, I thought.

And then I found something even better. A stack of old check registers for, like, the last twenty years. Mrs. Wegliecki spent between forty-five and sixty bucks a week on groceries, she paid her gardener thirty bucks once a month, and she was punctilious about gas, water, and electric. Flipping through 1997, however, I noticed recurring regular payments to a Dr. Chandra Pritha. In fact, it turned out to be payments made once a week for two years, fifty-five a visit. Had to be a cheap shrink, right? Then, six months before Farnswell got his job as an air steward with Skyblu, a whopping four thousand eight hundred thirty-five to Sunland Clinic. I looked it up online—took me a while. It was called Sunland/Tujunga Private Clinic now. An understanding temporary environment focused on non-traumatic re-entry from psychotic and depressed states. A loony bin!

That old bitch must have been lying to us the whole time, I thought, sitting there in the cafeteria, eating our pie and shoveling shit faster than a felon. But why would she lie to us? She didn't have any money, so nobody was going to sue her. I tried to put myself in her head. What mattered to her? From the pictures, Jimmy. And maybe what people thought of her. And him.

If she admitted that her precious Jimmy was a whacko, and that she had always known he was a whacko, then there could be some hate talk. People might very well blame her for not advising Skyblu before they issued him an employee ID that got him through the security procedures and allowed him to sneak on a plane filled with innocent people.

God, you'd think once you dragged your sorry ass to an old-folks home to live out the rest of your days, you could be free of the lead weight of public opinion. But no. People get older, but they don't change. Mrs. Wegliecki had spent her life covering for Jimmy, and she kept it up after he died.

Which reminded me, I should make sure that pie hadn't killed her. I went up to my room and found the bottle of pills the old soldier had given me, still in the pocket of my jacket. How was I going to find out whether there was something in here that shouldn't be in here? Until I did that, I could hardly begin to find out who had poisoned her.

The most I could do is identify who had a motive.

Oh crap. I felt my stomach clench. The Wegliecki archives were great for VJ's case, but really bad for Dan. It put a lot more comparative fault on Skyblu for not finding out about Jim Farnswell. Worse, though—much, much worse—it meant that Dan had a great reason for wanting to beat us to Villa Flora, to make sure we didn't get our hands on this stuff.

I nearly broke out in a sweat when I remembered that the guy on the phone had given his name as Cartwright. Dan's last name was Boatwright. Was Dan the guy on the phone? Was Dan the guy in the red car? His car isn't red, it isn't a BMW Z4, I argued with myself. I argued right back, too. Maybe he had two cars, maybe he used a friend's car for illegal activity.

He was a very ambitious guy. Even ruthless. Wong had said so, and he had no reason to lie to me about that. Would he go this far to win a case? It seemed incredible, but I remembered him talking about his new firm, his big chance with Brunswick Insurance. How it could lead to a ton of other work, if this case turned out well for him.

Maybe the check registers were the thing that the pom-pom man was looking for. Maybe Dan was the pom-pom man. But the pom-pom man was almost certainly the one who had shot Burton—rubbed out Wegliecki—that made Dan—I rubbed my cheeks with my hands. This couldn't be happening. Not really. I thought of those eyes, as sweet as rock candy, that little sideways smile. Dan, the guy who was close to his parents.

No, here's an even better reason it can't be Dan, I told myself. Dan couldn't possibly have beaten me back to my house the night the movie died. Dan couldn't be the pom-pom man. I felt better until I remembered Dan on the cell phone trying to get through to someone who couldn't get reception. Like we can't get on Mt. Washington.

Had he been trying to warn my attacker that I was coming home?

I grabbed a beer out of the fridge, popped it open, and then poured it down the sink when I realized it would certainly make me barf if I drank it right then.

Back up, I commanded myself. If Dan had gotten me out of the house to let his accomplice ransack the place, all he had to do when the lights came up at the movie theater was take me somewhere to get a drink or something. I'd have gone with him, right? I felt better and was sorry I had poured the beer away. I opened the refrigerator again. No more beer.

Back to the pills. How do I get them tested? If I gave them to half-brother Joe to let the LAPD test them, would he do it? Not without an open case, I guessed. And if they opened a case, they might see all the arrows pointing towards Dan. The arguments that convinced me he was innocent might not convince them.

I couldn't sit still. I would have liked to take the dog for a run, but Violet and Bosco had the dog. I had to wait until VJ got back from court and, believe me, it was a long wait.

When I finally got her on the line, at 5:43, I found it hard to contain my excitement. "I think I found out the reason they paid. I've got it here. You've got to come over. It's big. Huge. I think I did it."

VJ's calm tones soothed me right down. "Belt up, you silly bint, what are you on about?"

"I've found some great stuff, VJ, really, I did. I found out what Mrs. Wegliecki could have told us, only she didn't, and she wasn't going to, so even if I'd gone back in time, it wouldn't have made any difference, so it's not my fault. But she should have told us. She didn't have the guts."

"Okay, you're raving, and it's not at all entertaining or informative."

"Come on, you've got to see this."

"I was going to relax a little this evening. De-pressurize, think about what evidence I'm going to put on in rebuttal."

"Okay but wait till you hear," I said and explained what I had found.

"The photo, we'll never get in," VJ observed. "We don't know who took it, or when, or where; don't really even know it's James Farnswell then, do we?"

"Well, of course, it's him," I began, but she cut me off.

"And too prejudicial. After all, a schoolboy Halloween costume—but these check registers, now, they give me a place to start."

"A place to start! Why aren't they the place to finish?"

"Because, Fifi, I still have to prove what these payments were for."

"It's obvious," I howled in frustration.

"I need a bit more than your perception of what's obvious. I can probably set this up, though. At least call the doctor, find out her specialty at that time, ask her if she had such a patient. Same with the clinic; that'll be even easier to establish. Both the doctor and clinic are likely to keep records, even back that far, which they are not likely to want to turn over. But really, all I need is sufficient fire to have placed Skyblu on notice that there was smoke. After all, we don't have to prove Farnswell was crazy. His dramatic final gesture speaks for itself. We have to prove that Skyblu should have known he was crazy before that."

"Yeah, I think we can safely sell the jury on the 'Farnswell was crazy' theme."

"On the other hand, there is no way this is what got Wong and crew his bonanza. For one thing, it doesn't explain why Grund paid the majority of the settlement. Sorry, Feef, it's good, but they had an atomic weapon."

✳ ✳ ✳

147

It came to me in a dream.

Maybe it didn't actually come to me in a dream.

But when Sketch woke me up the next morning, before I had even opened my eyes, I had the idea. I found the number I needed in a pile of miscellaneous crap I had carted home from Colchester Casualty, waited until 9:23, and called.

"Forensic Laboratories of Orange County."

"Hello there, this is Carlotta Anelli, I'm with the medical liability claims department of Colchester Casualty," I announced, trying to sound as much like a bloated nymphomaniac as possible, given the vast differences between Carlotta Anelli and myself. "We are investigating a pharmacy malpractice claim and I need some lab work done." I gave her the fake information on my imaginary claim, right down to a phony authorization number for her to bill to Colchester's account. I wasn't really in a position to front the $3,424 charge. I bargained with myself to shave my bills to Colchester over time to make it up. I guess what I'm saying is that I cheat, but I don't steal.

That night I woke up to the "pop pop pop" of gunfire from somewhere down on the flats, Glassell Park, or Cypress Park. Maybe Frogtown. Two or three minutes drive and a world away from my safe mountaintop refuge.

Sketch woke up, ears alert, and barked softly. I gave him a pat, and he lay back down.

It happened once a month or so, the gun shots echoing up the canyon. I always checked the time just in case somebody died and it mattered when. A detective in a tweedy coat would ask me, "What time did you hear the shots, Ms. Cutter?" And I would reply, "It was 3:31 exactly." I smiled at my foolishness and drifted off back to sleep.

* * *

I got to the courtroom in time for the morning recess. VJ gestured me up to counsel table. "Don't look over at the expert," she commanded, and my eyes were irresistibly drawn to the elephantine lout in the ill-fitting suit. He was bending over whispering to Jan Porter, and I could see his shirttail had worked its way loose and was hanging down below his jacket.

"I said, don't look," VJ's jaw clenched.

"Sorry. What's up?"

"Lon Green. He's terrible." VJ murmured.

"Terrible? You mean terrible for us?"

"No, I mean terrible for Grund. He was decidedly weak on direct, and his manner is off-putting." She flicked her glance over to the jury. "The Golden Girls look disgusted and the Ditzy Blond was trying not to laugh."

VJ then proceeded to serve up Lon Green flambé. She challenged his credentials, pointing out that one of the schools he claimed to have attended hadn't existed at the time, and that one of the articles he claimed to have written had been published some three years earlier by a popular Romanian terrorism expert who routinely made the talk show circuit every time a bomb exploded in a crowded market.

Credibility shredded, the man was sweating so much he coulda filled up the LA River. VJ started in on his opinion testimony.

"You have opined, have you not, that locking doors are unnecessary in private charter jets?"

"That's right." He mopped at his forehead—which was roughly the size of Denver—and shifted uncomfortably in his seat.

"Because—let me be sure I have this straight—only foreign-born Muslim extremists have any desire to use airplanes as weapons?"

"That's not exactly what I said."

VJ didn't make the mistake of asking him what, exactly,

he had said, but changed up on him. "Although I understand your main opinion to be that it would cost too much."

"That's right."

"Are you aware that the United States has spent over one trillion dollars on fighting Muslim extremists in Iraq?"

"I don't know the precise number."

"But you admit it's around a trillion dollars?"

"I said I don't know the precise number."

"But you know it's around a trillion dollars?"

"I guess."

His recalcitrance had given VJ the opportunity to say "a trillion dollars" three times. I smiled. Mr. Grund, I noticed, had pretty much turned to stone.

VJ continued to pummel him with statistics. How much time per year air travelers spent extra to get through security lines. The budget for Homeland Security. The projected cost of 9/11, man-hours lost, price tag to rebuild, lost opportunities. Each question had to be repeated two or three times before the grudging "I guess." The guy was a slow learner.

Then VJ pointed out a simple arithmetic error Green had made in his calculations. Mr. Grund could restrain himself no more and slammed his palm down on the table. The jury swiveled in that direction like spectators at a tennis match.

"It was a rout." I told VJ afterwards. Mrs. Rayburn added, "You creamed that big boy good."

VJ shook her head. "It was a walkover. A giveaway. Hardly brilliant lawyering on my part."

"Still feels good though, doesn't it?" Mrs. Rayburn asked.

VJ shot her a sideways look. "I guess," she replied.

VJ had asked for one day to put on her rebuttal evidence, but it didn't take more than two hours from start to finish. I had tracked down the custodian of records of Sunland/Tujunga Private Clinic and served him with a subpoena to show up in court on Friday. The doctor who had treated Jimmy was long gone, out of state and out of subpoena range, but the records would be better anyway. After so much time, there was little chance of the doctor remembering anything useful.

"How'd it go?" Bosco asked me when I got home Friday evening.

"Like we had planned it that way. The big surprise witness right at the end. The Sunland/Tujunga records were full of everything we needed. The cat that was found gutted and burned. A kid he tried to set on fire. Uncontrollable screaming matches. The importance of keeping him on his medication. And best of all, a diagnosis of antisocial personality disorder."

"Boatwright must have crapped his pants."

I winced. Dan hadn't asked me out that weekend, though. In fact, he was a little curt when I approached him during the lunch break. "Not going to be able to see you this weekend. I've got to prepare for the closing arguments Monday." That's what he said. Not sure what he meant.

Chapter Eighteen

"Ladies and gentlemen of the jury." Dan stood up to give his closing argument. VJ had said I didn't have to come down today. There was nothing more I could do. But I couldn't stay away. This was on my own nickel, and Dan looked sweet in a navy blue suit with a red and white tie.

"This is my final opportunity to address you, to tell what I think before you tell me what you think, which is of course the only thing that matters here in this courtroom. Now you've already heard from plaintiff's counsel, Ms. Smith here, and she's awfully good, and you're going to hear from her again when Ms. Porter and I are done talkin' to you. As the judge explained, the plaintiff's lawyer gets two chances to talk to you. But I only get this one chance."

Dan was right, VJ had been good, addressing the jury with confidence and setting forth all the evidence in a logical way, reminding the jury of favorable testimony they may have forgotten about. But it was clear, in his first few minutes, that Dan was raising the bar. His accent had thickened, gone from a plate of buttered grits to molasses-glazed ham and sweet corn and fresh lemonade and sun-ripened melon from the garden. My stomach growled. It was 11:32 and I hadn't had breakfast.

"Other people's money is real easy to give away, I know that," he said. "Got a guy killed here, no fault of his, I'm not sayin' it is. But is it the fault of my client, either? Did plaintiff prove to you it was my client's fault? That's what you got to decide. You're all sympathetic people, I know that. Good people. But you need to be fair people here today because our system of justice, which is the very foundation of our country, doesn't let you give away other people's money based on sympathy. No, you have to do some hard work, and it's tedious work I'm asking you to do, just like a soldier in the army might have to do weeks or months of tedious work before going into battle. Your work here today is just as important as the work of a soldier, and just as hard."

The jury looked rapt, and I didn't blame them. Here was a guy that might, maybe, have tried to kill me, and I still wanted to be close to him. Of course, I reminded myself, he didn't try to kill me. I had proved that to my complete satisfaction. Hadn't I?

"See, your duty here today is to go back to that jury room and read all those instructions, each and every one, and then read the verdict form, from top to bottom, and decide every issue, every question. And when you do, I think you'll find that Earl Rayburn was a hell of a nice guy. I think you'll be real sorry about what happened, but that the fault for his death lies with Jimmy Farnswell, and nobody else. That my client had no way to know what demons Jimmy was fighting, no way to know about the torment going on his mind."

Dan paused and walked back to counsel table, picking up a few sheets of paper which he held up high for the jury to see, and incidentally giving me a brief view of his face.

"You've heard tell about a doctor that saw Jimmy years ago, that recommended a rest in a place where he could get help. Help he apparently needed, according to this report right here. But what didn't you hear? You didn't hear that my client ever knew about that doctor, ever heard about Jimmy needing some help."

I squirmed in my seat, but only a little. VJ had warned me not to ever let the jury see when the other side scored a hit. The jury wasn't looking at me, anyhow.

Dan's closing was a compact sixty-three minutes; he was obviously of the school that believed the jury's attention span was no more than the hour given to most television dramas.

Judge Stein glanced at the clock. "It's a quarter past noon. Time for the lunch break. We will begin again at 1:45 sharp. I mean that. Court adjourned." The gavel rapped, and we all stood up. Out of the corner of my eye, I saw Yarborough on the other side of the aisle, a row back.

As soon as Judge Stein had disappeared into his chambers, I slid over to the door to the courtroom, as if I was waiting for VJ. Yarborough didn't bother to glance at me as he swept past, but he stopped dead when I said, in a low voice, "Hey Mr. Yarborough, I've got a copy."

"What did you say?" his glare was a little unfocussed, his usual glare for unimportant people who might momentarily delay him on his way to the rest room.

"I said, I got a copy. I thought you'd like to know." I held his eye. The glare snapped into focus.

"You—" he spluttered.

But before he could express his innermost thoughts on the subject, the jury started to stream out, passing, as they had to, directly between us. I smiled and kept the door open for them. Yarborough had no choice but to do the same on the other side or risk appearing boorish. He couldn't quite manage the smile, and by the time the last juror had nodded his thanks, VJ, Mrs. Rayburn, Dan, and Jan Porter were lined up at the door as well. I grabbed a stack of files from VJ and followed her out.

We set up in the cafeteria again, but VJ declined to eat. She wouldn't talk either, which made time drag. I finished my yogurt and we were back in the courtroom at 1:33. Yarborough came in at 1:40 and made a move as if he was going to come talk to me, but I stared ahead and pretended I didn't see him. He hesitated long enough for the clerk and the court reporter to come in, and then it was too late.

Porter was not as wise as Dan. Her closing was a rambling two and a half hours, not including two bathroom breaks. The jury was nodding long before her final comments, a not very inspiring "And that's why we ask that you not award anything against my client, but if you do, the value of this case cannot exceed five hundred thousand dollars." Mr. Grund stared angrily ahead and clenched his fists on the table. Just in case the jury didn't notice how crappy Porter's closing had been.

Judge Stein stifled a yawn and looked up at VJ. "It's 4:15, Ms. Smith. I'd like to finish the closing today and let the jury start deliberating first thing in the morning."

VJ stood up. I thought to myself that the best strategy would be to go after Grund, given Porter's weak defense, and leave Skyblu and Dan more or less alone. I figured that's what VJ would do. I was wrong.

"I'll be brief, your honor." VJ walked close to the jury box, and put her head down for a moment, maybe fifteen whole seconds. The tension grew thick. She raised her head and her voice rang out, really loud, but not shouting. How does she do that? I mused.

"Mr. Boatwright asked you not to base your award on sympathy. We're not asking for sympathy! How dare Mr. Boatwright suggest that my client has come in here like a beggar asking for your charity! No, ladies and gentlemen, make no mistake; we are asking for nothing but justice. Yes, by all means, read the instructions, each and every one, but there are only two questions you must decide. First, but for the negligence of Skyblu and Grund, would Earl Rayburn be alive today? And if so, then what amount of money can you award to Mrs. Rayburn that will send a message loud and clear to our aviation industry that this must never happen again?"

VJ's voice dropped back to normal, but the jury had woken up again.

"You've all been to the airport since 9/11; you've seen the security in place, suffered the long lines. You know our commercial airlines are safe. But that's not where the next threat is coming from, my fellow citizens."

Oh good one, VJ's British accent could be a real asset, but you gotta let the jury know you really are American.

"No, the next threat is going to be a private jet, just like this one. Only it won't be brought down by a poor man who had no wits left to lose; it will be brought down by a terrorist. And the fallout won't be a hapless trailer park; it will be an office building or a school."

"Objection," Dan and Porter were both on their feet. This time Dan didn't yield. "There's been no testimony—"

"I beg to differ, your honor, this is precisely the testimony of Skyblu's own expert, who told this jury that the approach used by private charter companies in designing security programs was to flag terrorists."

Judge Stein scratched his bald spot as he flipped through his notes. "That's right," he said, reading from the yellow pad. "He said, 'the risk we foresee is the risk of foreign terrorists, and we exert—or is that expend—yes—expend our resources to prevent the catastrophe of a private jet being used like a missile, aimed at office buildings or school.' Objection overruled."

VJ lifted her chin, her only acknowledgment of triumph, but it was enough. "So the danger we are facing here is not an unknown freak danger, it is a recognized danger, that someone, for motives we all find crazy, even if we don't understand or predict the precise nature of the craziness—"

"Objection!" This time only Porter jumped up. I saw Dan's nearly imperceptible wince, as if he knew what was coming.

"This line of argument is wholly irrelevant, and unduly

inflammatory, your honor. This case is about one man who was mentally ill. Terrorists are not mentally ill," Porter declared.

"I beg to differ," VJ remarked with seeming casualness. "Perhaps my esteemed colleague has a greater understanding of these fanatics who destroy innocent human beings in the name of God. If that's not mental illness, I don't know what is."

Judge Stein frowned. "Look, we give a lot of leeway on final argument. I'm not going to tell an attorney how to argue his or her case, but I am going to remind Ms. Smith that she only has about fifteen minutes left, because we're finishing closing arguments today and I really don't want to have keep this jury late."

"I have no intention of keeping the jury late, your honor. I would very much like to continue." She looked a question at Porter, daring her to object again, and letting the jury know who was to blame if they were kept late.

Perfect, I thought. Now VJ has made the trial about preventing terrorism, and has subtly aligned herself with the churchgoing jurors, including Bible Thumper, without alienating the not-so-religious Juror Number Eight. And Porter was not-so-subtly aligned with terrorists, of whom there were none on the jury. Yes, perfect.

"The defense wants you to accept that a security system aimed only at terrorists is a reasonable security system. But how are we going to know our foreign terrorists, I ask you? Are we just going to accept what prospective employees put down on the application? They say they're from Guadalajara and we just accept that?"

Juror Number Twelve, the one who could be a libertarian, nodded so hard he looked like a bobble head. Judge Stein gave an eyebrow signal to VJ. Enough of this argument, move on.

Victoria paced in front of the jury box. "You heard Mr. Boatwright admit, with great candor, that his client had no idea that Mr. Farnswell had spent several weeks in a psychiatric institution. Several weeks. In a psychiatric institution. His client had no idea! The question for you, my fellow citizens, is why didn't Skyblu know this vital and easily ascertainable fact? Yes, the records themselves might be confidential, but the fact of the confinement should have been uncovered."

VJ wrapped up by reiterating her points against Grund, how cheap—relative to wholesale death and destruction—it would have been to include the locking cockpit door.

Then she paused for the big finish. "And how much was Earl Rayburn's life worth? To him and his wife, beyond monetary value. But you have to put a value on it, because the reality is that no amount of money brings him back, and giving an award to his widow is all you can do. Now, it's true that as a retiree, his future earnings weren't in the millions. But I ask you to think about that. This man worked hard all his life—good, honest labor—and this was his reward time, his golden time, to kick back and enjoy life. You might say he was robbed of the very best years of his life. No, he was no high roller, but I have to ask you, how much was it worth to Mrs. Rayburn to sit on the side of the creek by her husband's side, maybe doing a little fishing, maybe sharing a beer and a laugh with friends? How much was it worth to her to get that goodnight hug every night? How much to be with him when she went to hospital to see his first grandchild?"

Here, her voice broke a little and, right on cue, Juror Number Three watered up. VJ put the price tag at seven million, hoping for three million, happy with two million.

The judge dismissed the jury and they took no time fleeing the courtroom. I avoided Yarborough by walking up to counsel table as soon as the jury was dismissed and the judge had left the bench.

"Great job, Veej. I thought you were gonna lay off Sky-blu, go for the easy kill."

"The easy kill wouldn't translate into lots of dollars, Fifi. I thought about it, but I had to get the jury feeling strongly to get the numbers up."

Yeah, maybe, I thought to myself, or maybe VJ had gone into competitive overdrive when Boatwright had made such a good showing. I walked with her and Mrs. Rayburn down the hallway. They agreed to meet there again tomorrow, to be sitting on the benches in the hallway when the jury arrived in the morning, when they went to lunch, when they left for the night. Letting them see how much the case meant to Mrs. Rayburn.

"You don't have to come, though, Fifi," VJ said kindly. "Babysitting a jury is hard duty." I nodded and patted VJ awkwardly on the shoulder as we exited the courthouse. I put on extra speed walking down to the cathedral where I'd parked, and felt pretty safe as I passed under the bells and headed towards the escalator down to the parking.

The huge hand clamped down on my shoulder as I leaned over to work the balky lock on the Squire.

"What the hell did you mean?" Yarborough's baritone boomed in my ear. I whirled around to face him, my throat drying.

"What do you mean, what did I mean?"

"No bullshit. You said you had a copy." He looked at me shrewdly. "A copy of what?"

Since this was precisely the question I couldn't answer, I stood there with my mouth hanging open. Yarborough seemed to grow taller.

"Look, I don't know—" I was interrupted by the sound of running steps echoing in the parking structure.

"Fifi, Fifi!" I truly hadn't realized I would ever be that happy to see Bosco.

"Oh excuse me," he panted, as he got close. "I didn't mean to interrupt."

"Not a problem, Bosco, we were just done talking."

Yarborough turned on Bosco, appraising him as if he

was trying to decide if he could take both of us on. Which he totally could. He was taller than me riding Bosco piggyback and weighed more than the two of us and the Squire combined. But he didn't try because the cathedral security guard chose that moment to ride down the escalator and make his rounds.

As Yarborough backed away, I finally got the damned door open. I hopped in and opened the passenger side for Bosco. As soon as he got settled, I smartly backed out and scooted up to the parking kiosk.

"So what are you doing here?" I asked as I gave my ticket to the bored attendant.

"Who was that guy? I've seen him before."

"That's Yarborough. You know, the guy who's vice president of claims. He insures Skyblu, Dan's client. He's the one who retained Dan to defend the case." I handed over the requisite fourteen bucks, pained to see a lone twenty left in my wallet.

"What was he doing talking to you?"

I debated whether to explain to Bosco, then gave him an abbreviated version. I didn't know what was going on, but it involved the case. I wasn't sure that what I told Bosco wouldn't end up with Violet, and that what Bosco told Violet wouldn't end up with Wong and Chu, or that what Wong and Chu knew they wouldn't tell Yarborough. I could end up looking stupid. Stupider than usual, I amended as I caught a glimpse of the Squire in a store front window. Or it could even be dangerous.

"What are you doing here?" I repeated.

"Violet and I went to see the gallery, you know, to drop off the portfolio. But then Violet had to do some shopping, and she dropped me off at the courthouse so I could get a ride home with you. I just missed you at the courtroom, ran into Dan, who was still packing up. He told me you usually parked down here."

It took me a few seconds to see that this cleared Dan.

Probably cleared Dan. I mean, if he was in it with Yarborough, he wouldn't have sent Bosco to find me, right? I felt better for a second until another disturbing thought struck me.

"At the gallery? Bosco, I hate to remind you, but you don't really have a show going up at the gallery. You made it all up, remember? To get laid?"

"I know that, but the young assistant there didn't. He's a real nice guy, name of Trevor. In fact, Trevor didn't want to admit to us that his boss hadn't told him about the show, so when Violet explained, he acted like he knew all about it. And then he took it upon himself to confirm some ideas with Dante Wildman, who apparently didn't want to admit that he didn't remember who I was."

"How could he remember who you are? You don't exist."

"I exist!"

"As a photographer you don't exist! As anyone Dante Wildman would ever have met, you don't exist!"

"Apparently, I do exist, because Trevor said so. And I'm telling you, Fifi, he had some really awesome suggestions about the publicity and the themes. The show is called 'Wildman and the Legacy of Grace.' Of course, I won't be the only Wildman student featured. But, really, it's an honor to be associated with this show. That Trevor's got quite an eye. I see him going far."

I was speechless.

✳ ✳ ✳

As we rounded the bend toward home, Sofia Canyon falling away to my right, Bosco yelped. "Rita!"

"What?"

"Rita!"

"What?"

"Oh man, this girl comes up to me just as I'm leaving the courthouse. She's pretty, you know, but dressed in a black suit and with her hair pulled back and she hugs me and says how long it's been since we've seen each other and to give her a call. I knew I knew her, but I just couldn't remember her name. You know how it is when you see someone out of context? Even someone you know really well? You see them in a different place or dressed different, and I just couldn't remember her name. It's Rita, the girl from the New Year Eve's party at that actor's house in Hollywood."

"Rita," I repeated. What Bosco said was true. When you see people you know out of context, you know you know them, but you don't know where you know them from. That's when I got it. The couple I had seen outside of Work Out World. The couple who had startled Burton. Different hair and clothes. But it was Porter and Yarborough. Her red hair down, his baldness disguised with that perfect Helmet Hair wig.

Janet Porter was supposedly a great trial lawyer. Wong said he didn't think she'd been really trying. Of course, this was before he settled with her, when he still hated her. But, still, it was a specific thing he had said. Not that she was nasty, sneaky, or obnoxious, all things lawyers say about their opponents on a routine basis. He said she wasn't really trying.

Brunswick was in financial difficulties, faced with the more culpable defendant in a big case, but having a small percentage of the insurance on the minor defendant. What if Yarborough had used his influence to get his girlfriend appointed by the ICARUS consortium as defense counsel for Grund? What if she was throwing the case?

That had been the scheme.

So why settle after the trial had begun? Because Burton saw them. Burton, the document clerk, figured it out. And then Burton died. Yarborough? Who else?

But there was a videotape of that touching moment. A videotape Reg Wong himself had watched. Maybe it had taken him a while to realize what he'd seen, but eventually

he had. Then he noticed that Janet Porter's trial perfor-
mance was strangely lacking. Maybe when his expert was
excluded, he got desperate.

That's what pom-pom man had been looking for. My
copy. I can't believe it, I had actually been telling Yarborough the truth.

I hastily explained my reasoning to Bosco, and we
ransacked the house as soon as we got home. "Where the
hell could it be?" I moaned, hours later. We don't have a lot
of stuff in the house. We'd searched everything we did have
three times.

"They got it," Bosco concluded. "Somehow, sometime,
they came in here and they found it."

"Then why was Yarborough so exercised today, when
I said I had a copy? If they already had it, he'd know.
Anyway, the tape is just a tip-off. The important thing now
is, we know. We've figured it out."

"So VJ can use the information to force a great settlement, too?"

I would tell VJ. Of course I would. But I knew my friend;
this wasn't the kind of information she had hoped for. This
wasn't like identifying a great witness or uncovering the
smoking-gun document. VJ Smith wasn't going to blackmail
opposing counsel into settling the case. And she wouldn't
want me to do it for her, either.

Chapter Nineteen

The phone rang.

"Hey, Fifi, it's Dan." As if I wouldn't recognize his voice.

"Hey, you did great today."

"Thanks, I felt like it went well. But VJ came back strong. This is the hardest part, you know. Sitting around waiting. It could be days. And I really should be there. I'll bet VJ's going to be there, huh?"

He was fishing. I ignored it. "Well, what are you doing tonight? You want to come over?"

"Oh Fifi, I'd love to, really, but this trial has gotten me so far behind on my other cases, I have to head back to the office. I'll probably be there really late."

"Okay, not a problem," I lied.

"Listen, though, you got any plans for the weekend?"

"Actually, I was going to do some investigation on a case I have."

"You work almost as many weekends as I do."

"Ha. I have to. It's the only day the guy isn't going to be there."

"You mean is going to be there."

"No, I meant isn't. Trust me, you wouldn't believe me if I told you."

"Try me."

I related the Saga of Wade. It hardly needed embellishing. "I called him on Wednesday and said I had a 1968 Jag that was making a pinging noise, and Wade Brockett was the only one I would trust to look at it. He ate it up and told me to bring it in, any day but Saturday. He was leaving the shop in the hands of his little brother and taking the day off to go watch monster trucks. At least I think that's what he said."

"I don't get it though. If toilet-photo guy isn't going to be there when you go, how are you going to confront him?"

"I'm not going to confront him. I happen to know that for a complete jerk-off asshole grease monkey, he keeps very good records, and I intend to take a peek."

"Fifi, don't do that. It's dangerous."

I warmed to Dan's concern. "I'll be okay. The brother's never seen me, and it will only take me a minute or two."

Dan argued some more, but my plan was simple and foolproof. He finally gave up.

"I can't tell you not to do it, but I don't like it. What time do you think you'll be home?"

"Oh, I'll be home by one o'clock, one-thirty at the latest."

"Well, how about I pick you up at six? We can drive out to Huntington Beach, walk on the sand, see the sunset. I know a great little Italian place there with an ocean view."

Giddy delight bubbled up. I crushed it down, keeping my voice moderately enthusiastic. "Sounds great. See you then—"

"I can't wait."

He can't wait. I smiled as I put the phone down. He can't wait.

Thursday and Friday passed with me glued to the phone. Either VJ or Dan would call me with the verdict; probably whoever prevailed would call first. I wondered for a moment who I was rooting for here. Either way, I was going to have to celebrate with one and commiserate with the other. Unless the jury put all the blame on Grund. That would be perfect.

Every time the phone rang, I had to swallow my heart to get it back in place. But most of the phone calls were of the hi-my-name-is-Stacey-and-I-have-an-important-message-from-the-message-center variety.

Finally, on Friday evening, VJ called. "Hey, thought I'd check in. No sign that this jury is anywhere near a verdict. It's a hard jury to read," VJ informed me. "The Golden Girls smile at everybody. The Accountant frowns at everybody, but more at me than Boatwright. The Enigma ignores everyone except the ditzy blond."

"What about the Plumber and the Old Hippie?"

"Oh, they're solidly in my camp. But I think the Hispanic guy may have turned against us. He can't meet my eye."

"Maybe you intimidate him, VJ. You are freakishly tall."

"He nods good morning to Boatwright, I noticed. Your boyfriend's been there both days too, with his laptop. He sits on the bench right across from me. It's so irritating."

I remained silent.

"They don't act as if they've been having violent disagreements, though. You know a jury that's going to hang; you can usually see it coming. But not always. Your dad used to tell me, a jury verdict is always what it seems like it's going to be, except for the times it's not."

That sounded like Pop. I told her the same thing I used to tell him.

"It's going to be okay, VJ."

"I hope so. I would die if I had to try this thing again. Do you know how long it took? How much it cost the firm? Or worse, what if I just lose outright?"

"You can't lose, somebody was at fault."

"Yeah, James Farnswell, according to lover boy."

Bad turn of topic. I quickly backtracked. "They're not going to hang. They're going to come back with a verdict on

Monday. They probably just wanted the weekend to think it over. To think over the great big old award they're going to give you."

We talked for a little while longer, VJ repeating herself, me trying to assuage her worries. I finally said good-night. I toyed with the idea of asking her to come with me to Wade's the next day, but given her state of mind, I didn't have the heart. I'd have to get somebody, though. I couldn't do it by myself.

* * *

"Bosco, I need you to do something for me today," I said as soon as Bosco, the lazy slug, had made his Saturday morning appearance. He was a little earlier than usual; it was two minutes to eleven. I was sunning myself on the front porch as he came out to walk the dog.

"That's so funny," he replied. "I need you to do something for me, too."

"I need you to go with me to Wade's car repair place in Eagle Rock. I need you to distract the brother while I look up the file on that Caddy." Having previously shared my general thought processes with him, Bosco needed no further information to decline.

"No way, I'm not doing it. It's illegal."

I probably shouldn't have laughed, but really—

"Anyway," he went on, "I told you my plan; it's a much better plan."

"Me going out on a date with Wade? That is not a much better plan. It's a horrible, inconceivable, very bad plan."

"It's not illegal."

"It should be. And this isn't illegal, either, not really. Wade's Car Repair is a business establishment open to the public, so there's no breaking and entering. And if I'm caught, I can just say I needed a little more information to complete my report, and Wade told me to help myself to anything I needed."

"Except Colchester has already paid the claim. Based on a report you already submitted."

"Details. If I'm right, Wade will hardly be in a position to complain."

Bosco's attention was distracted as Sketch strained against the leash, intent on squirrel murder in the first degree.

"And if you're not right?" he asked when he finally regained control of the slobbering beast.

"I'm right."

Bosco sighed. "Okay, but I'm going to pretend I'm not with you, okay? And if you do get caught, I'm not sticking around."

"Fine," I shrugged. "Now what was it exactly you wanted me to do for you?"

"Call Trevor and pretend to be my agent and negotiate my cut for the show."

"That's illegal," I told him.

"No it isn't."

"Okay, then it's just pointless. Bosco, there is no show."

"That's where you're wrong. Trevor is trying to pull it together for the second week in May. I have to get ready."

My eyes widened. "Get ready for what? There isn't going to be any show, Bosco. As soon as they contact Wildman they're going to realize that they are being totally snowed. It's going to get very ugly and I, for one, want no part of it."

"You can give a false name. In fact, I insist you give a false name. Something preppy, like Bunny Terwillager."

"I'm not going to tell anyone ever that my name is Bunny Terwillager. That is the stupidest name anybody ever—"

"It's not as stupid as Fifi—"

"Hey, your name is Bosco—"

I finally had to agree, as it was getting closer and closer to noon and I needed Bosco's assistance on my end. I made the call, identified myself as Veronica Van Bruner, and got

Bosco forty-five percent, after mailing and framing costs, artist to help defray the costs of the cheese cubes, olives and sauterne, which even I know is a crappy deal, but my motivation to negotiate really hard over fictional commissions which would never be earned from a show which would never be held was, let's say, weak.

The important thing was I got him into the Squire at 12:04 and we were a block from Wade's Car Repair at 12:11. I pulled to the curb and got out. Bosco slid over to the driver's seat. The plan was for him to park on the lot around the east side of the building, as close to the street and as far from the office as he could. He would drag Wade's brother out of the mechanic's bay to look at the car, and I would just walk up to the office, the door to which was on the northwest corner, walk on in, get what I needed, and be gone before Little Brother Brockett knew what hit him.

The first part worked perfectly. As I approached the office door, I could see across the open bay and through a large, grimy window to the outside of the building. Bosco and LBB, and a couple of hot Latina chicks were oohing and ahhing over the old car. I kept my head down and slipped into the office.

Facing the bank of mismatched file cabinets, I started to have my first qualms. Wade had taken the file from the top left, I remembered. I pulled the drawer open, wincing as the rusty runners screeched. I held my breath, ready to run, but heard a burst of laughter. I blew out and started to search.

It took me several minutes of riffling to find the date I needed, and a few more seconds to find the invoice for the Caddy. I checked the VIN number. Right. And stapled to it were Xerox copies of the pink slip and a check. The buyer was Jesus Hernandez. The name rang a bell. Oh yeah, Hernandez Used Cars, on Figueroa and 43rd. Wade had gotten eleven thousand dollars for what had been written off as worthless salvage. I stuffed the papers down my shirt.

As I turned to leave, I heard a noise from the back. I froze. There it was again.

"Wade?" I called out.

There was no response. I tiptoed to the glass door separating the office from the bay, upon which the talented Brockett brothers had painted EMPOLYEES OLNY FROM THIS PINT ON. Hadda hope they were better at car repairs then spelling. It was really hard, peering around the letters and through the window on the other side, but I could make out Little Brother, who was now ass up into the hood of the Squire.

As I turned back I noticed a narrow door that I hadn't seen before on the side of the bank of cabinets. I listened intently. Was that breathing? My mouth dried. I slowly inched away from the evil little opening, back toward the front door of the office. The door to freedom. I turned and had my hand on the knob, poised to bolt.

I didn't make it.

* * *

Return to consciousness came slowly, in bits and pieces. Dancing purple lights chased away coherent thoughts. Thoughts like I'm blind and there's a little man whaling away with an ice pick right behind my eyes and what's that smell? And what if I puke? Puking right then would be the absolutely grossest thing that ever happened to me as I realized my mouth was duct-taped shut. I kicked out spasmodically, only to find my legs were bound. I went to grab at the bindings only to learn that my arms, too, had been bound, behind my back, tightly. I convulsed in a frenzied panic of very limited movement, claustrophobic fear overwhelming me. Until I heard the laugh.

It sounded muffled, as though it wasn't too far away but behind something. The sound chilled me. Was he—she—it—laughing at me? I couldn't hear that sound any more, but as I strained to listen I heard another sound, a constant shushing background sound, and a hum, and then, unmistakably, a car horn honking. It hit me. I was in the trunk of a moving car.

The knowledge, which should have terrified me even more, actually calmed me. I had a point of reference. It was a bad world, but a world I sort of knew, if only from TV.

TV taught me you were supposed to punch out the rear lights and wave at traffic, but that wasn't an option in my trussed-up state.

I concentrated on breathing deeply through my nose. The trunk smelled a little gasoliney, and that hospital smell clung to me. Chloroform, or something very like it, I deduced. Who would have thought Wade was an operator on this scale?

Several minutes later, my brain returned to almost normal and I discounted the chances of this being Wade's doing. This was way out of Wade's league. But it would have to be someone who had known I was going to Wade's, when he was out. Someone was waiting for me.

Who knew I was going to Wade's? Sadly, I could only think of two people. One was Bosco. The other one wasn't. I sobbed as quietly as I could. Until I felt the car slowing, turning, going up a bumpy surface for a long way. And then it stopped.

I heard the trunk open. I squinted, expecting blinding light, but it was just as dark with the trunk open. I sensed rather than saw someone looking down on me. The only thing I can say on my behalf is that I didn't wet myself. I almost did, but I didn't. I cried. I twitched. I flinched. I squirmed. And when two gloved hands came down to lift me out, I tried to beg for my life but all I could say was "mmmmppphhh."

I landed like a sack of laundry on a hard floor and tried to peer though the darkness to make out a face, but all I saw was a towering shadow reaching down to rip the duct tape off my mouth, which hurt like hell and made my eyes water even more.

The shape stepped back, passing like a ghost through a barely perceptible shaft of light, and I saw it was wearing a ski mask. The silhouette of an orange pom-pom bobbed quickly in and out of sight. Okay, I don't know that it was orange. That would, however, have been my bet.

I was on a cold, concrete floor. The air smelled musty, oily. Still trussed at ankles and wrists, comfort was unattainable, but I stretched out as far as I was able, trying not to make any noise. There was no way to know if I was alone until a sound like dried leaves rustling underfoot wafted over and made it past the ringing in my ears. Pom-pom Man was whispering on his cell phone.

I heard him leave, a door opening, then closing, and the sound of a key turning in a lock, three times.

I waited to see if he would come back, trying not to move for as long as I could take it. I was going for ten minutes but probably only made it to eight. My internal clock, the nagging bureaucratic tyrant I usually couldn't escape, had taken a vacation right when I could have actually used him. It was obviously night, but was it Saturday night or Sunday? It couldn't be later than that, I'd be much hungrier. And there was no way I could go for more than twenty-four hours without going to the bathroom, which I hadn't done. It had to be Saturday night.

Saturday night and I was going to die, I thought miserably, but before I could dwell on it too long, I realized that I really did have to go to the bathroom. In fact, now that I was focused on it, I didn't think I could hold it another second. All other thoughts were driven out by the basic animal need to let fly.

I braced myself up against a wall and started hopping. I ran into cartons of things and a large barrel of something, but it took me seven minutes to find a bucket. Seven minutes. My little bureaucrat was back I realized and just in time. Grateful I had chosen to wear a skirt, I conducted the operation with as much dexterity as it required. The relief was so tremendous that for an instant, I actually smiled.

Now that I had the wall-leaning, hopping skill perfected, I decided to explore the perimeter. I counted steps, actually hops. I was averaging four inches a hop, roughly nine hops to a yard. It took me just another few seconds to reach the corner and I started counting at the turn. I fell down once, crashing over an industrial ladder that was propped up against the wall, and forgot exactly where I was. As I lay there, knowing that the coroner would be examining the effects of that encounter on my shin, I had to make myself get up again. All I could think of was my Pop's grim face, the night before closing argument in a case where the key witness had recanted on the stand and his client had come off like a sneak. Pop was going to lose and he knew it, but he gave me a painful little half smile and said, "Fifi, I'm going to go down swinging."

"Go down hopping," I said to myself as I scooted back over to the wall.

There was a garage door where, presumably, the car had driven in, heavy and padlocked. I turned with my back to the lock and felt it, but it was firmly in place, and it felt as though a chain had been looped from one end to the other.

I found the regular door, too, the one my kidnapper had gone out of. I rubbed my cheek up against it. Metal, smooth. I took a chance and banged my head on it, too, as softly as I could. Seemed pretty thick and didn't give.

Resting every ten minutes or so, I finally lapped myself. The building was a rectangle, the length about four times the width. The dimensions were between thirty and forty yards on the long side, say ten yards on the short sides. Very approximately. Added to the fact that there didn't appear to be any windows, at least not at my height, and the walls were concrete block, I guessed I was in an industrial neighborhood far, far away from anywhere I wanted to be.

Discouraged, I hopped back over to the corner farthest from the pee bucket and slumped down. I was winded and my arms were starting to ache really bad. I tried to concentrate. The building was some kind of a garage or warehouse. I couldn't be sure. The one thing I was sure of, there was no way out.

A wave of chloroform-induced nausea rolled over me. I slumped down, lying on my side. The floor was icy cold, but damned if I didn't doze off for a while.

I woke up, with my shoulder sockets burning like twin chemical fires. I had to get my arms free. I knew I should explore the center of the room. Maybe there would be something sharp, something sharp enough to cut the rope. If it was rope; it felt more like plastic-covered wire but, still, maybe it could be cut.

Dizzy and exhausted, I was unable to stand upright without the support of the wall, even for a short hop. So I scooted belly down into the center of the room. There was a lot of shit in that place, big, heavy, not-sharp shit that was of no use to me. Cartons piled up and sacks of things that smelled poisonous. I finally ran into a metal box on rollers. Hoping it was a portable tool chest, I tried to lean up against it and open the drawers with my hands, but of course it slid away. I landed heavily on my butt. Another bruise for the coroner to figure out.

It took me four minutes to catch my breath and at least twelve minutes before I found the tool chest again. This time, I leaned against it with my back, slowly rolling it towards the wall. It took three minutes to get it wedged in place. By this time, my arms were screaming in agony, and my ankles had started protesting as well.

I fumbled at the top drawer, it felt like there were nails and bits of things in there, but if I tried to explore too deeply into the recess with my hands, I only ended up closing the drawer with my back.

The second drawer simply would not open.

I gave up and tried the third drawer down. It opened easily and my numbed fingers closed around a saw. It was thin and not particularly sharp, but it would do.

I lay panting, the saw in my hands, when I heard footsteps. My heart leaped up and I scooted manically back to where I thought they had left me. In truth, I had no idea of which direction I was going. My one thought was to get away from the tool chest. I shoved the saw under a carton on the way, praying that I had hidden it well enough if they turned on the lights, but with no time to make sure.

I heard the unlocking of all three locks as I scrambled to find a place against the wall. A flashlight played over the space to my right. I devoured the brief glimpse of my prison, the concrete floor confirmed, the color of the wall, yellow, the cartons I kept bumping into, ordinary cardboard boxes.

"Where the fuck—? Oh there she is."

I blinked as the glare of the flashlight hit my face. I had meant to pretend I was still unconscious, but couldn't pull it off. Fear and pain were wringing me out. Dully, I recognized the voice. Yarborough.

"Christ almighty, what did you do to her? She's filthy."

I hadn't considered the effect that sliding around on a warehouse floor would have on my appearance. Apparently, it wasn't an improvement.

"And she's awake." He snapped at his companion. "Now what?"

I sensed, rather than saw, the companion grab Yarborough by the arm and drag him back out. The locks turned again. The footsteps receded, accompanied by angry voices.

Again I waited ten minutes and then slid back into crawl mode. The problem was, of course, that I had no idea where the important carton was; the carton under which I had hidden the saw.

I nudged aside box after box, until I became certain that I was checking the same three cartons over and over again. I was unable to orient myself.

I finally gave up, trying to ignore the fact that I didn't smell so great. The crap that coated the floor, was now coating me, mingling with terror-induced sweat, and sour mouth. There isn't a personal hygiene product strong enough to help in this situation.

I tried lying on alternate sides, relaxing my arms as best I could, breathing slowly and deeply, and blinking into the dark.

The sound of Yarborough's voice echoed in my head. He cared that I saw him. That was good, it meant that "Plan A" wasn't Fifi-assassination. Of course, now that I had seen him, that might change. "Plan B" might be Whack Fifi Now.

But from what he said, Yarborough wasn't exactly in charge either, at least not of my fate. "Now what?" he had asked. Good question, Baldy, good question.

At least an hour passed before I saw it. Not so much light, as a softening of the darkness. Dawn had come. It was Sunday morning.

The warehouse was actually much bigger than I had hop-counted it to be, and much higher. The roof was at least two stories high. I could just make out a few grimy skylights far above, ruthlessly filtering the light. This was a major industrial building, and it was old.

Able to make out the vague outlines of objects, even dimly, was a huge help. At least I could rule out cartons I had already checked. After twenty minutes, as the light grew stronger, I found the carton and the saw. For a moment, I was delirious. Until I realized I still had to use the saw, with my hands behind my back.

I scooted back over to the tool chest. It was my plan

to stick the saw upright into the drawer, close the drawer to hold it in place, and rub my wrists against it. Stupid, fucking plan. It was impossible to wedge the saw tight enough. Every time I tried to get enough friction to cut the cord, the saw clattered to the ground. I started to sob in frustration and nearly came apart when a voice came out of nowhere.

"If you bring it over here, maybe I can hold it."

I twisted around, my heart was beating so fast I thought it would explode right out of my chest. I didn't see anything.

"Up here."

I looked up and gagged. There was a human figure hanging from the ceiling, bound by the wrists, arms extended overhead.

"Why didn't you say something sooner? Omigod, are you okay?"

"No, I'm not okay. What the fuck do you think? My arms are about to be pulled out of my sockets. I've been here since noon yesterday. And I haven't had a cigarette in all that time. And I didn't say anything because until the light came up, I didn't know who you were. From the way you peed, I thought you were a guy, a really big guy. And I sure as hell didn't know what the fuck you were doing."

It was Nadia, Burton's girlfriend. The rope that held her was long. Her toes were maybe six inches above my head, if I had been standing under her. Getting her down or me up there was going to be tricky.

"I was trying to find something I could use to cut my hands and feet free. I mean what else would I have been doing? And I found something, as you can see, only now I've got to find a way to hold it in place."

"Figure something out, and do it now. How much longer do you think I can hang here?"

I looked up at her, eerily swaying in the air, and felt sick.

"Hey Nadia, don't panic, now, don't panic. What can we do here, let me see, maybe I can push over that big carton. If I get it under you at least you'll be able to sit on it and get the pressure off your arms, okay?"

"Just do it, and do it quickly. I can't take this any more. I can't feel my fingers." Her voice was still tense with vexation, but fading.

I hopped over to the tallest box I saw, really more of a packing crate, and started pushing. At first it didn't move, but when I squatted down and used my leg strength, it started to inch along the floor. It was empty. I needed about ten feet.

I got about half way there when I hit a snag, an unevenness in the floor. I gave the box a backward lurch.

"Shit!" Nadia screamed, in a strangled way. I turned and watched as the crate toppled over, landing on its side directly under Nadia, but several feet below her flailing feet.

"You moron," she hissed. "That was the only box big enough. Now what?"

Panting with exertion, I couldn't answer her. I tried to give her an apologetic look when I noticed, in the growing light, that the ladder I had tripped over during my first foray was about ten feet to the right of Nadia.

"Okay, there's only one way to do this. I have to get my feet free first."

"Nooo, that will take forever, I can't wait, I can't wait, I can't wait, please save me, please, please." Nadia was losing it.

"Nadia, listen. I think I can hold the saw in my hand and bend my ankles up. If I can walk, I can climb, and if I can climb, maybe I can get you down."

"Maybe? Maybe? Oh God." She started to sob. It was hard to listen to, so I tuned it out. I concentrated on contorting myself into an advanced yogic position, grasping the saw with one hand, and rhythmically working the cords that bound my ankles. I quickly realized that they were not wire, just a stout plastic. It was agonizingly slow, but eventually the saw snapped through one strand and the length of cord crumbled at my feet. The sensation was beyond anything I had ever felt, the mother of all pins and needles. One foot crumpled beneath me as I tried to stand. I kicked at the floor until, with an agonizing rush, all feeling returned.

I hobbled over to the ladder, slowly, gently, pushed it along the wall, careful not to knock it over. I positioned it next to Nadia and started climbing up, the saw clenched in my hands. About five feet up, I swayed and almost fell. Nadia wasn't even looking at me, she had her eyes closed and was twitching with fear and pain.

"Nadia, you've got to listen to me, now, really you need to listen to me. Hush now, girl, hush. I'm almost there. Listen to me. Here I am, I'm getting closer, closer, I'm almost at the top, almost there. Just focus now, you've go a job to do, for both of us. Okay?"

I kept up the patter until I had reached the level of her hands.

"Here we go. I'm going to turn around now, and you get the saw out of my hands. Nice and easy."

I heard her voice right behind my ear. "Why can't you just cut me down now? Then I'll cut you free. I really don't think I can do this, Fifi. You gotta get me down now."

"No can do, Nadia, this is the only way. You understand? You have to take the saw in your hands and just hold it firm. Do you hear? Hold it firm while I get my hands free. Then I'll cut you down.

"I don't know if I can, I tell you, I've lost all feeling in my hands," she whimpered.

"Nadia, this is the way it has to be."

I gingerly turned around, not looking down, and leaned back, extending my arms as far as I could behind my back. Her fingers responded and she gripped the saw.

"Okay, now you got it? You got it?"

She didn't answer, but I could feel the saw blade against my wrist.

"Start sawing." I gritted my teeth. An eternity passed. I felt the cords give. Almost there.

"Oh shit, " Nadia cried out as the saw clattered down to the floor. "Oh sweet Jesus, shit, Jesus, help me."

"Stop, stop, Nadia, wait I think I got it, I think I got it." I strained mightily and the cord snapped.

My arms swung out to my sides, and searing pain shot down from my shoulders to my wrists. I lost my balance. It was bound to happen. To the accompaniment of Nadia's hoarse, staccato shrieks, I fell off the ladder and onto the crate, slid off the crate, landed on the portable tool chest, skidded several feet, and thudded heavily to the concrete floor.

I cracked my head and twisted an ankle but I had no time to appreciate all the new injuries, as Nadia was gabbling, "Get me down, get me down, get me down."

I scrambled around, found the saw and darted up the ladder again. She didn't calm down until I was working away, my arms screaming in protest at each jab of the saw. The rope was thick, but it looked old. Fourteen minutes of sawing and the last strand snapped, sending Nadia hurtling down. She landed much easier than I had, more or less on her feet. I climbed down the ladder and watched her writhe as she rubbed her arms and hands.

I wanted to just sit back and revel in being free, but I knew we couldn't. They weren't going to forget about us.

Trying to blast through the cinder block walls was a no-hoper. I examined the door again; it was as impenetrable as it had originally seemed. I peered at the seams and hinges. I know that a person can, theoretically, take a locked door off the hinges, but this didn't seem to be an option here, not without power tools. And someone who knows how to operate power tools.

Despair crept up and breathed on my neck. I had to brush it off. Come on, I told myself, I'd been gone all night. Wouldn't Bosco be missing me by now?

No, he would think I made it back home somehow, and he wouldn't care how, and that I'd gone out on my date with Dan and stayed the night at Dan's house.

But, here was a better thought. Let's assume Dan had nothing to do with this. Maybe he went to pick me up, I wasn't there, and he's been frantic ever since. Maybe he called the cops. Maybe the whole city was looking for me, every spare man called on duty, my face all over the TV.

Or maybe not.

I dragged the ladder over to examine the top of the door, hoping for a little, teeny space I could stick a crow bar or something like a crow bar in and get a little leverage. I climbed up and what I found was way better than a teeny little space.

"Hey, Nadia, what do you make of this?"

"What," she whimpered, not even getting up.

I ran my hands over the flat patch, about one and half foot square, over the door. "I think there used to be a window here. Like they plastered it in."

"So?"

"So plaster isn't cinder block. And it's been through an earthquake or two. It's pretty cracked." I was getting excited. "Find me a hammer thing."

Nadia slowly got up and then, with more energy, started looking around.

"What about this?" She held up the handle of a broken dolly, about four feet long, made of iron. Perfect.

Well, not perfect. Perfect would have been somebody else to swing the hammer. But by alternating chipping and pounding, I made a dent. And then a hole. And then, with one final swing, the plaster square crumpled. The light flooded in and I poked my head out.

We were in a neighborhood of warehouses, at least as

far as could see. A pockmarked macadam road was directly beneath me, running into a huge chain-link gate to the right and curving out of my sight to the left. Directly across the road was a much newer building, a metal prefab job that would have been much easier to escape from. Other industrial-looking buildings blocked my view.

"Where do you think we are?" Nadia asked.

I shook my head. "I have no idea. We could be miles away from civilization, or a Starbucks could be just around the corner. Probably not too near a freeway, though. I don't hear anything." Then I did hear something. A car. Coming up the road.

"Quick, quick, up and out," I ordered Nadia, at the same time struggling through the opening. I heard her on the ladder behind me. I got my butt through the opening and perched, half in, half out.

It was only about twelve feet to the ground. Suddenly, it seemed like a hundred. I froze. My head was pounding and my ankle was swelling and all I could think of was to protect the extremities from further harm. I was unable to jump.

Nadia took care of that with a vicious jab to the kidneys. I pitched out of the opening, landed on the bad ankle and a previously uninjured wrist, and curled up in the fetal position. Nadia landed neatly beside me. I reached my hand out for some help up, but she took off like a purse-snatcher.

I pulled myself up as the car swung around the corner. Yarborough! He was alone, but I had no illusions about my ability to outrun him. I allowed myself to hope that Nadia had been thinking along the lines of "If I stop to help Fifi, we'll both be caught, but if I get away, I can call the police and save her, too." It wasn't much of a hope, but I clung to it.

Yarborough slammed to a halt and got out of the car slowly. "Where is it?" he growled. "You tell me right now."

"The copy?"

"Yes, the goddamn copy."

I flinched, but kept my voice calm. "There isn't a copy. I just made that up."

"You liar. That two-timing black-haired bitch told me she had a copy."

I assumed he meant Nadia. The description fit. "Well, maybe she has one, but I don't."

Yarborough advanced, still moving very slowly. I backed up. Putting weight on my ankle hurt like hell, but it was bearable. Through my own pain, I saw that Yarborough was not only moving slowly, he was listing to his left.

"You hurt?"

"Shut up," he growled, still advancing. His clothes were torn and bloody, I realized. There was something definitely the matter with his knee.

I started to feel marginally better. Overpowering him was still out of the question, and he was between me and the road out. But maybe I could get away if I detoured around the back of the old warehouse. I ran, or rather ran-limped, away from Yarborough. He ran-limped after me. If he didn't have a gun, all would be well, I thought.

He didn't have a gun, and yet all was not well.

The sharp, terrifying bark of a large dog trained to kill reverberated from somewhere way too close. That dog was out and on the prowl and looking for someone to maul.

I debated hiding behind a stack of large barrels propped up near the perimeter. A watch dog probably had a good sense of smell. Not that a really good sense of smell was strictly necessary given the state I was in. I veered away from the fence and back toward the south end of my erstwhile prison when a form suddenly lunged from an adjacent alleyway, a frothing-at-the-mouth, black-and-tan German Shepherd, with psycho-killer eyes. I screamed and pressed myself against the building, trying to be flat.

The beast ducked down in a half crouch. His eyes locked onto my face, every hair on his body quivering with impersonal rage. He dropped a fraction lower, tensed for the spring.

I stopped breathing. A drop of saliva formed on the corner of Fido's mouth, quivered and plinked to the dirt. At that moment, Yarborough came lurching around the far corner.

He barreled toward me, scudding to an ungainly halt when he caught sight of man's best friend.

The dog began to pace, still holding himself low and coiled to spring, left, right, left, growling deep in this throat, looking first at me, then at Yarborough.

I started edging back toward the corner of the building, toward Yarborough. I drew even with him.

"You're crazy," Yarborough whispered, barely moving his lips. "You can't outrun the dog."

I couldn't believe he handed me that beautiful straight line. "I don't have to outrun the dog, Yarborough. I only have to outrun you." I darted past him, pushing him off balance on the way by. Fido lunged.

At that, Yarborough lost his head. I'm not blaming him; he'd obviously had a very rough night. But he turned and ran the other way, toward the chainlink fence blocking the road. I think he had some idea of climbing over it, but I didn't stay to find out. I heard snarling, and then screaming, and then the sound of bone being snapped. Then some more screaming.

I gathered all my strength, shoved the pain away, and galloped clumsily down the potholed road to freedom. I was hoping for a Starbucks, but after twelve agonizing minutes I settled for Pepe's Taco House.

I caused quite a stir when I came panting up to the counter, shaking, filthy, my hair all finger-stuck-in-light-socket. There were maybe twelve people sitting at picnic tables and standing around.

"No homeless people here. Vamos!" the walleyed, beer-bellied proprietor shouted.

"Not homeless," I gasped. "Una persona rica, rica, muy rica."

"Una persona loca," he waved his spatula.

"No, no loca. Kidnapped, held for ransom, escaped."

The small crowd began to gather around me. Mostly men, but there was one woman who looked a little like a goat, in dungarees and hair clips. Something about her; she might believe me.

"Please," I turned to her, "you've got to help me. You've got to call the police."

The mention of police caused several of the Hispanic men to slip out the door, much to the annoyance of the taco stand's owner, who began muttering. But it worked on the woman. Homeless people rarely ask for the police to be called. She opened her capacious bag and pulled out a cell phone.

"I'm gonna call the cops," she said. "Is that what you really want?"

"Yes, yes, yes, oh yes. And tell me where we are."

"City of Industry."

Just then the door opened again and Nadia came stumbling in. The goat-like woman looked uncertainly at the two of us, now starting to suspect a sorority initiation gone awry.

Nadia stopped, open-mouthed when she saw me. "You got away?"

"Yeah, no thanks to you, you jerk. What the hell was that all about? You just left me there."

"I had to escape. You were injured. I could hardly carry you. Hey, I was going to call the cops when I escaped. I'm here, aren't I?"

I had to admit she was here. I turned back to our benefactor.

"Please call the police," I begged. "My name is Fifi

Cutter. Nadia here and I, we really were kidnapped. We really did escape."

"Was you raped?" one of the men asked, way too eagerly. I ignored him.

The woman still hesitated. Out of the corner of my eye, I saw a red car, a BMW Z4 come up the road. I grabbed Nadia and pulled her to the ground. Now everyone was openly staring. We slowly got up.

"Don't call yet," Nadia said shakily, glancing at me. "Listen, Fifi, I gotta talk to you." She dragged me outside. I was sputtering.

"Now she's never gonna call the cops and whoever that Mexican guy is in that goddamn BMW Z4 is going to realize we escaped in about, oh, four minutes and then he's going to turn around and come back out—"

"Shut up," said Nadia. "This could still be worth money. Big money. They think Steve made a copy of some old VCR tape. I don't know what it is and I don't know where it is, but they thought I did. Look, I know that Steve was into something when he was killed. Something he thought was going to make us rich. I didn't know then, but it had to be this tape, right? That's why they kidnapped me, they kept asking—I mean, that's why they kidnapped you, isn't it?"

"I guess," I shrugged.

Nadia grabbed me. "Where is it? What is it a tape of?"

I pictured myself outside Work Out World. Had I really gotten Yarborough and Porter on tape?

I looked into Nadia's face. "I have no idea what the tape was of, Nadia, but I do know there is no copy. I just made that up." I gave her my most open, sincere, slightly rueful, smile.

"You're a lying sack of shit," she hissed.

"I'm not lying," I protested, but it was no good. She wanted to believe there was a copy worth millions, and that's what she was going to believe. There might even be a copy worth millions, if I could just remember what I'd done with it.

"Listen, cut me in and I won't tell the cops. I swear to God, Yarborough will pay anything for that tape. Wong got sixty million for the original. We could get a tenth of that and it's six million dollars!"

"You do realize that Yarborough probably killed your boyfriend, don't you?"

"I know," Nadia looked momentarily dampened. "But Steve would have wanted me to be rich. Whatever he was doing, he was only doing it for me."

I half believed that.

"Anyway, I got some bad news for you about Yarborough. I don't think he's in a position to be paying for the tape." The Z4 roared back down the road. Pom-pom man, wearing his disguise. He didn't slow down. I wondered if he had Yarborough's body in the trunk. "Go home and forget about the whole thing, Nadia. Except don't go home. Or to work. Call in very sick. Take a vacation. Go stay with the friend who lives the farthest away. That's my best advice."

"Hey, chicas, you wanna ride? I going up to LA now. I get there in time for evening mass." A kindly looking Salvadoran man, slurping on a Coke and munching an enchilada, came over to us. "I gotta truck, you ride in the back, okay? 'Cause you don't smell so good. You know."

"Thanks, but no," Nadia said shortly.

"If you think that woman is going to let you use her cell phone now, you're dreaming," he said, then introduced himself as Hector Garcia.

"Thank you so very much, Hector, I would love a ride to LA in the back of your truck." I gladly left Nadia to her devices, and followed him to his truck.

Hector let me off at Union Station, where I caught a Gold Line train, for which I did not pay. I walked up the hill. It took forty minutes, because I had to stop and rest every ten feet. Bosco wasn't home, nor was Sketch. I had to break into the house.

I needed to call the cops. But first things first. I took a hot shower and washed my hair. Then I fell onto the pool raft, the sound of a wet, relentless crunching, and a man screaming, echoing in my ears.

Chapter Twenty

I didn't wake up until Monday morning.

I went over what had happened in my head and rose, stiffly, from the pool raft. I peeked out and looked down at the end of the hall. Bosco's door was closed. I still had to call the cops.

But second things second. I was beyond starving. I made myself some all-natural macaroni and cheese with canned organic peas, the last remnants of my shopping trip to the health food store that seemed so long ago.

Which reminded me that this time I really had lost my purse, and it occurred to me that I probably should cancel my credit card. Priorities. Call the cops, then call the credit card company. As I approached the phone, I saw there was a message on my answering machine. With shaking fingers, I punched the button.

"Hey Fifi, Dan, here. I am so sorry. I have to cancel tonight. Believe me, I don't want to. But Mr. Yarborough called; his boss is in town to monitor the verdict. Jim Simmonds is the president of claims; he's very high up in the company. Mr. Yarborough has another engagement scheduled for tonight so he wants me to take Mr. Simmonds out to dinner."

Another engagement? Is that what they're calling felony kidnapping and attempted murder these days?

"God, I hope you understand. It's a great opportunity for me to solidify my relationship with this client. It

189

could mean a whole lot of business for the fledgling firm of Daniel W. Boatwright. I'll make it up to you, I promise. Jeez, honey, I wish you were there so I could talk to you in person, make sure you understood. Don't be mad at me. OK? OK. Bye."

I sat down at the kitchen table with my face in my hands. Ohmigod, he called me "honey." I had totally wronged him. I'm a horrible person. There I was, practically accusing him of conspiring to kidnap me, when he was thinking of me and trying to get in touch with me.

Trying to get in touch with me to cancel our date, sure, but still, he wanted to talk to me. He called me "honey." That's the important thing to remember here. I played the message over again. And then once more.

I felt groggy and slow. I had to pull myself together. I needed help, and climbed up the stairs to Bosco's room and knocked on the door.

"Bosco?"

No answer. I opened the door. His bed was empty. He couldn't have gotten up earlier. It was only 9:46 by the bedside clock.

They got him, too. I lost my breath and felt dizzy and then a jolt of adrenaline kicked in. I ran down the stairs to the phone, and started punching in nine one one. Where could he be?

The question was answered, seconds before my call was, by a big face lick. Not Bosco, Sketch. Bosco was right behind him.

"Sorry I didn't leave a note, I spent the night at Violet's. Hey, how was the big date? Oh my God," Bosco stopped short, catching sight of the lump on the side of my head, the bruises on my arms and legs, and the ankle wrap. "Jesus, Fifi, what the hell happened? Parachute didn't open? Or is that the way you and Dan—"

"Shut up." I cut him off. "There was no date."

Bosco looked thoughtful. "Well, then, I hope he looks worse than you do, Feef."

"Dan didn't do this, you idiot. Didn't you happen to notice I disappeared from the gas station? Weren't you just a little bit curious about what the hell happened to me?"

Bosco brought a bottle of beer over to the table and sat down. "It's so funny you should say that. I was curious. Very curious. It's just that I ended up taking Rosita and Carmen out for a spin in the Squire. Wally and I were trying to see if we could get the brakes tightened up. Hey, I'm really sorry, I know we took kind of a long time. We stopped for a bite to eat, that pizza place on the corner of Figueroa and 43rd. You know the one. They take forever, but that dough, it's so flaky, I think it's worth it."

I listened in semi-disbelief.

"Thing is, when we got back and you weren't on the corner like we planned, I figured you'd gotten tired of waiting. How'd you get home?"

I glared for a full twenty seconds before replying. "I got home the roundabout way, you inconsiderate cretin. Let me tell you about it. The first leg of the journey I spent in the trunk of a car, and then I was delayed for a while, tied up in a warehouse all night, and then I ran for a mile with a slathering, rabid monster dog after me, and then—you'll love this—I got a ride in the back of a pickup truck. And then I took the Gold Line. And then I walked all the way up the frigging hill, with my ankle swollen to the size of a soccer ball. That's how I got home, Bosco. BUT THANKS FOR ASKING!"

✳ ✳ ✳

"I'll drive with you down to the cop shop," Bosco offered, when we finally stopped yelling at each other. "You have to report this."

"I know. I've been trying to report it since I got up."

"Fifi, look," Bosco chugged back the last swallow of beer and carefully placed the bottle on the table. "I gotta ask, did anyone other than Dan know you were going down to Wade's?"

"Just you," I admitted.

Bosco concentrated on arranging the beer bottle, the salt and pepper shakers, and the sugar bowl into a perfect square. "This might be hard, Fifi. I know, but you gotta see that Dan tipped off the kidnappers, right? How else would they know where to find you?"

"He didn't. You're wrong. Listen." I played back the telephone message. "See, he didn't know I wasn't home. He didn't know."

Bosco shook his head. "Aw, come on. That call could easily be a bluff. Designed to fool the police when they came to investigate. They'd think the fact he called you showed he didn't know anything had happened. He could just be smart, Fifi. Some people are."

"A bluff?" I didn't want to admit that the idea hadn't occurred to me. "Bull. Nobody could sound that natural. Anyway," I realized with relief, "he has an alibi."

"He says he has an alibi."

"I thought you said he was smart," I challenged. "If he was smart he would know that his story would be checked out. If the police ever did get his message, they would check with this Simmonds guy."

"Who might be in on it. Yarborough certainly was. They work for the same insurance company. He was Yarborough's boss."

"Well, they would check with the restaurant. The waiter. The maitre d'. The valet. Everyone can't be in on it." That last was said a little desperately. I mean, everyone couldn't be on it, right?

"Besides, I didn't say he kidnapped you. I said he passed the information along to someone else who kidnapped you.

And speaking of Yarborough, don't you think the police are going to want to talk to anyone with information about how an insurance executive ended up mangled trying to claw his way over a chainlink fence into a paper goods warehouse? Even if you're right about Dan, which you aren't, it won't do him any good if it looks like you're covering up for him."

"He's innocent until proven guilty," I replied, the truculent response of all defenders of the probably guilty.

Bosco looked sad. Not super-sad. More other-people's-problems sad. "I don't see how he could be innocent, Fifi," he said. "I'm sorry. Fact remains, he's the only one who knew where you were going to be on Saturday."

"I've got an idea. Why don't we just let the police figure this out." I reached for the phone. "I'm calling Joe."

Joe was at the station and I got right through.

"Fifi who?" he said.

"Joe, stop it. This is serious." I relayed my misadventures while Joe switched into professional mode. When I finished, he said, "You need to report this to the San Fernando station. Eagle Rock's in their territory."

"But I just reported it to you," I protested.

"I know, but I'm not going to be the one investigating it. They'll want to hear directly from you."

"Can you come with me?"

Joe sighed. "I'm interrogating a suspect in a triple murder gang shooting in twenty minutes. You've already lost 24 hours since the kidnapping occurred. Tell you what, I'll call over there when I'm done, and make sure they're taking you real seriously."

"Why wouldn't they take me seriously?" I asked.

"I'll call over there," Joe repeated and hung up.

"I'm going down to the station," I told Bosco. Just then, the phone rang. I picked it up.

"Fifi, I'm so sorry. Really, really sorry. Are you mad

at me? Of course you're mad at me. How mad? Goodbye forever mad? Or a dozen long-stemmed roses mad?"

I found myself unable to reply.

"Not-even-speaking-to-me mad? Are you there? Fifi, are you there?"

The urgency in his voice stung me back to life. "I'm here, I'm here. Dan, listen, I'm not mad at all. It's just something happened last night."

"What? What? Something bad? I hope it's not too bad."

"No, actually I guess I'm okay."

"What do you mean, you guess you're okay?"

The moment of truth, I realized. Tell? Don't tell? Trust? Don't trust? I should trust Dan, I decided, but when I spoke, what I said was, "Don't worry, Dan, I just had a touch of the twenty-four hour flu. I'm better now."

"Poor you. Listen, I gotta go. Jury came back with a question."

"You go and take your jury question. I'll be fine."

Bosco wandered back into the kitchen as I was saying good-bye. He stood in front of me, tapping at his wrist and miming "When are you going to get off the phone? I have to call Violet before we go."

I disconnected and gave Bosco a shove. "You are so rude. And so wrong about Dan." I believed it when I said it, so I said it again, louder.

"He was the only one who knew where you'd be," Bosco insisted.

"Yarborough could have had me followed. That's totally likely to have happened."

"It's not the least bit likely to have happened. May I remind you, Dan is Yarborough's lawyer."

"I am well aware of that. Listen to me. We are going to the station now. But we are not mentioning Dan. Promise?"

Bosco promised, which was worthless. He took the phone from my hand and punched in a number.

"Violet? What are you up to?" I heard him coo as I went to the laundry room to pull a clean shirt out of the dryer, only to find my clothes piled up, still damp, on the ironing board. Except my black spandex skirt, which I found still in the dryer. It was, in fact, dry. But had been shrunk to the size of a headband.

"Bosco, you retard. Why did you take my clothes out of the dryer? I need a clean shirt. You have to look respectable when you go to a police station. And what did you do to my skirt?"

"I hadda do a load. I need a clean shirt for tonight. No, nothing, babe, I'm talking to my sister."

"Hey, my skirt!" I yelled.

"Sorry, about the skirt, I missed it when I threw my stuff in and turned the heat up to high. You know how spandex sticks to the roof the dryer. It's okay, it'll stretch out. No, don't worry, sweetie, Fifi's just obsessing about some laundry. Yeah—yeah—maybe therapy would help—you are so right about that."

I looked back in the dryer and found two shirts of Bosco's, a T-shirt from Harvard—God knows what sick joker gave him that—and a Hawaiian shirt of indeterminate vintage. I went with the Hawaiian—it was brightly colored and had little Hawaiian dancers all over it. Kinda cute. I brought it upstairs and tied the loose ends of the shirt in a knot, revealing only a sliver of midriff. I shoved myself into the skirt. I grabbed a pair of black patent leather pumps. The four-inch heels would give me some height and make me more credible.

Joe had promised to call, but I needed the police to take me seriously. After all, if Yarborough was still alive, he needed to be locked up. And whoever his accomplice was certainly needed to be locked up. And that person was not Dan, I told myself. I had blurted out the 24-hour flu story only to save time.

As soon as I saw Dan and could talk to him, I'd tell him

the whole thing. If the cops don't show up at his door first. I just wouldn't mention Dan at all, I thought. No reason to. No reason at all.

Except Bosco would be blabbing, "All Dan All the Time." I stared out my bedroom window at the Squire in the driveway. I had to ditch Bosco, I realized.

I calculated my chances of sneaking out without him catching me. I could do it. Stealth and speed. I didn't even stop to look in the mirror as I tiptoed downstairs, carrying my black pumps in my hand.

I shouldn't have worried. Bosco was still on the phone with Violet. "No, she wouldn't make that up," I heard him say. "She's kind of weird in a lot of ways, but she's pretty truthful."

I slid silently out the front door. Starting up the Squire was far from silent, but by the time Bosco figured out what was going on and ran out of the house, I was rounding the corner.

The station was right on San Fernando, an industrial corridor strung along the foot of Mt. Washington; barbed-wire fences and windowless buildings.

I parked in front of the modest stucco box, next to a black-and-white. I leaned against the car to put on my shoes—whoa, the heels were higher than I had thought—and stalked up the concrete stairs. I entered into a small, square, windowless space, with a desk at right angles to the door. "Excuse me; I need to report a crime."

A young—make that very young—black guy in a uniform looked up at me from the keyboard he was hunched over. He kind of stared. I rubbed my nose to make sure I didn't have a booger hanging out.

"Um, c-could you please have a s-s-seat," he stammered, gesturing toward a hard bench running alongside the outer wall. He cast his eyes down as if he was too shy to look at me. I don't usually have that effect on males.

I rubbed my nose again and checked to make sure

all my buttons were done. It was then that I realized the pornographic nature of the little Hawaiian dancers decorating Bosco's shirt, a detail I had missed in the dim confines of the laundry room. I didn't waste a second wondering why Bosco had a pornographic Hawaiian shirt, but I did, for the first time, realize the unfortunate effect that high-heeled black pumps, which look so sharp with a pinstriped business suit, have when paired with a pube-hugging micro-mini. I tugged at the skirt, crossed my arms over my chest, and approached the desk.

"Excuse me. I was kidnapped."

"You were kidnapped?" he gasped, darting a startled glance at me. I suspected irony, but saw none in his face.

"Yeah, I was kidnapped. And I'd really like to report it to someone."

The young cop licked his lips nervously. I gently leaned in and spoke softly, if deliberately. "I'd really, really like to report it," I read his name tag, "Officer Shaw."

Officer Shaw began slapping around at various piles of papers on his desk, finally coming up with a clipboard. "I can log you in, but I can't t-t-take a report."

"Why not? It's easy. You don't have to ask any questions. I tell you what happened. You just write it down. See what I'm saying? Easy."

If a black guy can blush, Shaw blushed. "This is k-k-kind of my first day." I believed him. His voice cracked when he said it. I sighed. God was just fooling with me now. I picked up a pen and handed it over.

"Here, start writing."

He took the pen, not touching my fingers, and concentrated on the form.

"Wh-what's your name?'

"Fifi Cutter."

Shaw froze. He paused for nearly ten seconds, a long time, and darted a glance at the narrow expanse of skin showing below my shirt. "I'm sorry, miss—ma'am, um, miss—" he mumbled, "I need your r-real n-name."

"Fifi Cutter." I repeated.

"Oh." He paused and then wrote it down. "S-sorry, I thought maybe that was your—um—stage name."

I'd have slapped him in the head, but as soon as he realized what he'd said, he slapped himself. Not as hard as he should have, but good enough.

"S-sorry," he whispered. "Um— When did the c-criminal activity t-transpire?"

"The c-criminal activity t-transpired—dammit, Shaw, now you've got me doing it. The kidnapping took place Saturday. I was held overnight at a warehouse at the City of Industry."

Officer Shaw slowly wrote in the date and then turned back to his computer. I waited. He finally turned back to me. "I'm sorry, but there's no Fifi Cutter reported missing." He blinked miserably.

I poked him on the shoulder. "Hey, I'm reporting it now. Got it?"

"But you're not missing now."

I leaned across the desk. "Okay, forget it, Junior. I would like to report this crime to someone who remembers Saturday Night Fever. Do you think you could get me someone who remembers Saturday Night Fever?"

Shaw bolted from his chair, and fled into the back room through an open doorway. A few moments later, an older Hispanic man with a gray walrus moustache stuck his head out. He gave me a cold stare and ordered me to have a seat. "Someone will be with you—"

"Shortly," I finished.

I slumped on the bench for forty-three minutes before the Hispanic man came back out and ushered me with unnecessary roughness into the back room, a surprisingly large honeycomb of partitions and desks. He plopped me down on a grimy swivel chair at the nearest cubicle, a shelf of cigarette-burned melamine between me and a tired looking woman of ample proportions. From her accent I though she might be from Tennessee. Her name tag said "Donegal." She was pinkish, with mouse-colored hair, and her uniform was way too tight for all the chicken-fried steaks and brisket she'd been eating. A Kay Jewelers diamond was embedded into her left-hand ring finger.

A slight atmosphere of antagonism settled between us before I even had a chance to say anything. Something about the way she held her chin down and sat back in her chair, as if I smelled bad. I could have understood that if she'd been talking to me yesterday, but right now I smelled like sandalwood soap and a spritz of Acqua de Parma.

After asking for my name and the date of the crime, Donegal invited me to describe the incident. What she actually said was, "Why'nt ya'll tell me what really happint." I looked around to find out who else she included in "ya'll" but there was just me.

I gave her the short-story version, carefully leaving out any mention of Dan.

"You was kidnapped in broad daylight from Wade's, right there on Colorado Blvd, yo' brutha not twenty feet away and he don't notice nothin'?"

Arkansas. That was it. "Half-brother."

"Does that mean he's a half-wit?"

"No," I lied.

"But he didn't notice nothin'?"

"He was working on his car and talking to some other people."

"Why would anyone want to kidnap you, you tell me that, Miss Cutter? Was it yo' boyfriend?"

"No, I'm not presently dating anyone." I flashed on Dan and my hands convulsed. I kept them on my lap, out of sight.

"Well, couldn't be for ransom, you surely don't look rich." Officer Donegal leaned in with a smirk. "You jist don't have that certain *je ne sais quoi*. Know whut I mean?"

"Actually, although this will come as a surprise to you, I took French in college, and I know exactly what you mean. You are stating your no doubt expert opinion that I do not have style or breeding and are, rather obliquely, referring to the fact that I'm black." I affected my most Bennington tone.

"Not a'tall, not a'tall. Fact is, I didn't even know you wuz black," she snickered. "I was referrin' to yore attire."

"The shirt is a loaner," I replied with as much dignity as I could. "I didn't have time to do laundry yesterday, since I was kidnapped. As I believe I may have mentioned. Which is, if I could bring you back to the point, why I am here."

Officer Donegal leaned back and said, in her best bored-cop voice, "So why do you think somebody took the trouble to kidnap you, Miss Cutter. Do you think it's 'cause you went to college and took French and all?"

"No, I don't think that, Officer Donegal." I reached down deep for the self-control it was going to take not to rip out every wispy hair on that big hillbilly's head. "The other woman who was kidnapped, Nadia—she's white, if it matters, by the way—she thinks it has to do with a VCR tape that her boyfriend had."

"Who's her boyfriend? Is he white too?" Her voice dripped with sarcasm. "Maybe I can talk to him?"

"Yes. I mean, no. I mean, he was white, but now he's dead."

Officer Donegal tilted her head. "Let's get this straight. Her dead boyfriend told her about an old VCR tape he used to have? And that's why you guys were kidnapped?"

"Look, I didn't say that. I don't know why I was kidnapped. I just said that's what she said."

"You got a last name for this Nadia? A phone number?"

"No, but I know the address. She lives at the Altadena Arms. And you should be able to get the phone number and last name pretty easily. Her boyfriend, Steve Burton, was just killed there a few weeks ago. He was shot. You must have an open file on it. Somewhere."

Officer Donegal stood up. "Wait here."

And I did. I waited another thirty-eight minutes. Officer Donegal returned, brushing powdered sugar off her ample bosom and slurping coffee.

"Your brother called," she announced. "He is really your brother?"

"Yes, he's my brother."

"Umhmm. Well, I found your Nadia."

"Oh good. Did you talk to her?"

"Yes. I did." Her pale blue eyes sparked with malice. "She says she doesn't know what the hell you're talking about."

I did a dry-spit take. "She what? That's ridiculous. You must have talked to the wrong person. The wrong Nadia."

"Nadia DeMarco. At the Altadena Arms, 1232 Sweetwater Street, Apartment 4-2. Live-in girlfriend of the late Steve Burton. Unless this Burton guy collected girls named Nadia, I'd say I got the right one."

I was momentarily stunned, even though I shouldn't have been. Nadia had made it clear she was going to try to play Mega-Lotto. She didn't want cops. But Nadia wasn't my only proof.

"You must, at least, have gotten word of Mr. Yarborough, though? Somebody would have found his body by now."

"Right. Some dog ate some guy in the City of Industry. And you sat there and watched?"

"No I didn't watch, I was running for my life."

"How could you see him get et if you wuz running for yore life?"

"Well, I didn't actually see—"

"Umhmm. Well, Ms. Cutter, I hate to disappoint you, but as far as I know, we haven't had any reports of a dog eating a guy. Not lately."

"It's kind of a deserted area. It's possible he hasn't

been found yet. Would you even get a report like that? I mean, you know, it's out of your geographic area and they wouldn't necessarily know you'd be interested in a dog mauling, right? It's not like the City of Industry cops would know it was connected to a kidnapping from here? Right?" I cleared my throat. "Maybe you could just check with the police from the City of Industry?"

Officer Donegal stared at me, arms folded. Then she stood up, hovered over me briefly and thudded off back down the corridor. Fifty-one minutes later, she came back, looking even less pleased with me.

"No dog-eaten guy anywhere in Industry," she announced.

"Look, did you check the hospitals? Maybe he didn't die. Maybe somebody saved him."

"I checked the hospitals."

I sighed. "It was probably the pom-pom guy. I saw him drive out. He probably had the body in the trunk."

"The pom-pom guy?"

"I call him that because he was wearing a ski cap with a pom-pom on it," I explained. "When he attacked me at my house."

"He attacked you at your house? You didn't say anything about being attacked in your house. You said you were kidnapped from Wade's Auto Repair."

"OK, see, this was before."

"Before when? You're changing the story on me? I'm trying write a report here."

"Listen, Officer, I'm sorry if I'm keeping you from your Hometown Buffet, but I was the victim of a serious crime."

"Did you jist call me a redneck?" Officer Donegal's chins jutted out.

"If the overalls fit—" I replied.

"Did you jist imply that I'm lower class?"

"I wouldn't say lower class," I smiled. "Let's just say, 'differently' classed."

"I think we're done here, Ms. Cutter."

So many racists, so little time.

Chapter Twenty-one

When I got home and told Bosco, he yelled at me for going without him and suggested we visit Nadia DeMarco ourselves. But by then it was almost 5:00. I'd blown a whole day waiting around that stupid station.

"She works at that club, the Back Room. I don't know exactly when they open, but I'm guessing she probably leaves for work pretty soon."

I called Dan back. Didn't get him. I wondered about the jury question, was it good or bad? For who? I called to report to Joe, but he was out on surveillance.

We drove over to Nadia's the next day, not too early. Chances were she wouldn't be up before eleven. Hostessing at a blues club would keep her up until the wee hours of the morning, or at least that's what we figured. Bosco insisted on bringing Sketch. I was kind of off dogs since the events of Sunday, but I reminded myself that Sketch was not a slavering mankiller, and he had saved my life, more or less.

I was thinking out loud when I turned into the parking lot at 11:13. "The way it had to be, Burton saw Yarborough and Porter. He worked on the case as a document clerk. Maybe he went to deposition or to court sometimes and saw them. He knew who they were. It would take him awhile to figure it all out, but from what Nadia said, he was working on it. It would be easy to find out about Brunswick's financial troubles. It made it to the news. It would have been the subject of rumors."

"You're saying he tried to blackmail Yarborough? And that's why he got shot?"

"Seems like it."

We left Sketch in the car. It wasn't a hot day, but I rolled the windows down an inch and tied his leash to the door handle. I didn't think anyone would steal the Squire, and if they did, we could probably run after them and catch them.

Bosco banged on the front door. No answer. He tried again, and then again. Still no answer.

"Maybe she spent the night somewhere else." I peered up at the fifth-floor window as if there was any way I could see into the apartment at that angle. Stupid.

"That would be pretty cold, Fifi. Burton's only been dead like a week."

"You're really not in a position to be criticizing other peoples morals, Bosco. Anyway, I didn't mean it like that. I mean maybe she took my advice and departed."

We had turned to walk back to the Squire when Bosco veered to the left. There were very few cars parked in the lot, which formed an L around the front and side of the building. Most people would be at work. Bosco pointed to a gold VW bug with a bumper sticker "Blues at the Back Room."

"Look at this."

"Her car?"

"Gotta be, don't you think?"

"Well, maybe not, maybe it belongs to a neighbor who goes there because he knows Nadia."

"Guys don't have gold VW Beetles, Fifi."

"OK then, it's a girl neighbor. It can't be Nadia. She doesn't know we're coming to see her. If she was here, she'd hear us."

"Maybe she's scared we might be the kidnappers."

We headed back to the front door of the Altadena Arms, but, without taking a tire iron to the front door, there really was no way in. I tried yelling again, but no one answered.

"We just have to wait until someone comes in or goes out," said Bosco. We waited another three minutes, which seemed much longer, but no one came in or out.

"Let's go," I finally said. We went back to the car and I unlocked it. Sketch had snotted up the windows during our short absence. "Great," I took a rag and started wiping. "Take him to pee."

Bosco held the leash as Sketch jumped out, but instead of trotting off obediently to pee, the dog stuck his nose in the air and started to sniff. When he darted off around the side of the building, Bosco lost his grip on the leash.

"Oh great, Bosco, can't you do anything right? Go get him. If he runs into the street and gets hit by a car, I doubt the owners are going to pay you for taking care of him."

Bosco ran off after Sketch.

"Stupid goddamn dog," I muttered to myself. "Stupid goddamn half-brother."

I looked around for a trash can to throw the rag away, but didn't see one. Annoyed, I followed Bosco and Sketch around the back of the building. Presumably there would be trash cans in the back.

There was. A big, green, metal one. A big, green, metal one with a body beside it; a body being enthusiastically licked by Sketch.

That dog will lick anything, I thought.

"Is it her?" I asked. Bosco nodded. I tried to think what to do. Since neither of us had a cell phone, and we'd already tried contacting someone inside the Altadena Arms, our choices were limited. Finally, I dragged Sketch away, locked him the car, and stood on the side of the road, waving frantically. About thirty cars went by in the space of eleven minutes, but one finally slowed and stopped. It had a USMC sticker in the window. A big, well-muscled, middle-aged man got out. He looked like he'd take my news in stride.

I was right. Corporal Earnest Checca, Retired, followed me to the dumpster, took a close look without touching anything, calmly agreed she was dead, and had his cell phone out before I could even finish the story.

"You two go out front, wait for the cops. I'll wait here," Corporal Checca gestured.

Bosco was happy enough to get away, but I hesitated. "Has she been dead long?" I asked.

"I can't tell without touching her. I'm sure the cops don't want me to touch her."

"Can you tell if she was shot?" I asked.

"Yeah. Twice, I think. Maybe more. I can only see the back."

"She was shot in the back?" We both looked down. Nadia was wearing a black shirt, but you could still see the bullet holes and the blood. I swallowed hard. Checca glanced with concern at my face.

"Look, you should go join your brother. Come on, get away from here. You can't help her now. It's going to take a while; the dispatcher tells me that most of the available cars are out at a violent domestic."

I nodded and started walking, sleepwalking almost, back to the front of the Altadena Arms. As I turned the corner, I noticed a glint in the narrow grass verge between the sidewalk and the building. I stooped and picked it up. It was a set of keys, with a silver N charm attached. I stared at them for a moment before slipping them into my pocket and running over to Bosco, who was sitting on the asphalt in the shade of the car. Actually, he was sitting on my jacket which he had placed on the asphalt. Sketch was draped across his lap.

"Get off my jacket, you dork. I think these are Nadia's keys. I think she dropped them."

"Or the murderer did."

"Right. The murderer." I squinted back at the unimpressive brick-and-glass edifice. It told me nothing. "Well, if he dropped them, then he's not still up there."

"Of course he's not still up there. She's probably been dead since last night. You don't really think she was killed in broad daylight, do you?"

"If you think about it, daytime would be the best time. That is, if she was shot up there in the apartment. We saw for ourselves. No one's home during the day."

"Either way, the cops are coming and it's too risky." Bosco shrugged. "Have a seat."

"I'm not going to have a seat, and I told you to get off of my jacket. I'm going up there."

"What are you, crazy? You get caught up there, you'll be a suspect. Or at least an accessory after the fact or an obstructer of justice or something bad."

"You watch too much TV. If I get caught, I'll just say—I'll just say—"

"Say what?"

"I'll say it's your fault for keeping me here talking when I should be hustling up there right now." I turned and legged it over to the front door. The extra-large key was obviously the front door key. I slipped into the entrance hall and darted into the elevator. When I got to Nadia's door, it took me three wrong keys before I picked the right one. Nadia had a lot of keys.

The state of the apartment told me most of what I needed to know. It was a mess, having been thoroughly ransacked. I carefully picked my way over upturned houseplants, the ruin of the sound system Burton had been so proud of, Nadia's clothes. The refrigerator door was open, the contents strewn all over the floor. The smell of soy sauce and ketchup was nauseating. The couch had been reduced to a mass of fluffy batting and shredded leather. Every possible thing was pulled out, thrown down, torn apart.

I searched for the phone and found the handset smashed. But the base was only cracked, the message light still blinking. I punched it on. "Nadia, you're late. Your shift started twenty minutes ago. This is a busy night. We can't take this kind of crap. You'd better be dead, because if you're not, you are so fired."

That had to be Nadia's boss at the Back Room. She hadn't shown up for work. Meaning she was killed yesterday. Maybe shortly after Donegal talked to her. Maybe because Donegal talked to her. Maybe because I talked to Donegal. Oh shit.

I pawed ineffectually through the mass of papers on the floor near the little hall desk and pocketed her address book. You never know. Any further exploration was cut off by Sketch's frenzied barking. I clambered over detritus to the living room window and saw the first of a line of cop cars turn into the parking lot.

I took the fire stairs, wiping the keys free of my prints and dropping them in a corner on the third floor landing.

No one saw me come out. All eyes were focused on Sketch, who apparently didn't love a man in a uniform. Bosco was in the back seat trying to calm him down.

I opened the door and got in. "The place had been totally ransacked. And she never made it to work last night, there was a message on the machine."

"Fifi, you know that Yarborough didn't shoot Nadia. Not unless he ran into a really good faith healer after you least saw him. Who does that leave?"

I dodged the question. "This is going to take all day."

It not only took all day, it took all three days. We were visited at home, asked down to the station, asked down to another station, asked to go back to the San Fernando Road station—which invitation I declined—and then re-interviewed at home. In the middle of the third day, I had to talk to someone. I couldn't call Dan; he was maybe the murderer, which I didn't believe, but he was still maybe the one. I couldn't call VJ, because she was sweating out the jury wait; weekends when the jury is out are torture.

I couldn't talk to Bosco because he kept dumping on Dan, and when he wasn't dumping on Dan he was all kissy-face with Violet.

Joe.

Chapter Twenty-two

Joe growled into the phone, "I'm on a stakeout."

"Oh come on, Joe."

"Fine, but I can't talk too long. I'm waiting for an important call."

"Hey, this could be an important call."

"Is it?"

"Well, not to you," I admitted. "But it's important to me."

"Go ahead," Joe gave me the world-weary cop voice, "but make it quick. I heard about Nadia DeMarco. And I heard you found the body."

"I did. It was awful."

"And Bosco was there?"

"Sure, he was there."

"And Bosco knew you were going to the store when your purse was snatched?"

"Sure, Bosco knew."

"And he knew about Burton?"

"Of course. What are you getting at?"

"Listen, Fifi, Bosco's been harping on Dan's guilt because Dan was the only other person who knew you'd be at Wade's, right?"

"Yeah, but like I said to him, it coulda been—"

Joe interrupted. "But Bosco knew it too."

That wasn't a question. I stared straight ahead. Sketch was idly licking himself.

"Okay, Joe, what you're saying is crazy talk."

"It's not. Look, when that guy moved in on you, I had a rap sheet run on him. Selling dope."

"It was oregano."

"Fraud."

"Okay, it was fraud, but it was oregano fraud."

"Drunk and disorderly."

"Oh, not that again, Joe."

"His rap sheet's as long as my arm."

"As long as your arm?" I asked skeptically. "Sounds to me like it isn't even as long as your—"

"Hey, hey, you watch it, girl. You don't talk like that, you got it? This guy is bad news, that's what I'm telling you. Bosco Dorff has no respect for authority, no regard for the rules. There is a history of reckless behavior. There is a driving over sixty-five in a forty-five zone—"

"Oh, bullshit. He doesn't even have a driver's license."

"And a driving without a license."

"OK, he's a bad traffic offender. Take away his license—oh wait, he still doesn't have one."

"You can't blow off that drunk and disorderly in public. It was just last year."

"It was in New York. Everybody's disorderly in public in New York, and I bet a lot of them are drunk. And this was a simple misunderstanding. Do we really have to go through this?"

"I know you got his version."

"Yes, I do have his version. Look, Bosco was having a martini, totally legal, in his own apartment—actually, I guess it was his girlfriend's apartment, but he lived there so he could drink there—only he wasn't alone, see, and he wasn't with his girlfriend, so she comes home and throws him out. It was not his fault that he was drunk in public. He meant to be drunk in private. And he wasn't disorderly, he was just upset. If anyone was disorderly, she was."

"Well, he was drunk outside, and that's what you're not supposed to be."

"Is that it? Is that what you've got?"

"He's not a good person, Fifi. You shouldn't be hanging around with him, and he sure as hell shouldn't be living in Pop's house."

Ah, finally, the real agenda.

"Joe, Pop didn't leave the house to you because you already have a house. Right? You have a house?"

"I have a house I worked for, Fifi. Did you ever stop and think what leaving you the house is really saying to you? It's Pop from beyond the grave telling you that you'll never be able to afford a house on your own."

Ouch! That was so far below the belt it was whomping on the soles of my feet. "Hey, you listen here, Joe." I heard a voice in the background, "Joe, hang up, there he is."

"Gotta go."

That went well, I thought bitterly to myself. So freaking glad I did that.

I was walking away when the phone rang. Joe's called back to apologize, I thought.

* * *

"The jury's back." VJ's voice was hoarse with strain.

It took me a sec to adjust. "Do you want me to come down?"

"That depends. Who will you be rooting for?"

"You VJ, you. I'll always root for a big verdict—and for you. You know that."

"I suppose. If I don't win, you don't get paid."

"Come on, VJ, I don't roll that way. I stick with my friends. You called me. You must want me to come."

"Oh, if you want to." Tension made her ungracious. I understood.

"I'll be there in twenty minutes. Don't let them start without me."

Seventeen minutes after putting the phone down, I was walking down the hall to the courtroom. Mrs. Rayburn was sitting on the bench outside. I realized she had never left, keeping vigil for all those days. I sat down next to her.

"How're you doing?'

"So nervous I could throw up."

I was unable to spout a platitude that might so quickly be proved wrong. I asked instead, "Not letting us in yet?"

"No, the judge let the jury go to lunch. He told 'em to make it snappy, though. The clerk had me wait here until the jury assembled."

I looked up at the sound of rapid footfalls approaching from my left. Dan.

"Fifi," he began, but was forestalled by equally rapid footfalls approaching from my right. VJ.

They each strode down the hall toward each other, wheeling their document cases, facing off like Wild West gunslingers.

They both got to the courtroom door at the same time and stopped. No one said anything.

The impasse was broken by the arrival of Skyblu's president, Czypieski, with Janet Porter on his heels, followed closely by Mr. Grund and Cissie McMull. The girl from ICARUS. VJ, Mrs. Rayburn, and I retreated to the bench across the hall from the courtroom. Janet and her entourage set up camp on the bench to the right of the door, Dan to the left.

As the jurors began to trickle back from lunch, the tension ratcheted up. First came the Plumber and the Accountant, heads down, not looking at any of us. Then came the three Golden Girls. The Old Hippie arrived alone, the Enigma right behind. They carefully avoided meeting our eyes.

We waited.

Just as I was checking my watch for the third time, I saw VJ's head snap to the left. I looked up to see the Bible Thumper approaching the courtroom, her red linen-like jacket flapping and her wispy curls bobbing. She slowed as she reached the door, and ducked her head. But before she entered, she quickly turned her head and gave Mrs. Rayburn a small, shy smile.

Porter looked incensed. Cissie McMull looked worried. Dan pretended not to notice. VJ and I huddled. What did it mean? Was it an apologetic smile? A don't-worry smile? Or just an embarrassed smile for being late to take her place? We discussed this for several minutes.

The clerk called us in to take our places, and time slowed down like a sports movie when the fat kid on the underdog team swings the bat in the big game, tied at the bottom of the ninth.

The clerk took the verdict form from the Accountant, and handed it to the judge. Judge Stein took his time reading it, while I concentrated on my breathing.

Judge Stein handed the form back to the clerk and asked her to read the verdict.

Her big moment. The clerk's contralto rang out. "We the jury, in the above entitled matter, hereby find as follows. Question one: Is defendant Grund Manufacturing liable for defective design in omitting locking security doors to the cockpit? Answer: Yes."

Mr. Grund gasped out loud and Cissie McMull threw him a warning glance.

"Question two: Is defendant Skyblu Airlines liable for negligently hiring James Farnswell and negligently allowing him onto the airplane with a loaded weapon? Answer: Yes."

I darted a glance over at Dan. He remained stoic. I was proud.

"Question three: If you answered both questions in the affirmative, what percentage of liability do you attribute to Grund and Skyblu?" I held my breath. Since the answer to this wouldn't affect VJ, I could wholeheartedly wish for Skyblu's percentage to be small. "Answer: Grund, eighty percent, Skyblu, twenty percent."

I heard Dan expel a slight breath. Now for the big question.

"What amount of damages do you find were suffered by the plaintiff as a result of the acts or omissions of defendants?"

The sadistic woman paused for dramatic effect. VJ became unnaturally still beside me. Mrs. Rayburn's eyes closed.

"Answer: one hundred thirty thousand for economic loss—" Oh shit! "—and twelve million in loss of consortium, emotional distress, and pain and suffering."

Oh, yeah!

✳ ✳ ✳

The courtroom discretely erupted. A reporter sitting in the back darted out. Mr. Grund slumped in his seat. Cissie McMull began scribbling notes like mad to Janet Porter, who stared straight ahead. Dan applied himself studiously to his calculator, as if he was too upset to figure it out in his head. VJ looked serenely ecstatic. Mrs. Rayburn looked bemused.

The excited whispers became frenzied murmurs, which became out-loud expressions of disbelief—joyous and outraged both. Louder and louder, until Judge Stein rapped his gavel.

"All right, that's enough. We're still in session here. Counsel, would you like to poll the jury?" He looked toward Boatwright and Porter. When Janet didn't respond,

Boatwright stood up and asked that the jury be polled. Predictably, each juror affirmed the verdict. Bible Thumper was beaming at us as if she had just adopted us. I beamed right back at the old dear.

"The jury is excused. We thank you for your service."

Janet Porter was the first to leave the courtroom. She walked like she had a ball and chain attached to her ankle, but was hoping no one would notice. Cissie McMull trailed her out.

Breathless, I darted after Porter and McMull. The insurance adjustor was pawing at Janet's arm, fiercely imploring.

"Janet, can we appeal? Do we have any grounds for appeal? Jesus, Janet, why isn't Mr. Yarborough here? We need to talk to him about this." Porter paid no attention. "Could you please hold up a minute? I'm upset, too, but we need to discuss this."

Porter continued her dreary march down the hallway. McMull stopped, put her hands on her hips, and snapped open her cell phone. She punched in a number and waited. Going to voice mail, I surmised. She hadn't noticed me behind her.

"Mr. Yarborough, wherever you are, you may be interested to know that the jury just came back with a verdict and it is not good, not good at all. I'm trying to get an answer from Porter about appealing, but she has decided to stop speaking to me. And may I take this opportunity to thank you very much for that recommendation, by the way. Call."

I didn't think the sunny Cissie had it in her. Well, I guess paying out over sixty million in settlement and then getting whacked for another twelve million would make even the cheeriest disposition a little grouchy.

But I didn't think Yarborough was going to be calling her back. My eye was fixed by a small headline on the front page of an LA Times being read by a lawyer waiting for his case to be called. He turned stiffly away when he noticed me staring, but it was enough. I got the headline, "Man Mauled By Dog In City of Industry." I could read the rest later, as I hurried back to Judge Stein's courtroom.

VJ and Mrs. Rayburn were over by the jury box, talking to the jurors.

"I thought that Ms. Porter was so stuck up," said one of the Golden Girls. "I couldn't go her way."

"God wanted you to win," said the Bible Thumper. "He told me He did."

"I thought it was very interesting," said the Plumber. "The whole idea of putting a dollar figure to a person's grief. I thought twelve million is about what I would put on my own grief for my first wife." He tilted his head. "Maybe more like five for my second wife. And to be perfectly frank," he lowered his voice, "I'd pay someone to kill my third."

"Companies like that, they shouldn't even be in business," said Juror Number Eleven. "Profits ahead of lives, that's what it is."

Dan was slowly packing up his briefcase, his head bowed. I figured VJ's daze of perfect happiness would last about ten more minutes before reality kicked back in. Dan needed me more than she did right then. I walked over to the defense table.

"Hey, sorry about that. It's not too bad though, is it? Not compared to Porter's client." He looked up at me. His smile was sadder than any frown could be.

"I don't like to lose, Fifi. I don't like it, and my clients don't like it."

I stood there awkwardly, trying to think of something to say that would make it better.

Dan read my mind. "Don't worry about it. It's not your problem. Look, I'll call you later. I gotta go talk to the jurors now." He waved me away.

"You don't want to talk to the jurors, Dan."

"No, I don't want to," he agreed. "But I have to. I have to learn what I didn't do right. For my own sake. For the client, too. We'll appeal, and if we win the appeal, we'll be trying this baby again."

That was bravado speaking.

"Alrighty, then, I'll be talking to you."

Dan grimaced in answer. I let him go.

I told VJ I'd call her later. She nodded, but I doubt she even heard what I said. Mrs. Rayburn had started to cry, and Bible Thumper and the Hippie were alternately hugging her. Enigma turned out to be a mild-mannered guy who did whatever the Ditzy Blond told him to, and Ditzy Blond had been incensed by the romantic tragedy of Mr. and Mrs. Rayburn's lost Golden Years.

I walked down Grand toward the cathedral parking, breathing in the perfect day, and stopped at the light. A white Mercedes passed into the intersection on the yellow and got stuck trying to make the turn. Cars honked, and I saw it was Janet Porter, tears streaming down her cheeks. She was human after all, I thought, as she maneuvered her Lexus into the flow of traffic.

She must know Yarborough was dead. I slowed my pace and thought about the inescapable fact that Yarborough wasn't the pom-pom man. The pom-pom man was someone who was prepared to go a lot farther than a middle-aged vice president of claims would go. Was the pom-pom man a tall statuesque woman? She was driving a white Mercedes, and I didn't think so. I had gotten close enough on two occasions to be sure pom-pom man was, in fact, a man.

What if Yarborough hadn't killed Burton? Burton had recognized Yarborough and Porter, sure. Had he tried to blackmail them? That fit with what I knew about him. But Burton hadn't known about the tape at first. He'd probably thought he was the only one who saw them. Judy the loud-mouthed receptionist might have told Burton about the tape. Who else saw the tape?

Reg Wong. I gave it to him and I told him I had a copy. But Reg was old. Do people really start killing other people in their late sixties? When they were already financially secure and had nice houses in the Hollywood Hills? And the pom-pom man was tall, strong, and—by all accounts— Mexican.

Or wait a minute. Maybe not Mexican. Maybe Asian. White people get Asian and Mexican mixed up all the time, at least at a distance. The organic grocery store was filled with white people.

What about that seemingly mild-mannered young man whose ambitions were cloaked in pinstripes and herring-bone? Norman Chu? Norman was a real-estate lawyer, and he could be the friend of Burton who had a gotten him a good deal on the apartment. To which Norman might have had a key, explaining how he could get into that secure building. Norman could easily be mistaken for Mexican. Norman brought the case to the firm in the first place, and stood to collect a huge portion of the one-third attorney's fee for the sixty million settlement.

Norman.

Chapter Twenty-Three

"How do I look?"

Bosco looked fabulous. Of course, he did. He always looked fabulous.

"Is that what you're going to wear?" I sniffed. It was Friday evening. The big opening at the gallery. A week had passed and life had returned to more or less normal. I had passed my suspicions about Norman Chu on to Joe, who had passed them on to the various members of the LAPD investigating Burton's and Nadia's murders, my kidnapping, and Yarborough's assault and possible manslaughter. Other state and federal agencies investigating Brunswick had also been advised. Brunswick stock had plummeted, but VJ's firm and Mrs. Rayburn got paid.

I still cared. I followed the cryptic stories that appeared, in the comfortable role of observer. All bruises, sprains, and cuts had healed. Dan and I were doing good. He was busy catching up on all the work he had neglected while in trial, and worried about Brunswick, his main client. But we were doing good, and I had invited him to Bosco's opening. He said he'd meet me there.

"You don't like it?" Bosco looked down at his black designer jeans, his silk-tweed jacket over a black T-shirt. "You think a button-down shirt would be better? I can't wear a tie; artists don't wear ties."

"Totally fake artists do."

At 6:15 Violet knocked loudly on the front door. I was unhappy to see her, but relieved Bosco hadn't yet given her a key.

"Did I mention Violet offered to drive us over to the show?" Bosco asked

I looked suspiciously at Violet. Since when had she been doing me favors? But she smiled brightly, if insincerely. "Come on, let's go. We don't want to be late, right? We need to be there before the doors open to make sure the arrangements are all okay."

I grabbed my all-purpose cropped-cut grey blazer and shrugged it on. Violet wrinkled her nose. "Is that what you're going to wear?"

Wordlessly, I stomped out to her car and got into the backseat.

Violet and Bosco followed, chatting animatedly. "I heard Martin Scorcese's going to be there," she said, sliding into the driver's seat. She kept it up all the way to Hollywood.

The gallery was a two-story white brick structure, nestled in between an office building and an upscale restaurant. There was no parking. The one space in front of the gallery had been reserved for Dante Wildman. Violet circled around, not offering to let us out in front. I notice things like that.

We parked in an Albertson's parking lot and walked the three blocks back. When we finally made it inside, my jaw dropped. Bosco's pictures were blown up to three feet square. In one, Sketch's mournful face peered down from the seat of a delivery van. In another, his skinny body was caught disappearing around the side of a warehouse. And in a particularly charming shot, he was seen, through a chain link fence, peeing against a rusty engine part.

It was what the dog did best, I reflected.

I looked closer and my blood ran cold. I knew that truck yard. I knew those trucks. I knew that warehouse in the distance. I'd been there all too recently.

"Bosco," I grabbed his arm and pulled him over. "How did Violet get you into this place to take pictures?"

"A client of Norman Chu's leases space for his trucks there. He arranged it."

"Bosco, look at that warehouse. That's where I was held."

Bosco stared. "So it *was* Norman Chu."

"Right. I'll call Joe tomorrow. Another piece of the puzzle."

"Now that the cops have started digging, it's only a matter of time."

"You admit now that everything you thought about Dan was totally wrong and I was totally right?"

"I'm not going to admit I was totally wrong. Dan might not be a murderer, but he is still a self-centered, inconsiderate workaholic."

"And Violet is what?"

I turned away from Bosco to face the far wall and lost my breath as I was confronted by a grotesque enlargement of my own face. Hair wild, makeup smudged, eyelids half-closed. The "practice" shot Bosco had snapped of me in the kitchen.

I whirled back on him. "You take that down. Right now. You can't show that."

"Yes I can. Trevor loved it. Look at the title. 'Young Woman Unmasked.' Trevor says it reflects the essence of sloth in the modern era."

"You asshole! I invited Dan tonight! He might actually come! I can't have him see me like that."

But Bosco was scooped up by Trevor to greet the arriving Dante Wildman. A tubby little man emerged from behind the wheel of a silver Lamborghini while an East European model type with legs to the sky swung out of the passenger seat.

I had no idea there was that kind of money in Dalmatian kitsch.

As Trevor escorted Bosco forward, I was amused to see Violet right behind them. In ten minutes she managed to insinuate herself into the publicity stills, right between Bosco and Wildman, smiling into the camera as the flash popped.

I planted myself next to the bar and waited for the bartender to come open the wine. The East European model was propped up against the wall on the other side, with, apparently, the same thought. The bartender saw our need and rushed forward.

A glass of Pinot Grigio firmly in hand, I circled the room, angling for my chance to bump into "Young Woman Unmasked" and knock it off the wall. A little self-help. We still had seven minutes until the door opened to the public and I was ready with the hip check when my eye was caught by the next photo, to the right. It was Wade on the toilet. I stared aghast. Bosco must have picked it up off my desk when he swept up the proofs.

"Bold, isn't it? Bosco has such magnificent artistic nerve, wouldn't you agree? I'm very proud of what he's been doing under my tutelage." I glanced over to the tubby man at my side. He was stroking his goatee and gazing with admiration at the super-enlarged image of the mechanic with his pants around his ankles. I stifled the "you've got to be kidding me" that sprang to my lips when I recognized my companion as Dante Wildman.

He gave me the patronizing look of the celebrity who realizes he's just been recognized by a nobody.

"The dog portraits are, if I may say so, a bit derivative of my own work. Only to be expected, I suppose; the student follows the master. But this—" He gestured. "It's truly original."

"Yes," I agreed. "It's truly original."

Wildman wandered away, to spout banalities at someone else. My train of thought was interrupted by a squeal from the group of black-clad art devotees rushing into the gallery as the front doors were officially opened.

"Trevor, darling, you have done it again. Magnificent," gushed an older woman with her hair swept up into spikes.

"Genius!" breathed a shorter woman whose hair was dyed magenta.

Trevor greeted the new arrivals with air-hugs, and a half an hour later, a crowd had formed, filling the small space. By 8:15 it was hard to walk around.

Dante, I noticed, had a constant circle of sycophants around him as he pontificated on his newest protégé. I saw one man, in a rumpled brown suit, writing in a notebook.

And Violet appeared to have accidentally gotten super glued to Wildman's rib cage. The East European model hovered two feet away, swigging from a bottle of the Cabernet. There would sure be a sound in the forest when that tree fell down, I reflected.

I turned to find Bosco, but couldn't get near him. His circle was almost as large as Dante Wildman's and included Trevor, clapping his hands archly whenever anyone uttered some trite compliment. Of which the night was full.

"The power of the composition—"

"The courage to show the human condition at its most debased—"

And of course, everyone who gathered around "Young Woman Unmasked" uttered the new catch phrase, "The essence of sloth in the modern era—"

I gritted my teeth.

Food was good, though. No cheddar cheese squares here. When I finally managed to elbow my way close to the buffet table, I was treated to warm figs with gruyere, spicy miniature empanadas, and sushi. I stuffed myself.

I brightened and waved when I saw VJ come in.

"Hey, Veej, celebration all around, huh?"

VJ's face doesn't reveal much, but I know her pretty well. That wasn't joy I was seeing.

"What's the matter?" I asked.

VJ shifted. "Nothing. Mrs. Rayburn is happy. She got what she deserved. The partners are ecstatic."

"But you're not happy."

VJ shot me a look. "I was advised today by the partners at my firm that I will receive a bonus of ten thousand dollars for my work on the trial."

I nearly dropped my figs and sushi. "Ten thousand dollars? You've got to be kidding! The firm made four million dollars off that verdict."

"I am very well aware of how much the partners will be taking home." VJ's tone was bitter. "Their perspective is that I should be glad for the chance to try such a big case at my tender age."

I snagged us two glasses of wine from a circulating waiter, and VJ made a wan attempt at art appreciation. "Young Woman Unmasked" got a ghost of a smile, but I wasn't surprised when she put her glass down, nearly untouched, and soon after departed, leaving me still watching the door for Dan.

By 10:10 I was trying to remember just how many glasses of Pinot Grigio I'd had when a tall figure towered over me. An extraordinarily handsome Asian man at my elbow. He was staring at me intently, but somehow not with admiration.

I felt unmasked.

"Do you want a drink?" he asked, in a harsh, slightly accented voice.

I'm not adverse to a gorgeous guys bringing me drinks, especially when I've already had too many. But this guy was out of my league, and I felt kind of like his wing man had pegged me for the ugliest girl in the room and had bet him five bucks he wouldn't ask me out.

On the other hand, I did want a drink.

"Sure," I said, and watched him go fetch it. The view

from behind was interesting but I would much rather have seen Dan walk into the room.

"My name's Fifi," I volunteered when Tall Asian Guy returned.

"I'm called Spider," he muttered grudgingly. He didn't say anything else, just stood there awkwardly and, it seemed to me, a little angrily. There was something not quite right about his eyes. I'd have dumped his ass right then, but I was tired of scuttling around with no one to talk to, looking pathetic. It wouldn't hurt, I reasoned, for Dan to show up while I was talking to this guy.

"So, what brought you here?" I asked.

"My sister."

Oh, that explained it, I thought. The guy has no interest in art and is only here because of sibling pressure. About which I know quite a lot.

"What do you think?"

"About what?"

I was nonplussed. "About the photographs."

"Oh. I guess they're okay." He looked around and his eyes fell on Young Woman Unmasked. "Is that you?"

I glanced over, unconcerned. "No." I replied. "I don't know who that is."

He looked at me suspiciously. "But you are Fifi Cutter?"

"Yes, that's my name." There was something weird about this guy. Was he, like, borderline retarded? After a few more awkward attempts at conversation, I gave up my plan to make Dan jealous. I didn't want to talk to this Neanderthal any more, no matter how good-looking he was. Even wandering around alone would be better than this.

I drained the glass. "Excuse me. I have to go to the restroom." I dashed off down a narrow hallway, turned left, and went down some stairs, following the helpful "Restroom" signs. The restroom was a pit—a unisex one-staller, concrete floor, no window, bare light bulb. But it served the purpose.

I felt so much better when I emerged. Then I felt awful again when I saw Spider standing right there. Then I felt really awful when I saw he was holding a gun. Pointed at me.

"What are you doing?" I asked, my wits in need of a reboot.

"I need the video tape," he answered.

"I don't have the video tape. I gave it to Reg Wong."

"Not that one. The copy. You made a copy."

Yeah, the copy Bosco and I had looked for, and couldn't find. What had I done with it? A vision rose before me of shredded papers, chewed-up sneakers, unrecognizable bits of plastic, long tangled loops of tape.

The dull realization dawned. "My dog ate it."

Chapter Twenty-four

He clipped me upside the head with a closed fist.

"Ow."

"Shut up." He grabbed me by the arm and dragged me out a back door into an alleyway where a black Lexus stood. He pulled a set of keys out of his pocket and waved me into the driver's seat with his gun, as he slipped over to the passenger side.

He handed me the keys and told me to drive.

"Hey, this is Violet Fang's car."

"Shut up." Spider gestured with his right hand, the gun, held low, still pointed at me.

He indicated which way I was to turn by jabbing the air with the gun. Right. Left. Right again. I felt ill, the Pinot Grigio threatening to come up. I thought it was over. I thought I was safe. Norman Chu must have figured out the cops were investigating him; he was a bright guy. And a careful guy. What was he doing this for? After all, he'd already gotten his money, probably safely tucked away in places no one could trace it.

And who was this guy? How was he connected to Norman Chu?

"Get on the 10. East, stupid."

I obeyed his orders, and we sped toward the downtown high-rise cluster, passing pockets of light, zooming in and out of darkness. We slid toward the great freeway collide, where the 10, 5, 110, and 101 meet. I thought longingly of my house as I wondered where he was taking me.

"Get in the left lane," my captor hissed.

Oh shit, I thought as I made the transition. We were going home.

Yeah, yeah, I know I had just been thinking about how much I wanted to go home, but not in this car, and not with this guy. He was taking me home because he still hadn't found the tape and thought I had hidden it at the house.

In the movies they tell you to get the bad guy talking. I wasn't sure why, and there was nothing about Spider that made me think he'd be an entertaining conversationalist, but I didn't have anything else going on, so I made myself give it a try. You listen, you learn; that's what Pop used to say.

I cleared my throat. "You know, Spider, with Yarborough dead and the case over, I really don't think the tape is your big worry right now."

"Shut up."

I glanced over. Spider had slipped his hood up over his face.

"That's a way better look than the pom-pom hat," I told him.

"Shut up."

He turned his face toward me. It was a perfect oval, high cheekbones, sensual mouth.

"You're Violet's brother," I realized, as I braked for the inevitable traffic jam through downtown. "You were the one behind the door when I was at Chu's office that time."

"I told you—"

"I know. Shut up. But what were you doing there? Norman was giving you orders?"

"I don't take orders from geeks."

"What were you doing there, then? Come on. I'll tell you where the tape is."

"You'll tell me where the tape is anyway."

"Eventually, sure. But how long do you think you have before Bosco notices I'm gone? He's very protective of me." I said it with a straight face and added, "You may as well tell me. You're going to kill me anyway." I was hoping for a denial, but I didn't get it.

"I had to talk to the lawyer." Spider's voice betrayed his sense of grievance. If I hadn't been so tense, I would have seen the humor in it. "That Norman guy. He was trying to do me out of my money. Said I couldn't be in the lawsuit. He made me sign a paper."

"Because you have a criminal record." I remembered the colloquy at trial when Dan was trying to question Violet about her brother. "Norman and Wong didn't want that coming out."

"It's my money."

Traffic slowed as we approached downtown. I idly contemplated the little family group stick figures affixed to the back window of the Suburban in front of me. Mom. Dad. Becky. Connor. Tilly. Why do moms and dads want the whole world to know their kids' names? I wondered. Was that really a good idea? With people like Spider around?

I tried again.

"It's not your money now. Violet got it all. You weren't a party to the suit. I heard that right in court." I was looking for an emotional button to push.

"Violet didn't take all the money. She's going to give me half. She promised, if I helped her."

I inched forward. Violet promised to give him half? That meant it was Violet who was behind all this. Not Norman. Violet.

Oh, Christ. Any hope of Bosco noticing I was gone evaporated. Violet would feed him a line and he would eat it.

"What exactly did you do to help her? Kill Burton? Is that what you did to earn your share?"

"Yeah, popped that punk. Ha."

"How'd you get in the building?"

"Burty boy let me in. I knew him from the club. We were good buds, him and me." Spider didn't see the irony.

"You killed Burton because Violet told you that you two had to be the only ones who knew Yarborough was banging Porter."

My hands felt icy, and I reached to turn up the heater. Spider stopped me with a poke from the gun barrel in my upper arm. I pretended I didn't notice.

"Let me see if I have this right. Violet walks in on Reg that day I was there. She sees Yarborough and Porter on the tape. She knows that Burton recognized them, and she also knows that Burton doesn't know they've all been caught on film."

Spider slumped further in his seat, like he was bored, but he hadn't told me to shut up again, so I assumed I was right and continued.

"Seems a little extreme to kill him at that point, Spider. What went down? He was going to get money from Yarborough to keep quiet about the affair? Yarborough married?"

Spider gave a little snort, which I took to be assent.

"Burton probably thought it was just a little bit of ordinary blackmail. He didn't see the big picture. Not like you and Violet."

I eased into the right lane. I knew the right lane would come to screeching halt where the 10 split off. Maybe I was just prolonging the agony, but if there was any chance I could, say, make eye contact with the occupant of another car, send a telepathic signal. But other drivers don't want to look at you, because then they might feel bad about not letting you into their lane, or cutting you off.

Spider grunted. "I didn't go there to kill him."

"Let me guess, you were just going to scare him?" Again, Spider missed the irony.

"Yeah. Just scare him into shutting up for a while. Violet said she needed time to think." Spider shot me an angry look. "She just needed time to think!"

"Sure, sure big guy. We all need time to think." I licked my lips. I didn't have too much more time to think. We had come to a complete halt. Spider hit the dashboard in impatience.

"Let me see if I can guess what happened next. Brunswick's financial condition hit the news, right? Violet gets worried. She runs some searches, just like I did. She found out about Brunswick and Heartland."

"Violet knows what she's doing. You don't mess with Violet." He said that with a pride that seemed to confirm my deductions.

"Once the trial started and Porter fell down on the job, Violet figured out that Yarborough and Porter were conspiring to throw the trial so Grund would end up paying the lion's share. That's way bigger than a measly extramarital affair. If that came out, man, it would be a career-ender for Yarborough. Maybe even jail."

"He was scared." Spider's voice held satisfaction.

"Judge Stein disqualified Wong's damages expert. Violet got desperate, put the screws on Yarborough hard. She told him to settle for the sixty million or she would tell all. Yarborough caved—as long as she agreed to his original plan to make ICARUS pay most of the settlement."

A settlement wasn't as good as a jury verdict for Yarborough, since it could be questioned and second-guessed. But it was better than the certainty of having the original plot revealed.

"So, Spider, tell me. How did Violet even know I had a copy of the tape?"

I thought at first he wasn't going to answer, but he shrugged and said, "Mr. Wong, he told Violet."

"Did it really matter so much?"

"Violet said you would figure it out. She said you were smart."

"She did?" Absurdly, I felt a warm glow. Compliments

from your friends are good, but compliments from people who don't like you at all are great.

"Let me get this right. You must have been watching the house when Bosco gave me the *Raiders of the Lost Ark* tape. You saw me put it in my purse." I was way creeped out by the thought that he had been stalking me. "Where were you hiding?"

"I wasn't hiding. I was right there, you could see me. Across the street, sitting on your neighbor's porch. They weren't home."

That's what I get for not being friendly with the neighbors, I thought. "You thought it was your tape?"

"It was just a stupid movie."

"*Raiders of the Lost Ark* is a great movie. You know, Bosco's seen it seven times."

Spider poked me again with the gun, urging me to the left lanes. I slowly merged.

"And the night I went to see *Queen of Minsk* with Dan," I continued. "Bosco told Violet I'd be out. She told you. Right?"

Spider didn't respond. I took that as a yes.

"And the same thing when I went to Wade's and you kidnapped me. Bosco told Violet. She told you." As Joe had said, Bosco was the only other person who had known where I'd be. I was going to tear Bosco a new one when I saw him again. No, I wouldn't be seeing him again. A new sorrow blistered up. I wouldn't be seeing Dan again, either.

Dan. I had to know. "Okay, Spider, I'm following it so far. But it wasn't you who went to interview Mrs. Wegliecki." I didn't say it, but I couldn't see Mrs. Wegliecki opening up to this dude and telling him all her secrets. That was Dan, just like we knew it had to be. Dan was a really good lawyer. He had probably done a much better job interviewing her than I did. He'd seen how she would try to help him, and end up sinking him when the truth came out. He probably found out about the hospitalization, too. Nothing sinister, just good strategy.

"So was it you or Dan who came to get her records?"

"Shut up."

"Okay, it was you. Why did you use the name John Cartwright? Were you trying to throw suspicion on Dan? Okay, sure, but you didn't think of it. That hadda be Violet's idea."

He gave me an insolent smile. He was enjoying our little game of Twenty Questions. He wouldn't admit anything; he'd been in and around the system too long for that. But he wanted me to know, because he was as proud of himself as if he'd just earned the fire-making merit badge.

"You killed Mrs. Wegleicki because Yarborough told you to?"

Spider's smile became a grin. I was close, but wrong.

"He didn't tell you to. But he was the only one who wanted her dead. Her testimony, if it came out, would kill Skyblu." I rolled it around in my brain. "Her testimony would support his decision to settle, but it would put all the liability on Skyblu. Cissie McMull isn't stupid, and for Mr. Grund it was way personal. If either one of them had known that Mrs. Wegliecki could testify to years of mental problems, Yarborough couldn't have even tried to put liability on Grund. There'd be a settlement alright, and Brunswick would be paying 100 percent. So Violet told you to get rid of Grandma Wegliecki, to make the deal happen."

Spider's face puckered up as if he was smelling something bad. "Legal shit."

"Right. Legal shit. How did you manage to poison her pills before we even talked to her?" I had a hard time picturing Spider acquiring a lethal substance, creeping into Villa Flora, finding the right room, finding the pill bottle.

And Spider reacted like he'd been scalded. "I didn't

poison her. I didn't poison nobody. I don't poison people. That's pussy."

That outburst had the ring of truth. "But you killed her." Traffic had picked up, but it would slow again where the 5 split off. I eased into the farthest left lane, to take advantage of the backup. "What did you do, smother her?"

He looked away. Another bull's-eye for Fifi. The old soldier's instincts had been right, but of course she couldn't see squat. I'd wasted all that money on a useless test. Getting Carlotta in trouble was small consolation.

"Great, Spider, smothering an old lady. That's not pussy at all," I muttered and got the heel of his hand to my head. An MTA bus honked as I swerved dangerously.

I took the next three minutes to gather myself for another go.

"Yarborough freaks out when he finds out you've kidnapped two people. Not his kind of crime at all. So you beat the crap out of him and killed him."

"I didn't kill him. Not my fault he got bit up by that dog."

"Fair enough," I conceded. "But what about Nadia? You shot her. Cold. She tell you she have a copy of the tape? That would be so Nadia. She didn't." I glanced over, but Spider just shrugged and pointed me to the exit.

I turned right at the bottom of the ramp. We were on a stretch of Figueroa severed from downtown by the freeway. A neighborhood with a distinctly Third World feel. Gritty little buildings, gated for the night, the street lights few and far between. I concentrated on the road, hoping to see someone, anyone at all. A tan pit bull slunk into an alley.

I peered down past the grungy clutch of apartments clinging to the hill on the left side of the street. My heart brightened and then leaped. Two signals away, the lights of a parked police car. No, two police cars! I sped up. There was hope, I thought. Thank you God, I promise I'll be a better person, I'll let Bosco get a dog, I promise I'll walk the dog, every day, I promise—

"Cops. Turn here." Spider gestured with the gun, forcing me to make a left onto Cypress, leaving my hope behind.

The neighborhood was residential and even more Third Worldly. Small working-poor houses with bars over the windows. No lights on anywhere, except at one tiny, stuccoed-over bungalow, where the glow of a TV illuminated the thin curtain. I latched onto that square of light, but I couldn't see anyone inside.

Savage graffiti, marking the territory of the Ave 43 gang, was splashed over every vulnerable surface—except where it was crossed out by the unintelligible marks of a rival gang. Young men taunting fate, and ending up with their own personal Baghdad.

We passed the chain link fence guarding the playground of a school—deserted, sinister in the gloom. The air was cold, way colder than the usual take-a-jacket-with-you-it's-hot-now-but-it-always-cools-off-at-night cold that Angelenos expect. Cold like a bitter, damp cold. If anyone in LA had ever walked, they wouldn't be doing it tonight.

It was weird. I should be crying. I believed he was going to kill me. I didn't really see what I could do about it. But I wasn't sad, I was mad. Not that different, I guess, from the way I usually feel, just more so.

The street narrowed from four lanes, to two, to don't-meet-anyone-coming-the-other-way. The tiny, twisted streets that protected my mountain refuge from the inconvenience of through traffic were now just places where Spider could put a bullet in my dome, kick my lifeless body to the curb, and drive away, a gruesome discovery for the kids going to school the next morning.

"Go home," Spider ordered.

Go home, he said. Not turn right. I knew he'd been there at least once before, back before he had a gun and was trying to kill me old-school with nunchucks. When we turned to avoid the cops, he must have lost the way.

How could I use this to my advantage? Detour a little to gain a little more time. I wanted a little more time.

I turned on a side street and approached the crossroad with Isabel Drive. Isabel became known as Avenida de Assasinos, after gang crossfire killed a little girl one night a few years back. I knew from the graffiti that the gangs were out, brewing their war.

Instead of turning right, I turned left.

"This the way? I thought you were supposed to turn up there." Spider peered at me from under his hood.

"Cliff Drive's out. Construction."

"You better not be playing me, bitch."

I stayed silent, my eyes straining ahead.

Bingo! Directly ahead I saw my guys. A shaved-head, sweatshirted bad-ass on my right and, on the opposite corner, two hooded figures standing tensed. You could smell the hate. The fear. Well, the fear was probably all me. These guys were battle-ready.

I slowed down.

"Speed up, you stupid shit!" Spider saw them, too. He slumped down and pulled his hood even farther over his face. Lovely.

I did what he said. I sped up and as I passed the dude with no hair, I mad-dogged him, staring right at him, my formidable eyebrows lowered. As we drew parallel, I raised my left arm to the side of my head so Spider couldn't see. I made a fake gang gesture with my hand.

Chapter Twenty-Five

I ducked under the dashboard, clinging to the steering wheel with one hand. Out of the corner of my eye I saw Spider raise his gun. No-hair dude and his two enemies would see that gun, too. If he'd had a can of red paint and a large brush Spider could not have painted a bigger target on his head. Both sides fired. The noise was volcanic and I lost control of the Lexus, which careened about a block before smashing into a line of parked cars. A minute and a half later, and lights started going on in the houses on Isabella. It took that long for the people to wake up and realize it wasn't a nightmare, or at least not their nightmare.

It didn't take me any time at all to realize I was hurt. Bad. My arm felt like it was on fire; I choked back a scream and sunk deeper under the dash. Spider's face, what was left of it, was slumped over in the seat, inches from mine.

I closed my eyes and gritted my teeth until I heard the wail of sirens, coming closer and closer and then stopping. It sounded like at least three cars. I wondered if I needed an ambulance. There was too much blood in the car, and too much adrenaline in me, to know how badly I was hurt.

I looked out the window at the heavy night sky. A dim shape appeared, but from my vantage point I couldn't see much more than a menacing shadow. I attempted to raise my head and the shape disappeared.

"Driver's alive." I heard a shout. "Watch out! He may be armed." I recognized the voice. It was the Coalminer's Daughter, Officer Donegal.

"Hey, wait, help me. I'm not armed. I'm not armed. I'm hurt."

Silence. I felt like I was in a dream, where you want to move, but can't, want to talk but nobody hears you. Like Pat Tillman must have felt.

"Officer Donegal, Officer Donegal, it's me. Help." I was blubbering.

"Hush up. Everybody be quiet. I'm trying to hear." I heard what sounded like Officer Donegal smacking somebody. The din quieted.

"Officer Donegal, it's me," I repeated. "Fifi Cutter."

"College girl?"

"I'm hurt."

"Now is this what your parents spent all that money for to send you to Harvard?"

"Bennington," I corrected. "Now would you please get me out of here? The other guy's dead."

"Put your hands where we can see them, College Girl."

"I can't move my arm." The tears flowed as I gasped for breath.

"No," I heard her bellow. "No one go near that car. Somebody in there has a gun."

"It's not me," I whispered, losing strength. I blinked, trying to retain consciousness.

"I said, don't go near that car!" the Coalminer's Daughter was screaming. "I said—"

There was an eternity of twenty seconds before some brave soul jerked the car door open, reaching in with strong arms and gentle intentions. It still really hurt, but I was soon laid on the ground, a blanket under my head. Officer Shaw, the stuttering newbie, smiled down at me.

✳ ✳ ✳

My arm was broken and my ankle was sprained, but the rest was cuts and bruises. The cops interviewed me in the hospital and I came home the next day. Bosco picked me up in the Squire.

"We have a little problem, Baby Sister."

"We? We don't have a broken arm. I have a broken arm."

"I mean the car," he advised me as we pulled into the driveway. "I'm going to have to give it back in two weeks. The owner leased it to be used in a movie. Set in the Fifties. I think it's going to be called The Big Orange."

"The Big Orange what?"

"Don't know. Let's focus on the problem here. I haven't fixed the brakes yet."

"Of course you haven't fixed the brakes. You don't know how to fix the brakes. You were never going to fix the brakes. Tell him you couldn't get the parts. That's not untrue, since you don't even know how to get the parts." I snort laughed. "Or even what parts to get."

Bosco gave me an exasperated, "I told him that. He kind of got mad. Now he wants his money back."

I exhaled. "Bosco, you didn't tell me that he paid you. You jerk. How much?"

"Five hundred bucks. But I already spent it. That night at the Back Room was expensive. Man, do you know what they charge for drinks? Come on. Be a pal."

I held up my hand, the one not in a sling. "I am not giving you five hundred bucks. I have a better idea. Take it to Wade Brockett. He'll be happy to fix it for free."

"Why would he do that? 'Cause he likes you so much?"

"No, 'cause I caught him in his insurance scam. He's been totaling out cars that only need minor repairs, buying them for scrap, and then selling them. Tell Wade I'll rat him out to Colchester. And make him give you a loaner."

"Fantastic." Bosco helped me out of the car. "You going to be okay here alone while I go down there?"

"Yeah. Just get me upstairs and give me a pain pill."

Walking up stairs was agony. I fell heavily onto the pool raft and Bosco tucked me in. He gave me a Vicodin and a glass of water. I drifted off, and when I came back I saw VJ sitting cross legged on the floor next to me.

"How are you?" she asked, her voice soft.

"I'm okay." I grimaced. "Gonna be okay anyway."

"I can't believe I got you into this. I feel so bad."

"I can think of a number of people whose fault this is, VJ, and you're not even in the top five."

VJ smiled and rubbed her forehead. "You could so easily have been killed. It seems unreal."

"But I wasn't killed. I killed him, that son of a bitch."

VJ looked at me sideways. "You're not upset?"

"I'm very upset about this," I waved my cast. "But you can't seriously think I'd be upset about icing that asshole. He smothered an old lady for God's sake."

"I know, I know. You were justified and it's been ruled self-defense."

"It *was* self-defense," I snapped.

"I just thought you'd be more upset."

"Boo hoo. That make you happy?"

I could see VJ suppress her retort. Making allowances for the invalid. Nice. "I'm glad you're well," she said carefully. "It's just that everything seems so horrible lately."

"What are you talking about? Bosco's a star. I got a boyfriend. You won the trial. Sure, the partners skunked you, but you can talk to them, can't you? Aren't they reasonable people?"

A long pause filled the room. Finally, VJ said, almost under her breath "I don't think I can stay there, Fifi."

"Stay where? You mean stay at the firm?" I shrugged. "You don't have to stay there if you don't want to. We done got freed, remember?"

VJ lifted her hands. "Your father gave me a chance."

"Well, if I know Pop, he didn't do it to be nice. He did it

because you were a top graduate of a good law school with mad debating skills."

"I still owe him."

"Maybe so but you can't repay him. He's dead."

That made her wince. I continued in a more conciliatory tone. "If Pop could want anything, which he can't, he'd want you take control of your own career, VJ. He liked his partners fine but that doesn't mean you have to. You hear me?"

VJ nodded. "It's just not been the same there since your father passed away. I feel like I'm not really wanted, for one thing. Nobody's exactly mentoring me. And the attitude is different now too. It's all about the paycheck."

"Um, well, yeah. They're lawyers."

"Your father was a lawyer. He cared about—"

"Don't say justice," I laughed.

"Okay, I won't. Not justice exactly, but the quality of the game. You know, if both lawyers are trying hard and the rules are fair and the judge isn't a drunken despot, then justice will be aided."

"Most of the time," I amended.

"Do doctors save all their patients?" VJ countered. "I don't expect perfection. Really, I don't."

"What do you expect?" I asked, curious.

VJ shook her head miserably. "It doesn't matter. Even if I subscribed to their money grubbing theory, it's obvious I won't be rewarded there. I've got to go."

"What are you going to do?"

She was silent.

"VJ, what are you going to do?"

"We should talk about this later. You're hardly in any shape to be holding me up."

"I'm not going to be in a better mood, later." I promised. "What are you going to do?"

"Well, if you must know, I was thinking of opening up my own shop. My own firm."

"Really? The law Offices of Victoria J. Smith?"

VJ cast her eyes down. "Not exactly. I may take on a partner. You know, it's really hard to be solo. You can't take a vacation, for one thing. And we were thinking about Cabo for Christmas, remember?"

"Yeah I remember. I got some bucks now I got paid, and Cabo would be sweet. But you have to find a partner. That's not easy, it has to be someone—" I stopped myself. She couldn't mean that, I thought. But then she wasn't looking at me.

"Dan? You and Dan?"

VJ jumped to her feet and turned her back to me. "We're just in the talking stages. But you know, his firm is in trouble. Brunswick may go under, and even if they don't, he's kind of tainted among insurance companies. He may have to switch to the plaintiff's side." She turned to see how I was taking it. Answer: not so good. "Nothing's been decided, Fifi."

"Wait a minute. Weren't you the one who called Dan the enemy?"

VJ showed astonishment. "But the trial is over." As if that explained everything. And for her it probably did.

"Oh Fifi, you don't look good. I'm so sorry. I shouldn't have been talking about it. You need rest. You need sustenance, at least. What can I get you?"

I closed my eyes and emitted a low groan. "A Pinkberry ice," I whispered.

VJ was out the door and down the stairs on her way to the closest Pinkberry in under forty seconds. I'd think of something else for her to get me by the time she got back.

✳✳✳

It was like that for several days. I felt like a queen, with a pool raft as a throne, VJ dancing attendance, Bosco keeping me fed on macaroni and cheese and microwave burritos, and Dan making the occasional special appearance.

The theoretical law firm of "Boatwright and Smith LLC" cast a shadow, but I tried hard to shush the little voice that said it might not be a good idea for my stunning, accomplished unattached best bud to be in daily proximity to my boyfriend. For one thing, I argued, VJ only dates guys taller than she, and Dan is an inch shorter. Three inches shorter when she's wearying heels which--let's think it through—she would mostly be wearing at work.

For another, Dan still worked pretty much all the time. While I was more than satisfied with having a conceptual boyfriend, VJ would probably demand a real relationship.

And then there's the Colonel and Miss Dolly. VJ is from a loving home and she would really care if Dan's parents hated her. But I'm totally used to parental disapproval. My mother channels Joan Crawford.

On the sixth day, I was re-reading my David Sedaris collection and eating Doritos when there was a knock on the half-opened door. Expecting one of my regular retainers, I crammed another handful of chips into my mouth and mumbled "Cub im."

It was Joe, with Sketch on his heels. I sat up and chewed fast.

"Nice dog."

"Yeah. He's not ours though. His owners are going to pick him up soon." I reached over and patted the dog on the head.

"Bosco let me in." Joe looked like he was going to say more on the subject of Bosco, but I gave him pleading eyes and he relented. "He said to tell you the car would be ready by Friday." He paused. "I guess it's good he's taking care of stuff like that for you." He looked over at me again. "That was pretty scary, what all you've been through."

I pulled off a modest shrug, "Shucks."

"You wanna talk about it?" Joe leaned against the wall and looked down at me. He has my same big, heavy-lidded eyes, and he's not afraid to use them.

I squirmed out of his gaze. "Yeah," I said. "I want to know when you're going to arrest Violet. I gave the cops my statement at the hospital. They should have more than enough."

Joe sank down to the floor, disturbing Sketch. "We're still looking at it, Fifi. But I read your statement. I'm not sure—that is, the DA isn't sure—that he can prove she did anything criminal."

"Are you kidding me?" I struggled to sit up. "She and her crazy fool brother killed four people and tried to kill me. That's five people. I can testify against her. I will testify. You can't stop me from testifying!"

"Hey, lie back down. Take it easy. And think about it, Fifi. Even by your own account, Spider didn't really say anything incriminating against her. Even if he had said something, and you could testify to what he said, we couldn't use it."

"What do you mean? Why not?"

"Look. We've done our homework. Spider got his nickname for a reason. I have his juvi file. His father was never around, his sister was in the US, and Mrs. Fang doted on him. His momma's been protecting his ass since he set fire to his elementary school. When he was eight. Mrs. Fang shipped him off to join Violet here, which worked out great for everybody except the poor guy he knifed in a street fight. He was thirteen when he was charged with attempted murder. The Fangs hired the best shrink expert they could find to testify that Spider was mentally retarded. He got put in a special facility. Stayed there for two years."

"He was a little slow," I acknowledged. "But I wouldn't say he was retarded. He probably just had a language issue and didn't test well."

"I'm sure you're right. But on the record, he's mentally retarded. The DA thinks the shrink's report is enough to keep out anything he said to you as evidence against Violet. If he even said anything. Which, from your statement, I don't think he did."

I replayed the conversation several times in my head, before I grudgingly admitted, "You're right. He never specifically said she put him up to it."

"Not so retarded, was he?"

I groaned. "Please tell me she's at least going to have to give the money back."

Joe shook his head. "Maybe yes, maybe no. According to what I read in the paper, Brunswick and ICARUS are looking at their options. But I don't know how far that's going to get them. I mean, think about it, girl."

"I see what you mean. It was a Brunswick employee who engineered the settlement, and it was authorized by Heartland, the claims-handling service owned by Brunswick."

"Yeah. So here we are. Bosco's girlfriend almost kills you, and she's a millionaire. Believe me, I want to see her in cuffs and a jumpsuit as badly as you do."

I pictured Violet in the cuffs and jumpsuit. It was a good picture. But Joe was being unfair. "She's not Bosco's girlfriend any more. She dumped him for Wildman at the show."

"You really think Bosco didn't have anything to do with this?"

"Joe. That is ridiculous." We stared at each other. He dropped his eyes first.

"I'm just saying," he muttered.

"Joe."

"Alright." He was silent for several seconds before he wandered over to the window. "I helped Pop move in here after he left your mother."

"You mean after he abandoned me?"

"Pop didn't abandon you."

"He wasn't there. What would you call it?"

"You were practically grown. And you gotta admit it, Fifi, your mother, she's a hard woman."

"And yo' momma so fat, she beeps when she backs

up. What, are we throwing the dozens here?"

"I'm just saying Pop woulda been happier if he hadn't left Momma in the first place."

"Pop was never happy. No, I take that back. He was happy for about five minutes after he won a case. Then he was all miserable again until he was trying the next one."

"You didn't know him before." Joe sighed and rubbed his head. "I don't want to fight with you, Fifi. It's not an even match anyway, with you lying there all banged up like that."

"Hey, I could be in a coma and it would be an even match."

Joe half smiled. "Okay. I'm going to go now. But you should at least think about maybe giving Bosco his eviction notice. He could get a job, get his own place. You don't need what Bosco brings to the party. If he didn't live with you, maybe you could get yourself a boyfriend."

"I have a boyfriend."

"Really? I don't see him. You almost get killed, your boyfriend should be here."

"He's busy."

"Busy doing what?"

"He's a lawyer," I admitted.

Joe crossed his arms. "A busy trial lawyer who's never there for you? Could you be more transparent?"

"Don't start that with me," I warned. "So he's not here right now. He just finished a big trial and he's got lots of work piled up. It's not a fair test."

"Fifi, I got news for you. Relationships aren't about fair, and life isn't a test."

"What, are we on the Hallmark channel?"

"Think about it," Joe said over his shoulder as he walked out the door.

"I'm not going to think about it," I called after him.

* * *

I didn't think about it either.

I thought about a lot of other things instead. Like Sketch. His owners came to pick him up and I watched out my window as a little girl came running up the side walk to throw her arms around him. Sketch bounded out of the house at warp speed, knocked the little girl flat on her butt and kept on running. Bosco and Mr. Sketch's Owner prowled the neighborhood for a half an hour before finally tracking him down. He was diving for sushi in a koi pond on Ave. 47.

I thought some about Wong. VJ told me Reggie boy lawyered up and dealt, trading immunity for what he knew about the video tape. Truth for freedom. Except, as it turns out, not so much truth.

Wong stuck to his story that he didn't know anything about murder or kidnapping, and as for extortion, well, according to Wong's lawyer, it wasn't really extortion in the way ordinary people think of extortion. It was more like free trade. Wong also insisted that Violet didn't know a damn thing about it, so my other thought is that the DA got a lousy deal. He'd have been better off trading Manhattan for beads. Okay, so Wong had to give up his bar card, but he was an old guy who was retiring anyway. You don't need a bar card to play shuffle board.

I thought venomous thoughts about Violet who had become an anointed tabloid princess. I couldn't even limp into the CVS without seeing her face on the cover of some rag, right next to the impulse buys at the register. She totally moved in on Wildman, poor guy, and even elbowed out Sparky the Dalmatian, becoming the new face that adorns note cards and calendars.

Thanks to Wong, Violet will never be prosecuted, she's keeping the money and now she's writing a book. I swear

249

to God if there is anything at all about me in that book I'll have VJ sue her so fast her hair extensions will spin.

And when I finally got out of my cast and back to work, and passed the San Fernando Police Station, I thought a little bit about Officer Shaw too.

Officer Shaw wasn't too busy to save my life. I notice things like that.

After clerkships with the CIA and the Dade County Attorney's Office, Gwen Freeman graduated from the University of Virginia Law School, and joined a law firm in Los Angeles, where she specialized in insurance law. More recently, she has represented death row inmates, and was successful in obtaining relief for the longest resident of California's Death Row.

An artist of note, Gwen shows her work in galleries nationwide and has a loyal cult following. Her work has been featured on the sets of *Frasier*; *The O.C.*; *The Sweetest Thing: American Pie II*; and *Daddy Day Care*.

Gwen presently lives with her husband, daughter, two dogs, five cats, 217 birds and a raccoon in a 100 year old restoration project, one hill over from Dodger stadium.